Jesse stared directl[...]w you something. Some[...]

"Something in the [...]"

"I tried to go to the police today, but that didn't work, so we thought we'd show it to you." His hands were in his pockets, then they were fidgeting, then they were shoved back in his pockets.

"And this something is what you were worried about this morning?" Liz asked Brad.

Brad nodded and added hurriedly, "But it's not our fault. We just found it. That's all."

"What is it?" Tawny whispered, picking up the vibes.

Jesse slid her another look, weighing his answer. Liz would have preferred Tawny not be a part of this, but apparently the boys welcomed her involvement. At least they weren't telling her to get lost, like boys their age were wont to do if an invader entered their territory. No, the boys accepted Tawny as part of the package.

"It's a dead body," Jesse suddenly admitted, his matter-of-fact delivery snapping Liz's head around in surprise. In an oddly mature voice, he added, "Looks like somebody shot the guy full of holes and left him down by Humming-bird River . . ."

Books by Nancy Bush

Published by Kensington Publishing Corporation

No Turning Back

NANCY BUSH

ZEBRA BOOKS
KENSINGTON PUBLISHING CORP.
http://www.kensingtonbooks.com

ZEBRA BOOKS are published by

Kensington Publishing Corp.
119 West 40th Street
New York, NY 10018

All Kensington titles, imprints, and distributed lines are available at special quantity discounts for bulk purchases for sales promotion, premiums, fund-raising, educational, or institutional use.

Special book excerpts or customized printings can also be created to fit specific needs. For details, write or phone the office of the Kensington Sales Manager: Attn.: Sales Department. Kensington Publishing Corp., 119 West 40th Street, New York, NY 10018. Phone: 1-800-221-2647.

Zebra and the Z logo Reg. U.S. Pat. & TM Off.

First Printing: January 2018
ISBN-13: 978-1-4201-3863-4
ISBN-10: 1-4201-3863-4

eISBN-13: 978-1-4201-3864-1
eISBN-10: 1-4201-3864-2

10 9 8 7 6 5 4 3 2 1

Printed in the United States of America

Prologue

Barney Turgate had never been known for his mental skills or his ambition, but that didn't mean Barney was unsuccessful. Lord, no. Closing in on the big 4-0, old Barn was not only entering another decade, he was finally about to attain the prize he'd diligently sought his entire life: a windfall.

Not just any windfall, mind you. No penny-ante dream had taken all Barn's stamina, cajolery, good looks, and limited brainpower. This was it. The top. The apex. The zenith. The ultimate.

And it was almost within his grasp.

Tonight, as he waited in the forest, shivering in the early evening chill that made the Northwest's summers sheer pleasure during the day and brisk to the point of teeth-chattering at night, Barney huddled in his Columbia Sportswear navy anorak with the red, zip-out, fuzzy lining and contemplated his new beginning.

Ha! It had been a long, long time since he'd felt this good. Inside there was a warm glow, kind of like he'd consumed his first pitcher of beer and was being hit on by one of the cute waitresses at the Elbow Room.

Old Barn had been a football player in his younger years. Halcyon days. Ego-boosting, cheering crowds. His face all over Woodside High's yearbook. He'd had the pick of the girls, then. Cheerleaders with bouncing breasts and Crest toothpaste smiles. Pseudo-intellectual-type women who orated politics and did his homework on the sly for a date to Homecoming on the Barn's arm. Most of them put out without so much as a meow, too. Yep, Barn still had it as he turned the corner to middle age; as a young man, he'd been a regular Romeo.

But times had changed. Life was a bitch, y'know? Barn had failed at college, failed as a real estate agent, and failed as a husband and father. It had been a long, gradual, limping decline, but even with his limited neuron-firing, Barn had glimpsed the future and it was dark, dark, dark.

Then, six months ago, everything changed. At first it was just a whisper he'd overheard. A plot too good to be true. And *legal*! Well, sort of. Barney Turgate might not be a speed demon when it came to mental gymnastics, but he was a bulldog, and when he got hold of an idea he chewed it around in his mind and chewed it and chewed it until it was soft and sweet and palatable. He'd known this one was good before he swallowed.

A smile quirked the corner of his mouth. He couldn't wait to crow about it! Ha! Wait 'til them bastards down at the Elbow Room heard about Barn and his newfound fortune. They'd be singin' a different tune now as they threw back their pints of Bud and choked on a few peanut shells. Ha!

There were a few gals in Woodside and the surrounding Podunk towns who still thought a slap and tickle in the sack with Barn was worth something. Just wait 'til they got a hold of him now! It got him all stirred up just thinking about it, and he chuckled softly.

Snap.

Barney's neck twisted fast, his reflexes still quick. His eyes searched the surrounding trees and undergrowth, waiting for a shadow to emerge. He was pretty sure that had been a twig breaking beneath someone's foot. "Who's there?" he whispered harshly.

Instead of an answer, a heavy tread hurried his way, footsteps falling in rapid succession. Barn waited without much enthusiasm. It clearly wasn't the person he'd expected to meet because they would answer him back pronto. This was probably some stupid tree-hugger racing through the dampish wetlands to stop him from felling a rotten old cottonwood. That's how you had to do it now, y'know. In the dark when no one was looking. Otherwise there were permits and meetings and scenes with screaming idiots who thought even scrub trees were worth saving. Stop the developers! Stop the tree murderers! Ha! They were morons. All of 'em.

Barney grimaced. Oh, he knew all about it. This very place was just another real estate deal that had gone sour because some assholes didn't understand how important housing construction was. How was a guy supposed to make a living?

The newcomer crashed through the underbrush, spraying Barney with water droplets. "Hey," Barn bitched, squinting. His brows lifted in surprise. This wasn't no tree-hugger, he decided, checking out the guy's light blue denim jeans, black Nikes, and gray, hooded sweatshirt that pretty much obscured his face. Tree-huggers acted like they owned every goddamned plant in the world and were proud of it. This, then, must be the dealmaker after all.

"Well, it's about time," Barn complained. "I've been freezin' my nuts off waitin' out here!"

A black handgun magically appeared in the stranger's tight fist. It jumped from some hidden pocket as if on springs, then pointed straight at the Barn's softening gut.

"Hey!" he cried again, disbelief sending an alarm sluggishly to his brain.

Blat. Blat. Blat. Three shots in rapid succession. Barn staggered, his mouth slack with stupefaction. He saw the gun barrel lift again, a dark circle staring into his eyes.

Blat.

Barney Turgate expired in a wheeze and a thunk. His six-foot three-inch frame toppled onto the fir needle–shrouded pathway.

His assassin didn't linger. Deed done, the Nikes turned on the path and jogged into the soggy silence of old Barn's last soured real estate deal.

Chapter One

Beneath the waterlogged bough of a Douglas fir, Jesse Hart pursed his lips around a cigarette and pulled hard. Smoke burned his throat. The vision of a dragon mistakenly inhaling his own fiery breath filled Jesse's creative mind. Defiantly, he dragged down harder on the Camel until the tip glowed scarlet and his lungs filled to their cancerous limit. Exhaling, he couldn't quite help several soft, choking coughs. Gnashing his teeth, he tried again. By God, he was gonna smoke, and smoke with *attitude*. Even if it killed him.

Ten minutes later he ground the smoking butt beneath the heel of his boot. Wet mulch and leaves smoldered and sizzled. He loved the hiss of fire meeting water. He loved rebellion. Sixteen and ornery as a badger, Jesse glowered into the dark woods surrounding him and hoped like hell Brad was going to manage to sneak out of the house without thunking his head on the window again and waking up the whole goddamned neighborhood like last time. What a dumbass!

Water dripped from drooping leaves, remnants of this latest wash of rain that had pelted down like wild arrows from some wicked water nymph lying in wait in the heavens. Jesse listened. He'd ducked beneath the spreading arms of the huge tree and greeted the wild, furious rainfall with a boyish grin—the kind of smile he refused to let anyone see these days.

He ran a hand through his hair. Sun-streaked brown strands, straight as a stick, seemed to grow from a center swirl at the back of his head and fall bluntly to somewhere near his chin. He had to part the floppy bangs to see, accomplishing this action by flipping his head long enough to cop a clear view before the slick strands fell in front of his face again.

Jesse prided himself on being a throwback clone of Kurt Cobain, lead singer for Nirvana and Jesse's personal hero. In memory of Cobain, a victim of suicide, Jesse wore vintage Nirvana T-shirts and played his music as loud as his father allowed—louder, when he could. The more the room throbbed, the more tribute was paid to the Seattle band that—in Jesse's biased opinion—still epitomized the misunderstood anguish and heat of his generation. No Pop 40 sterile music of today's so-called artists for him. His music icons were *artists*.

Closing his eyes, Jesse swayed his head to the dripping symphony around him. *I'm so happy, 'cause today I found my friends* . . . Nirvana lyrics. Cobain had been a master.

Jesse could admit he was a bit of a bad apple. Since moving from L.A. the year before, he'd been in a series of scrapes ranging from a suspension from school for cursing at a teacher to grand theft auto. Okay, the car thing was just a joke on a buddy of his, but having a cop for a dad really screwed things up. The excuse, "I'm sorry. We were gonna bring it back," just didn't cut it when your father had to explain it to the rest of the department (if you could call it that in this godforsaken nowheresville!).

What a bunch of crap. It wasn't like Dad was any big deal here, but Woodside's Finest sure as hell treated him like he was. Apparently Detective Hawthorne Hart's reputation preceded him: he'd been an ace shot with a police unit associated with the LAPD and even the residents of Woodside, Washington—two hours south of Seattle—knew it.

Jesse grimaced and spat. Dad hadn't been the same since the shooting. It shouldn't have happened. It was unfair, and it totally pissed Jesse off that the damn incident had sent him and his father to exile, far away from his buddies and life in sunny California.

'Course if they were still back home, Jesse never would have met Tawny Fielding and that would have been a crime. If there was ever a girl worth knowing, it was Tawny. Not that he could touch her. She was way out of range. But he could say hi in the halls and she always smiled and said hi back. Brad had jabbed him in the ribs and giggled once and Jesse had been forced to snap him in a headlock and yank the numbnuts around.

The cool thing was, this summer had been something of a breakthrough for him where Tawny was concerned. He'd actually stopped by her house a time or two, and she'd seemed kind of glad to see him. 'Course he'd always been with Brad, but he sensed she was warmer to *him* than his buddy. Maybe he was crazy. After all, she was a total good girl, and he was aligned with the losers. You couldn't attend Woodside High and not know where you stood. Jesse had shown up there last fall, looked around, and immediately refused the company of the football asses and computer nerds. Good God, it was hard to find decent friends.

Tawny . . . She was gorgeous. Damn near perfect. And she was always smiling. That was the first thing he'd noticed about her. Her smile. Jesse might not do a lot of it himself these days, but he could appreciate its simple beauty and honesty and be drawn to a girl whose joy was reflected on her bright face and curved lips.

Just thinking about her made him hard.

Jogging footsteps suddenly crashed through the underbrush, sounding like a clumsy ox on speed. "Jeezus, Brad." Jesse nailed him when his best friend came into view. "Why don't ya take out a full-page ad?"

"What's your problem?" Brad swiped rain from his own lank, near black hair. His cut was identical to Jesse's, but he was bulkier, with a good-natured freckled face. Brad had to work extra hard to look cool and cop an attitude.

"Gimme a smoke," Brad said, shaking water out of his hair like a wild dog.

"Damn it," Jesse muttered, but he handed his friend the pack and Brad fumbled for his own lighter.

While Brad smoked, Jesse ran his tongue around his mouth and didn't like the way it tasted. Smoking was a bitch any way you looked at it.

"So, what are we gonna do?" Brad asked "Wanna go scare the Ryerson twins?"

"Nah." The Ryerson twins tattled and shrieked and ran around like Donald Duck on acid. Jesse was tired of terrorizing them. Didn't life have any meaning anymore?

"You thinkin' about stealin' something?" Brad suddenly guessed with a trace of fear and eagerness.

The truth was Jesse only had Tawny Fielding on his mind these days, but he couldn't share that with Brad. Brad saw girls as sluts or prudes—period. Up until he met Tawny, Jesse pretty much felt the same way. But he was experiencing something new here. A kind of lust mixed with respect and even awe.

It was a shitty way to feel.

"Come on," he said, impatient with his own thoughts. He pushed hard at branches as he furthered his way down the path into the vacant property along Hummingbird River. A wetlands. Saved by a group of chanting environmentalists who'd linked arms and chained themselves to trees.

"Where're we going?" Brad wondered.

"Who cares?"

Stumbling over an exposed root, Jesse suddenly fell to his hands. Brad whooped with delight. "Fuckin' smooth move."

Jesse suddenly whipped around and yanked Brad's leg out from under him. With an earth-shaking thunk, Brad landed on his butt, his mouth an "O" of surprise. Jesse howled with laughter. Brad swore pungently and jumped him, and the two boys wrestled and thrashed through the underbrush until they were both swearing, panting, and covered with wet leaves, fir needles, and muck.

"Shit, this is my favorite shirt," Jesse complained.

"You shoulda thought of that before you jumped me."

"You jumped me, asshole."

"That's 'cause you broke my butt."

Jesse half-laughed. Brad grinned in the darkness. And it was then that Jesse saw, in his line of sight, the sole of a shoe. He blinked. The shoe was attached to a leg, and it wasn't Brad's.

A straight shot of adrenaline hit his bloodstream—a total body rush. "Holy shit," he muttered, leaping to his feet and backing up so fast he slammed into a tree.

His fear infected Brad, who was up and beside him in

an instant. "What? Are you messin' with me? What the hell do you see?"

Jesse grabbed his friend so hard even Brad's duller wits caught on and he closed his mouth with a snap.

Jesse waited, half-expecting the body on the ground to rise up and arrest them or something. "It's a guy," he whispered.

"Where?" Brad craned his neck.

"Shhh!" He stabbed a finger in the general direction and Brad visibly started when he saw the shoe and leg. The rest of the body was presumably tucked in the under-growth.

Slowly, gathering courage but poised to run for their lives, the two boys parted the wet leaves and scraggly stems of the plants to reveal a middle-aged man. A very dead middle-aged man. The series of huge dark spots across the man's chest and the hole in his forehead were silent testimony. His eyes were open.

Jesse shuddered and stepped back. "Somebody wasted him."

"Let's get outta here," Brad murmured.

They backed up slowly, twisted, hit the trail at a half gallop and tore away as if the devil were at their heels, which he very well might be.

"Don't tell," Jesse warned.

"No . . . no . . ." Brad's teeth were chattering. Not a good sign.

"I mean it. We could get blamed."

"For killin' some guy?" His voice was an octave higher than usual. "Oh, come on!"

"I'm not gonna chance it," Jesse muttered. Another scene unfolded inside his mind. An imagined one, but the facts were real enough. His father taking aim, prepared to shoot to kill, his rifle pumping rapidly, bullets zinging into human flesh.

The cold breath of reality fanning his neck, Jesse tore away from the downed body of Barney Turgate. He ran and ran, Brad at his heels, and with the fervor of a religious zealot vowed never to smoke again.

A guy like him needed all the lung capacity he could get.

Chapter Two

". . . and then I told him he couldn't go. I said, 'You can't go,' and you know what Josh did then? He *swore* at me!" Deanne Martin said with controlled fury. "So, I told him, 'Get in the car.' He just stared at me. Never moved a muscle. And his friends just stood around and smirked."

Petite and well groomed, Deanne smoothed back her short brunette hair, crossed her legs beneath a sleek, black skirt, and waited, lockjawed, for a response. Her gaze rested on Liz Havers, who mentally compared herself to the furious woman and, as ever, came up short. Liz's hair was light brown, her eyes an unremarkable blue, and she spent most of her time in jeans and cotton shirts.

But not today. Not on work time. Carefully schooling her features, Liz glanced from Deanne to her son, who sat in a chair as far away from his mother as possible. As a child psychologist, Liz spent most of her time listening to similar problems. The boy, a rebellious teenager over six-feet who had to weigh at least twice as much as his mother, glared at Liz behind eyes dulled with disrespect.

"You shoved me," he reminded his mother sullenly.

"You said, 'Get in the car,' then you shoved me at the car and I banged my head."

"And then Josh just left with those boys," Deanna finished, her gaze fixed on Liz. "I'm lucky he agreed to counseling."

Liz glanced at Josh. He wore a baseball cap backward over hair dyed a shade between red and magenta. She'd counseled a lot of kids his age. There wasn't much that surprised her anymore, though once in a while some creative youngster did manage to make her jaw drop. Once in a *great* while.

"What's going on, Josh?" she asked him.

"Nothin'." He glared at her before turning his attention to the straggling laces of his black Nikes.

"His dad's coming to pick him up on Friday and Josh is going with him no matter what he says." Deanne's voice rang out. Josh shot her a filthy look.

"What are you and your dad doing this weekend?" Liz asked him.

"Nothin'."

"Nothing?"

"Nothin'." He hesitated. "Besides, it'll be stupid, whatever it is."

Deanne shot Liz an exasperated look that said, *See what I mean!*

Communication breakdown. "What's a typical weekend with your father like?"

Josh rolled his eyes and refused to answer. Deanne seemed to take this as a cue to belittle her ex and, as a byproduct, Josh. "Robert spoils him. Buys him all kinds of gadgets and just plops him in front of the TV. He never takes him anywhere."

"You don't know!" Josh exploded.

"Well, it's true." Deanne rushed on to Liz. "Josh used

to love the arts. Theater, music, painting. I've got pictures he made when he was in kindergarten that are just amazing. You'd be astounded."

The past tense of that remark echoed throughout the room. Her regret was so deep, Josh couldn't help but make the comparison: good, then; bad, now.

"But his father doesn't appreciate the arts. Business, business, business. And football." Her lip curled. "He could name you every player on every NFL team, but he can't remember birthdays and he never remembered his own anniversary! At least that's one date he can forget now. I certainly have."

"Can we go?" Josh demanded in a loud voice.

Before Liz could respond, Deanne glanced at her slim gold watch. "We're five minutes late already. Great. Now I'll be in trouble at work." Gathering up her purse, she said, "Same time next week? Oh, I'll have to call you. I've got some important meetings. I might have to reschedule. Josh, hurry up!"

She practically stepped on his heels as he sauntered out of Liz's temporary office. Before she disappeared into the hallway, Deanne shot Liz one more glance of *Can you believe this?* as if she were the only parent on earth who had ever spawned such an undesirable offspring.

Liz sighed, closed her eyes, and ran her hands through her shoulder-length hair. She itched to get out of her cotton slacks and blouse and into a pair of well-worn jeans. She had so much to do, so many problems of her own to solve, and Deanne and Josh's troubles brought them all too close.

Switching off the lights to her office, she sat in semi-darkness, contemplating, though it was only ten in the morning. She had another appointment at two and a house call to make in-between.

Her job could be rewarding. Her job could be heart-breaking. So much of the time kids and their parents just couldn't bridge the gap. Parents were frustrated; teenagers were anxious and insecure. A deadly brew with sometimes tragic consequences.

Josh just wanted things his way, and his mother wanted to punish his father. And so it went.

Locking the door, she left her nondescript office and drove through a torrential summer downpour to a drive-through coffee shop, a cute tucked-away place called the Coffee Spot, then to the little house she'd purchased this past spring. Balancing her coffee, purse, and a briefcase with notes and papers, she dashed through the rain into the kitchen. Small and cozy, it was a haven. Her favorite spot in the whole world.

Dropping everything but the coffee, Liz stood at the front window, passing the scorching paper cup holding her latte from hand to hand. Newly hired by Woodside's school district, she would start as Woodside High's resi-dent psychologist this coming fall. For now, she saw a trickle of patients whose parents were desperate for some kind of counseling right away. It helped her limp finan-cially through the summer, though producing a steady income was the least of her problems.

No, all of this was just window dressing, for Liz Havers was on a mission.

Squinting her eyes, she gazed inward to her own troubled soul. Too much time had passed. She'd left it all too long. Yet she'd been working for this half her life.

My son. My sixteen-year-old son.

She'd moved to Woodside to reconnect with the child

she'd given up for adoption not long after her own graduation from Woodside High.

She breathed deeply several times. Air in, air out, air in, air out. Relax. Nothing else could have dragged her back here. Not even the pleas of her best friend, Kristy Fielding, who was having her own personal difficulties and was raising a teenage daughter.

The opportunity to meet her son face-to-face both thrilled and terrified Liz. With more trepidation than expectation, she'd plunked down in Woodside two months earlier and begun the mine-filled process of reconnecting.

She knew where he lived. She knew his father. And she knew also how negative her reception was going to be when that meeting came off.

Her heart jerked painfully. She'd made a lot of terrible mistakes, but she'd been seventeen, for crying out loud! Two heaven-filled weeks with a man nearly a decade older than herself and she'd set herself on this unlucky course.

Briefly, she let her thoughts touch on that insane time and the wild love she'd felt. It had been infantile, delusionary, and just plain wrong, but the intensity of it could still take her breath away. He'd been so handsome and reluctant and soul-sick with longing and loneliness. A lethal combination. A seductive brew. A chemical explosion destined to drug her own level-headedness and send her down destruction's path.

Luckily, she'd made a life for herself since. She'd worked hard to get over the past and become the woman she was today.

She hoped to hell that counted for something.

Rain pelted against the windowpanes, an all-out storm. Liz passed the cup again and stared into the gloom. June twenty-first. Summer solstice. The longest day of the year and the most god-awful. Lashing winds, fitful rain, leaden, pewter skies, and a general sense of doom.

One could really learn to hate the Northwest. Though she'd grown up here, the last sixteen years of her life had been spent in Arizona and Woodside's weather had become a distant memory. Now it was back full-force, but Liz felt more disinterest and apathy than hate. It just took too much energy to loathe something beyond her control.

Should today be the day? she asked herself, mouth dry. Should today be the day she met her son?

Her phone buzzed, making her jump. Silently berating herself, she snagged it up, grimacing through the dining room windows to the torrent beyond.

"Liz?" a young, familiar voice asked.

Liz smiled. "Hey, babe, how're you doing?" Tawny, her friend Kristy's daughter, who just happened to be one of Liz's most favorite people on earth. She passed the latte once again. Lord, the cup was hot. She should have picked up a cardboard jacket for it.

"I'm just kind of hanging around," she responded, sighing hugely. Fifteen-year-old Tawny Fielding sighed a lot these days. "It's so dark."

"Summer's a blast, huh?"

"Just look at it!"

"I am. I am." Liz brought the cup to her mouth, attempted a sip of milk-laced coffee, and scalded her lips and tongue. She sputtered and fought a moan. Sometimes the Coffee Spot went overboard on the steamed part, blasting supercharged, boiling atoms into the espresso and milk and turning it into a nuclear explosion. Criminy, the stuff could melt the planet!

"Are you okay?" Tawny asked, as Liz choked and fought back a string of swear words.

"I just burned the top layer of my tongue off." Turning

from the window, Liz gently probed her lips and tongue, knowing she'd lost the ability to taste for the better part of the day. The hazards of preoccupation. Her brain just wasn't engaged. "How's your mom?"

Her friend Kristy had come down with some mysterious plague that kept her constantly feeling low and nauseous, as if she suffered from chronic flu. She had yet to be diagnosed, but Liz wondered if it might not be depression. The local weather could do it to you all on its own.

Kristy, who'd stayed in Woodside while Liz had fled from her past, had fallen in love with the first man she'd ever kissed and remained a native Washingtonian, constantly raving to Liz about the area as if it were Eden itself. Lovestruck Kristy married Guy Fielding, her first and only lover, and bore him Tawny, whose name was some kind of family moniker that had made Liz wonder from the beginning how sound Guy really was in the first place. It was a bitch to have her suspicions founded: On the eve of Kristy's thirtieth birthday, Guy ran off with an eighteen-year-old who turned out to be already pregnant with a baby girl.

The bastard had probably named her Tawny II.

"She's okay," Tawny said.

"Is she going to the doctor again?"

"She went yesterday. She's . . . tired."

"Tell her I'll stop by this afternoon. I've got to see one of my rebels and my last appointment's at two. Then I'm free."

"Okay."

"Maybe I can bring takeout by? Pizza, sushi, Mexican?"

"Pizza'd be great."

"Okay, I'll see you later."

"Thanks. Bye."

Liz disconnected. She was currently seeing several rather antisocial customers. *Tutoring* might be the proper word if she were a teacher. At any rate, one of them, Brad—The Brad Influence, a name one of his buddies' moms had chosen for him—was on today's agenda.

Gathering her purse, a woven bag she could sling over her shoulder, Liz slipped into tan suede toeless slip-ons, her most loved faded blue jeans, a beige tank top, and a denim overshirt. Sure, she liked to dress down, but she'd learned kids responded to her best if she was just herself.

There was, however, the rain. By the time she'd dodged puddles as she ran for her car, a black Miata convertible— top up today—her toes were squishing against the leather soles, the tan suede stained a ruinous dark brown.

A trip to the grocery store for nonperishables and she was on her way to Brad's home, a dark blue ranch with a cracked picture window and a diagonal of three diamond-shaped cutouts across the face of the garage door, the height of sixties fashion in the modern home. Rain ran sluggishly from a gutter that hung half a foot lower on the northeast side of the house, creating a pool on the grass below that was trying hard to spill over the edge of the cement drive. So far, the one-inch lip held the flood back, but as Liz climbed from her low-slung car and dashed for the porch, she calculated the driveway would be inundated by the time she ran back to the Miata.

She knocked loudly. Brad's mother was supposed to be home. Liz wasn't about to visit one of her students at home without another adult present. She'd been scammed by the best of them—kids with too much time, brain-power, and energy and too little self-esteem, recognition of cause and effect, and general sense of purpose.

They could be devilishly clever and oh so destructive.

"Hello, Mrs. Barlow," Liz greeted Brad's mother when she answered the door.

"Hi yourself," the woman greeted her. She and Liz were already well acquainted, though they'd only known each other two months.

The house smelled like dogs. Good reason. Two friendly-looking golden retrievers lounged in the front room alongside Brad, his younger brother and sister, and a clutter of video games, one of which was currently on screen. The sister and brother were playing and Brad was watching. Sort of. He seemed to be staring off into space, a throw pillow clutched to his chest, caught in some reflection of his own, which was unusual for the cheerfully reckless Brad Liz had grown to know.

"Come on, Brad. Ms. Havers is here and I don't want to waste my money on you watching that stupid game." Gina Barlow snatched away the pillow and, like a sleepwalker, Brad climbed to his feet and led Liz to a room off the kitchen that was designed to be something between a laundry room and a den.

Liz perched herself on what looked like a chair from a dining room set and Brad sat behind the desk in a swivel rocker. Gina left them alone, half-closing the door behind her. She knew Brad's counseling sessions were necessary, but she couldn't help resenting them a little. Most parents felt the same way, defensive of their own parenting skills because their offspring's behavior reflected poorly on them—or so they felt. Sometimes the way a child chose to be was their own decision, no matter what. It crossed all socioeconomic boundaries. But try telling that to an overworked, overstressed mother with no foreseeable options.

"What is it, Brad?" Liz asked.

He surfaced, blinking. "What?"

"What's bothering you?"

"Nothin'." A pause. "What's botherin' you?"

"You seem kind of preoccupied," Liz responded, ignoring him. Brad was great at counterattack, but not as swift at long-term defense. If she kept chipping away, eventually she could usually get to the root of things.

"I got things to think about."

"Anything you can share?"

He snorted. "Uh-uh."

"What have you been doing since school's been out?"

"Nothin'."

"Seen your friend Jesse?"

It was a simple question, not meant to require more than a yes or no response, but Brad startled, as if he'd been pinched. Jesse was Brad's good buddy, by Brad's own accounting, and on a good day Brad would tell her the "really cool stuff" he and Jesse did together; on a bad day, he'd simply grunt acknowledgment at his friend's name.

But today he'd reacted with nervous jitters, his teeth tearing at the corner of his thumbnail—heavy concentration for Brad.

"Yeah," Brad finally answered warily.

"So, what happened?"

"What do you mean?"

Liz spread her hands. "What did you do together?"

"Mom!" Brad suddenly yelled. "Can I have a bowl of ice cream?"

"No!" came the muffled response.

There followed a verbal skirmish between mother and son in which the rules appeared to be that neither would take one step closer to the other. They were content to scream from a distance until one ran out of breath. Gina Barlow folded first, with Brad still yelling at her to no avail.

He subsided into glowering silence. Intuition enfolded

Liz, a familiar sensation that was nine parts deduction and one part basic understanding of human nature. Teenagers weren't so different from adults if you took a little extra time to listen.

"Something happened with you and Jesse," she guessed. "You're worried and you don't know what to do, whom to turn to."

"Shut up!" Strong words directed at her, even for Brad.

"Is it something you did?"

"No!"

"Something Jesse did?"

"No! You don't know anything!"

"Why don't you tell me?"

"I—shit—no." He struggled. "We didn't do anything. Nothing! I'm not talkin' anymore."

"Maybe I should check with Jesse," Liz suggested.

"You don't even know Jesse."

"I could find out from your mom . . ."

Expecting immediate, strenuous objections, Liz was surprised when Brad merely frowned. Anytime before when she'd mentioned meeting Jesse, Brad had gone ballistic. It embarrassed him that he was seeing the "school shrink," and though Liz suspected Jesse knew all about it anyway—probably as a result of Brad's big mouth—Brad was adamant about keeping them apart.

Liz added reasonably, "Or you could just unload on me. It might help."

He shook his head.

"Is there anything else you'd like to talk about?" she tried.

"No."

She waited, watching the play of emotions across Brad's guileless face. The kid was an open book.

After a protracted silence, he said slowly, "If something happened that wasn't your fault, but you knew about it, and then you didn't tell . . ." He struggled to pick through the right words. "Well, could you be responsible? I mean, when it all came out?"

"In what context are we talking?" Liz eyed him closely. "Something with one of your friends?"

"*No*." He jumped to his feet, moving restlessly. "Let's say you found something you shouldn't have, and you didn't report it to the police."

"The police?" Liz's radar swung into high gear.

"Yeah."

"Give me a for instance."

He blinked rapidly, thinking hard, apparently unable to come up with something.

"Like you discovered one of your friends was selling drugs," Liz suggested.

"Yeah!" he exhaled eagerly.

Scratch that off as a possibility. He's too quick to jump to the bait.

Brad persisted. "So, if you didn't tell, what would happen?"

"To you?" He nodded rapidly. "As long as you weren't involved, nothing. Except a whole lot of guilt if your friend should get in over his head, and maybe even die."

Brad swallowed and looked past Liz to a blank spot on the wall. Inordinately thoughtful behavior for him. Something wasn't right.

"Could you tell me what the problem is? In total confidentiality," she added.

"There is no problem. I'm just thinking."

Try as she would, Liz couldn't get much more out of Brad about whatever was preoccupying him. She attempted a change of subject to keep him talking, but he wasn't interested in any way, shape, or form. Eventually, faced with defeat, she told him she'd see him the following week and, after a quick good-bye to Gina, raced back through the depressingly purposeful drizzle to the Miata. Yep. The rain had managed to flood the driveway.

Liz made her two o'clock appointment with Carrie Lister, a young girl who wore a perpetual snarl on her face and whose mother was even more impatient than Deanne Martin. Carrie was less communicative than Brad, and by the time Liz picked up the pizza and arrived at her friend Kristy's house, a small bungalow with a clematis-ensnared carport—Guy's one gift to his ex-wife—she was more than a little depressed. She sloshed through another flooded driveway, ruining any hope of salvaging her suede shoes, and concentrated on shaking off her mood. She had to be upbeat for Kristy, who may or may not have finally learned what her mysterious illness was, and she just plain looked forward to seeing Tawny.

Tawny. The perfect child. If Liz could have a daughter half as wonderful, she'd sign herself up for a dozen. She hoped her own son had turned out as well.

Soon, she reminded herself. *Very soon.* And with that last thought, she headed for the front door of Kristy's riverside cabin.

Chapter Three

The lady holding her purse strap with both hands could have been scripted out of a movie. Dowdily dressed, with sensible shoes, a small dark brown hat, and a grim mouth, she was a nightmare for an adventurous spirit— the absolute antidote for fun.

Detective Hawthorne "Hawk" Hart watched her step across the threshold of the Woodside Police Department's front door and thanked the heavens he wasn't on duty. He'd just stopped in to check with his buddy, Chief of Police Perry Dortner, who, unfortunately for him, *was* on duty when the lady appeared.

"Can I help you, ma'am?" Perry asked, grinning affably beneath a dusting of freckles and a shock of blondish red hair. Half the staff called him Opie behind his back, but as chief of police in this dusty one-horse town, he had enough of an iron will to keep them from saying it to his face.

Hawthorne's lips twisted in amusement as he accepted the cup of plain black coffee Perry, who'd just made a run across town to the Coffee Spot, handed him. Hawthorne narrowed his eyes against the rising steam, snorted at the frothy latte Perry'd gotten for himself, then glanced at the dried-up prune of a woman in front of them both.

"They took them all. My yews," she declared, biting off each syllable.

Perry blinked. "My-yoos?"

"My yew trees! A whole row alongside my drive. Both sides!" She turned on Hawthorne, glaring at him as if he'd voiced his thoughts, which were less than sympathetic to say the least. "Those hooligans ripped them right out of the ground and took off with them!"

Hawthorne eyed her steadily and silently. Not his problem. The issue had neighborhood yard war written all over it, and it bored him to his back teeth.

A far cry from what you left behind, he thought grimly. A shudder ran somewhere beneath his skin, reminding him of his own wretched fallibility. As a diversion from his own torment, he asked, "How many trees?"

"Twenty-two."

"Twenty-two?" Perry repeated. "Someone stole *twenty-two* trees out of your yard?"

The prim lady lifted her chin and nodded sharply twice. Hawthorne suffered a sudden vision of his ninth-grade English teacher. This time he didn't bother to disguise the shudder. "Twenty-two," she repeated precisely.

"You say they were ripped out of the ground?" Perry asked. "How big were they?"

"About eight inches in diameter. Not that big yet."

Her shoulders abruptly sagged and she looked as if she were about to cry. Hawthorne inwardly sighed. He had neither time nor patience for womanly histrionics. "Sounds like a prank. You'll find out who did it and they'll bring them back."

"I *know* who did it!" she reacted furiously. "It's those truants. Those boys! Brad Barlow and his other long-haired friend! They should be locked up like the criminals they are!"

Perry coughed into his fist and shot Hawthorne a sideways glance.

The woman glared from Perry to Hawthorne, sensing she'd hit a hot button but not caring what it was. "I want you to go arrest them. Right now! I want them locked away and I want my trees back!"

Brad Barlow and his other long-haired friend . . . With difficulty, Hawthorne fought the desire to defend his son because the boy sure as hell knew how to find trouble. But to steal twenty-two trees? That just didn't sound like Jesse.

"How do you know who the culprits are?" he asked.

She sniffed audibly. "I'm Mrs. Anita Brindamoor and I've known Brad Barlow all his life. That boy's been trouble since he was five, and his friend's even worse."

Perry stifled a choked laugh. Hawthorne's lips flattened. "We'll look into it," Perry told her, his shoulders shaking with suppressed laughter.

Anita Brindamoor glared at him. "Well, I want to see some action or you can expect me in here every day until those two hooligans are arrested!"

As if on cue, Jesse himself suddenly strolled through the front door, setting off the buzzer. Mrs. Brindamoor turned her whole body around to see the new arrival, then flushed burgundy with rage. Instinctively, Hawthorne moved forward to protect his son, but Anita Brindamoor got there first, shaking one small fist in front of Jesse's nose. "You thieving boy!" she cried. "I won't stand for it. This community won't stand for it!"

Jesse threw a baffled look at his father. There wasn't a lot of heavy-duty communication going on between father and son these days, but Hawthorne had no trouble reading him. With casual disdain, Jesse flipped his hair out of his eyes, then scowled down at the tiny woman with a supremely ugly face. She gasped in shock and Hawthorne inwardly groaned.

"Jesse," he bit out, but Anita Brindamoor showed her starch.

"You frightening young thief!" she sputtered. "You should be locked away forever!"

Jesse glanced at Perry and Hawthorne through strands of hair. "What did I do?"

"You talk to me, young man! Those were my trees. My property." She bristled with fury. "I've lodged a formal complaint and you won't get away with it!"

This time the look on Jesse's face was comical. He stared at her as if she'd lost her mind.

Relief flooded through Hawthorne. Jesse wasn't involved. At some level, he'd worried Anita Brindamoor might be right, but Jesse wasn't that good of an actor. His son could lie like a rug when forced, but he was clearly completely at sea over this one.

Anita Brindamoor wasn't nearly as convinced. She balled her hands into fists and shook from head to toe, as if the ground beneath her feet actually vibrated. Jesse, whose insouciance knew no bounds, watched this transformation with growing amusement—although Hawthorne had to admit his son's smile could be labeled maniacal for someone who didn't understand Jesse's twisted humor. Now the good lady's voice became a rising crescendo of indignation. "I plan to sue your family, young man! This won't be the end of it!"

"I'm so scared," Jesse drawled.

"Jesse," Hawthorne warned through his teeth.

"Well, I am. I'm scared shitless."

It was all Hawthorne could do not to grab his son by the scruff of his neck and boot him out the door. But that sort of action invariably backfired. The last time he'd grabbed his son, Jesse had simply disappeared for five days, so instead Hawthorne barked, "Sit down and keep quiet!" and kicked a chair in Jesse's direction. With a shrug, Jesse did as bidden.

With Jesse in a chair, and therefore below eye level, Anita Brindamoor unwound a bit, her ruffled feathers somewhat soothed. She even managed to momentarily unpurse her lips; Hawthorne could almost hear her jaw hinge creak, the movement so completely alien.

A bit of foil stuck out of Jesse's jean's pocket. A cigarette pack. The sting of betrayal ran through Hawthorne's veins; a familiar sensation. Everything Jesse did these days was an act of rebellion. Hawthorne, who'd hunted down and dealt with criminals for most of his adult life, knew the bitter taste of failure over this one half-formed adult. God's punishment? Probably.

It seemed to finally occur to Mrs. Brindamoor how odd it was for the object of her contempt to wander into the police station. Brow furrowed, she snapped at Hawthorne. "You already suspected him, didn't you?"

"No."

"Then why is he here?" She clasped her hands in front of her and waited, chin tilted.

Perry glanced toward the ceiling. His amusement irritated Hawthorne to his bones. The fact that Jesse had picked up on his father's annoyance only increased the sensation. Hell if he was going to explain that Jesse was his son.

"Jesse's father works with the Woodside police force," Perry enlightened her.

Mrs. Brindamoor's lips retightened. In a voice that could curdle milk, she declared, "The state of our country is even worse than I imagined. That young man has no respect for anything. I hope you all prove to be better lawmen than parents."

With that, she regally lifted her head and swept through the doors, her exit marred only by the last withering glare she tossed around the station as a whole.

"That went well," Perry said, grinning.

Hawthorne swore silently to himself.

Jesse asked in disbelief, "She thinks I stole some *trees*?"

"Did you?" Hawthorne bit out. It was bait, pure and simple.

Rebellion flashed in his eyes like blue heat. "Oh, yeah. I took 'em all. Thought I'd start my own little tree farm."

"Okay, okay," Perry attempted to appease, but once on a track Jesse wasn't easy to derail.

"They're in the backyard at home," he went on. "A whole goddamn orchard. But I won't stop at trees. Oh, no. I plan to move onto shrubs and flowers. I really like rhododendrons. Plan to take a dozen or two of those. Then maybe later I'll go roll up some sod. Yeah, and smoke it, too!"

Hawthorne reached out and yanked the cigarette pack from Jesse's pocket. He crushed it in one hand, his face granite. He'd had it with Jesse. His son's insolence and constant profanity were enough to turn Hawthorne violent. But memories always circled in the cauldron of his mind and his anger and frustration were swept into the spiral, losing power. He felt frozen, incapable, and downright helpless sometimes. "Was there a reason you stopped by?"

For the first time, Jesse showed some indecision. A

crack in the armor. A tiny view to the boy within his hard adolescent shell. He swallowed once and shook his head, clearly wanting to say something but unable, apparently, to frame the words. "Nope," he muttered, turning away.

"That right?" Hawthorne pressed, knowing it would do no good.

"Yep."

"Then why'd you come here?"

Jesse hesitated, then glanced at the crunched-up cigarette pack in his father's fist. A new scowl darkened his brow as he got to his feet and sauntered toward the door.

"Be home by six," Hawthorne ordered. "I want to talk to you."

Jesse lifted one shoulder.

"Be there," Hawthorne demanded.

For an answer, he received the nagging sound of the buzzer as Jesse strode through the door into the late-afternoon gray skies.

"You've really got a way with people, don't you?" Perry said, clapping Hawthorne on the back. "It's a gift."

"Shut up."

Perry grinned. "I wouldn't plan on seeing him at six, or anytime soon after."

"He'd better come home."

"What're you going to do when he doesn't?"

Hawthorne's jaw tightened.

"Yesiree, you've got your hands full with Hawthorne Jesse Hart, Jr." Perry's smile faded. "The kid needs a mom."

"Laura's dead." Hawk was terse. Whenever he thought back to that time, guilt took over. The only good thing to come from all the tragedy was Jesse . . . and based on his behavior lately, even that was debatable.

"Laura's car accident was a long, long time ago," Perry reminded Hawk. A moment of tension followed. Drawing a breath, Perry added, "It wasn't your fault. Just like that other business. It wasn't your fault, pal."

Then whose was it?

Like a familiar, unwanted relative, memories came back uninvited. Laura, his wife, pushed off wet, slick roads by a drunken driver.

But she'd been drinking herself, remember?

"Let me drive," he'd told her, holding out a hand for the keys, but she'd laughed and kept them out of reach. He'd let her climb behind the wheel, not wanting the fight. At the bend in the road he'd braced himself, watching in that eerie, slow-motion state while the car swung wide to the right and Laura, making up for her error, yanked it back and over-corrected into the path of another slightly inebriated driver.

Both drivers were killed outright, both passengers unhurt. He remembered standing in the purple twilight of a beautiful summer evening listening to the whimpers of the dead man's wife as she shook in his arms, the two survivors embraced in grief, while they waited for help.

Hawk surfaced from his reverie to find Perry eyeing him with compassion. Hawthorne rarely thought about Laura anymore, but "that other business" was very much his fault and thinking about it was far worse. "That other business" was why he'd come back to Woodside. "That other business" had separated him from his LAPD job, slicing through the umbilical cord of his work to set him spinning into space like some severed capsule.

"I think we both know where to put the blame," Hawk muttered.

"On circumstance, pal. On the perp. The one that used that kid as a hostage."

"I pulled the trigger."

"Your SWAT team did their job," he reminded him. "You damn well know it."

Because he couldn't stop himself, Hawthorne thought back now. The kid's name had been Joey and he was twelve, asleep in bed when a burglar stole into his room, running scared after bungling a job three doors away. Police were dispatched. The perp held Joey hostage on an upstairs landing, a gun to the boy's head. Hawk's team of sharpshooters crouched along the stairs. Everyone was screaming except Joey, who waited with huge, trusting eyes. The burglar cocked his pistol and a *thunk, thunk, thunk of* sharpshooter bullets hit him.

But one bullet hit Joey in the neck and he died. Not from the burglar's gun. Hawk knew it was his. *Knew it.* Though the department preferred to keep just whose bullet it was an internal secret.

"That's why I came back here," Hawk muttered hoarsely. "Need to put it behind me."

"For God's sake . . ." Perry clamped his jaw.

Hawk said, "Let me check out the yew story. I oughtta get through that one without killing an innocent victim."

"You're full of guilt-ridden bullshit."

"You just don't know humor when you hear it," Hawk said lightly.

"Yeah, well, I know when somebody oughtta seek therapy. Surprised it wasn't ordered."

"Just point me in the direction of Mrs. Brindamoor's yew estate."

"Okay, fine. Get outta here." Perry gave him a look. "And let me know how it works out with Jesse."

Hawk waited while Perry handed him the address. That was one reckoning he wasn't looking forward to.

* * *

Jesse slogged through rain puddles big enough to swallow Montana, fighting both the urge to ram his fist into the side of a tree and the equally strong need to break through the dam on his emotions and just plain cry. He did neither as he beelined his way to Brad's house, six miles away. He half-hoped he'd run across someone's bike so he could borrow a ride. Stealing wasn't really stealing if you meant to bring it back.

Halfway to Brad's he crossed the small bridge right before the loopy, tree-shrouded drive that led to Tawny's house. His steps slowed and he thought random thoughts, mostly about what he wanted and couldn't have. He walked to the first curve and glimpsed a car at the end of the drive. A sweet-looking black Miata convertible.

Black Miata convertible. Brad's goddamn *shrink* drove a black Miata. Brad had raved about the car so many times Jesse felt he knew every aspect of the vehicle.

Could there be two in Woodside?

"No way," he whispered, suddenly alarmed. Was Tawny seeing a shrink, too? What was wrong?

The shrink lady could be here for Tawny's mom, he reasoned. That made more sense.

Backing up, Jesse hightailed it the rest of the way to Brad's house. He could hear angry screaming practically before he reached the edge of the property. Brad erupted from the front door in a rage, Brad's mom on his heels.

"Don't bother coming home!" she yelled.

"I won't!"

"I mean it, Brad. This is the last straw!"

"I said I won't!"

"Jesse, talk some sense into him!" she cried upon spying him.

Jesse waited, curiously uplifted by this scene of domestic turmoil. Made his own problems look better.

"What the hell are you doin' here?" Brad greeted him.

"Wha'd you do?"

"Nothin'."

Jesse snorted.

"I called that girl in Texas."

"And?" Jesse couldn't believe how turned on Brad had gotten over a girl he'd chanced to meet over spring vacation who lived in Austin, Texas. Brad had gone bonkers over her Southern drawl, but Jesse'd caught the looks she'd slyly sent him and had wondered what her real agenda was.

"She was glad to hear from me," Brad claimed defensively.

"What'd you do?"

"Nothing."

"Bullshit."

Brad looked about to argue some more, but then he shrugged. "I guess I sent her a few things that . . . I bought with Mom's credit card."

"You swiped the card from your mom?"

"I was gonna tell her, but she found out before I could."

"You're such a jerk." Jesse laughed. "How're you gonna pay her back?"

"I'll get a job." He shrugged, but Jesse knew his friend; beneath the attitude, Brad felt bad about it.

"So, you're out of the house for now."

Brad nodded.

"Join the club." They started walking back down the road to town. "Your shrink's at Tawny's. I saw the car."

"Really?" Brad eyed him intently. "I had an appointment today. I almost told her. I kinda hinted around, and she said we weren't responsible for anything unless we did it ourselves."

"Yeah?"

"Maybe we oughtta tell."

Jesse considered. He'd gone to the police station today with a similar idea in mind. He'd wanted to talk to his father, but it had all gone to crap, just like always. Now, he ran his hands through his rain-soaked hair and drew a deep breath. His pulse beat light and fast. They could unload the truth and he could see Tawny.

"You'd get to meet her," Brad pressed. "She can tell you how nuts I am."

"Oh shut up. It's just therapy because you smoke, drink, and lie."

"And steal."

"Let's go to Tawny's," Jesse decided.

Liz sat cross-legged on the couch across from Kristy, who half-lay in an armchair and ottoman, dispirited and quiet, cuddling a cup of tea. For half an hour Liz had tried to make small talk with her friend to no avail. The music throbbing from somewhere down the hall suggested Tawny was in her room, but Liz had yet to see her.

Delicately, Liz brought up the subject they'd both politely skirted. "What did the doctor say?"

Kristy smiled wanly. "It's not confirmed yet, but they think it could be . . ." She breathed deeply, sending a chill of premonition down Liz's spine. "Ovarian cancer."

"Oh, Kristy."

"If it's true, I'm having surgery as soon as the diagnosis comes through."

"Good, good." Liz felt cold inside.

"So, then I guess we just hope for the best."

Liz nodded, her throat constricted. *Ovarian cancer.* She couldn't think. If that diagnosis were proved correct, Kristy's life depended on what stage she was in. If caught early enough, people could survive, but if the cancer had progressed and spread . . .

"Everything's going to be fine," Liz murmured. She wanted to comfort Kristy but felt awkward and incapable. Behavioral advice she dispensed with ease, but the ability to say the right words and offer crucial help at life-altering moments was an art Liz had yet to learn. It seemed to be almost genetic; you either possessed it or you didn't. Now, feeling totally inadequate, she rose to her feet and gave her friend a self-conscious hug.

"I find out for sure tomorrow," Kristy said, "but they're certain enough to start scheduling surgery already."

Liz squeezed her hand. "Have you told Tawny?"

"Not yet. You'll be there for her, won't you? I don't want her to be scared."

"I'll be there."

"Go see her. She's been waiting for you."

Like a sleepwalker, Liz found her way down the hall to Tawny's room. Her mind ran in circles. Of course Kristy was going to be okay. These things didn't happen to people you really knew.

Of course they did. *But not to Kristy!*

"Tawny?" Liz called in a voice she barely recognized as her own.

"Hey!" Tawny answered above the noise. Abruptly, the song ended. "Come on in!"

Gently, Liz pushed open the door. Tawny was flopped across her bed, thumbing through an old, dog-eared copy of *People* that sported Kurt Cobain's picture on the front cover. Liz stared down at the picture, a pit in her stomach, her heart beating so hard it felt as if it might burst from her chest.

"A friend gave this to me," Tawny said, catching Liz's gaze and closing the magazine so Cobain's image was fixed in front of their eyes. "He changed music, y'know."

"I've never . . . listened to him."

"Really? You should. He's dead now, though," she added. "Killed himself."

"Yeah . . . I know."

Tawny glanced up, aptly named for the goldish color of her eyes. Maybe Guy had gotten it right after all, Liz thought. "Are you okay?" she asked, examining Liz carefully.

"Yeah."

"Wanna listen to *Nirvana: MTV Unplugged in New York*?" She lithely scrambled from the bed, all legs and arms, and flipped a button on a CD player. "Why do you think he did it?" she asked as the music swelled loudly. "I mean, he had everything."

"I don't know." Liz sank onto the edge of the bed and gazed at Cobain's picture. Unhappiness . . . illness . . . despair . . .

"He was only twenty-seven."

"Only the good die young," Liz murmured. She felt as if she were in a dream. Shaking herself, she added, "I didn't know you were a fan."

"I've just sorta gotten into his music now. I sure wish I'd known about him way back when he was alive." Tawny wrinkled her nose and stretched her arms over her head. Five foot five with shoulder-length light brown hair and a smile to light up billboards, she was currently immersed in fifteen-year-old melancholy, a large part of which was undoubtedly attributed to her concern over Kristy's chronic illness.

Don't let it be ovarian cancer.

"You want to go to a movie later?" Tawny asked.

"Sure. What do you want to see?"

"What do *you* want to see?"

"Something funny. A comedy."

"Me too."

Tawny smiled and Liz gazed at her with a mixture of love, awe, and worry. Tawny was a lot like Liz at the same age, and it was both a pride and a thrill to watch her develop. Of course at fifteen, Liz had been more paranoid than Tawny, worrying to death over the heft of her thighs, the start of a pimple, what her friends thought of her, if a boy who wasn't a geek would ever look at her . . . Tawny was tougher, maybe because she was more secure, maybe because her generation had forged her that way. Whatever the case, Liz's own maternal instincts were on overload around her and she jubilated over Tawny's accomplishments and sank to the bottom of despair with her over her woes.

They were only seventeen years apart as Liz had just turned thirty-two. Though Kristy was near Liz's age, she sometimes seemed ten years older, almost a generation in itself, and lately Tawny had tended to turn to Liz before her own mother. Luckily, Liz, senses on alert, hadn't perceived any friction from Kristy. Now, however, she suspected Kristy had been too self-absorbed in her health problems to notice.

"What do you think's wrong with Mom?" Tawny asked, her bare feet sliding into a pair of tan sandals. "I mean really."

"She said the doctors will let her know something definite tomorrow," Liz answered.

"Yeah, but what do you think?"

"Let's not speculate. Please?"

Something in Liz's tone must have penetrated because Tawny's eyes searched hers for several long moments. Then she hunched her shoulders. "I just want her to get better."

"We all do." Liz got to her feet, easing toward Tawny. But Tawny sidestepped her. That's the way it was these days. Sometimes Tawny wrapped herself in Liz's arms for comfort; sometimes she couldn't bear the intimacy. It was a tough age, even for one as self-possessed as Tawny.

"You ready for pizza?" Liz asked.

"Yeah! We've even got salad in a bag."

Tawny skittered out of the room and Liz followed. Kristy sat in the armchair, her attention apparently on a late-afternoon television talk show. Tawny had pulled two bags of salad from the refrigerator and eaten two pieces of pizza double-quick, while Liz ate one and Kristy passed, when the doorbell rang. Tawny and Liz exchanged glances. Tawny shrugged, so Liz went to answer the door.

"Brad!" she said in surprise.

"Hey," he responded uneasily, glancing to the young man beside him.

The newcomer sported a hairstyle identical to Brad's, but that's where the similarity ended. Intense blue eyes peered out between brownish-blond strands of hair. A haunting familiarity struck some chord inside Liz. She gazed at him in unabashed curiosity and knew in an instant this had to be Brad's friend Jesse.

"We saw your car," Brad admitted.

"You're here to talk to *me?*" Liz questioned. She

couldn't pull her gaze from Jesse, who regarded her right back with the same interest and intensity.

"Yeah, well, we were kinda thinking that we should talk to you. And then we saw your car at Tawny's. Hey . . ." Brad added, glancing over Liz's shoulder to where Tawny had appeared.

"Hey," Tawny answered, looking from Brad to Jesse and back again.

"So, Jesse and I cruised by," he finished by way of introduction.

Liz had lost Jesse's attention to Tawny, but at the mention of his name, it reverted back to Liz. His gaze was frankly assessing and she realized he'd probably heard an awful lot about Brad's new shrink. She'd heard a lot about him as well, but for some reason, even with all the tales Brad had told her about Jesse, she hadn't expected to feel like she knew him so well.

Not that his appearance was expected. If she'd thought about it at all, she would have thought he would look like Brad. Okay, the hair was the same length, but Brad's was darker and thicker. Jesse's was sun-streaked and straight and added to his overall look of insolence. He reminded her a little of a young Brad Pitt, and that reminded her of something else that she couldn't quite put her finger on at the moment.

"You want to come in?" Tawny invited, glancing back worriedly toward her mother.

Jesse and Brad hesitated. Liz realized they really *had* come to see her. She'd privately thought they'd used her as an excuse to see Tawny.

"Let's not bother Kristy," Liz suggested, easing herself out the door. "I really want to hear what you have to say, Brad, but let's take it outside."

The rain had rescinded to a wet mist. When Liz tried

to close the door, she found Tawny on her heels. Deciding to let the boys choose if they wanted Tawny as an audience, Liz glanced at the sky. Dark, overcast, slate-gray clouds hovered ominously close.

Tawny shivered.

"You okay?" Jesse asked her, in a husky voice that sent a strange chill down Liz's back.

Something familiar . . . and dangerous.

"Fine." Tawny nodded.

Brad and Jesse huddled beneath the eaves on one side; Liz and Tawny stood together about five feet away.

"Would you like to go to my office?" Liz asked uncomfortably.

Brad glanced to Jesse for direction. Jesse's gaze flicked Tawny's way. Tawny waited, a delicate frown forming on her brow, as if she couldn't understand what in the world was going on. Liz could. Jesse had it bad for Tawny but was doing his damnedest not to show it.

Then Jesse stared directly at Liz and said, "We'd like to show you something. Something in the woods."

That husky voice. "Something in the woods," she repeated.

"I tried to go to the police today, but that didn't work, so we thought we'd show it to you." His hands were in his pockets, then they were fidgeting, then they were shoved back in his pockets.

"And this something is what you were worried about this morning?" Liz asked Brad.

Brad nodded and added hurriedly, "But it's not our fault. We just found it. That's all."

"What is it?" Tawny whispered, picking up the vibes.

Jesse slid her another look, weighing his answer. Liz would have preferred Tawny not be a part of this, but apparently, the boys welcomed her involvement. At least they weren't telling her to get lost, like boys their age were wont to do if an invader entered their territory. No, the boys accepted Tawny as part of the package.

"It's a dead body," Jesse suddenly admitted, his matter-of-fact delivery snapping Liz's head around in surprise. In an oddly mature voice, he added, "Looks like somebody shot the guy full of holes and left him down by Hummingbird River. We thought you oughtta know . . ."

Chapter Four

It was the cold seeping into Liz's shoes that woke her from the nightmare before her. Numbness had crept into every pore, and the tingle in her toes seemed just a part of the same surreal feeling. But like the sleepwalker she was, she awoke to an even eerier sense of displacement: The body before her was someone she recognized.

She'd seen him on the street. Was that yesterday or the day before? He'd been hard to miss because of his height and bulk, and he'd been blathering on about something to a blond woman who couldn't have looked more bored if she'd tried. They were outside a local watering hole: the Elbow Room. As Liz drove by, she could see the way he gestured and grinned, and at some level she'd concluded he was schmoozing this woman for all he was worth.

And now he lay on his back amid wet leaves and sticks and dripping rain, eyes wide open, staring sightlessly up at her.

Jesse's tense breathing somewhere near her left ear penetrated her fogged brain. Her stomach revolted and she just managed to hold down her dinner. She half-turned, every movement in slow motion.

"We didn't do it," Brad babbled again, eyes riveted on the body. He was farther back, behind Jesse, looking scared and panicky. White-faced, Tawny stood pressed against the trunk of a dirty pine. Liz's gaze sought her frightened eyes, found them, and tried to silently offer comfort.

"It's okay," Liz said.

"He's dead?" Jesse's question came from his sixteen-year-old mind. He still hoped he hadn't accidentally ventured into the real, adult world.

"Yes."

"Somebody killed him."

Liz hesitated. "Yes."

A frigid drip of rain slid down her neck and she shivered. Huddled inside her coat, Tawny made a frightened sound. Before Liz could move, Jesse was beside Tawny, a tall, brooding presence who neither touched nor looked at her, but offered support nonetheless.

Liz stated dully, "We've got to go to the police."

"No!" Jesse and Brad cried in unison.

"I said we didn't do it!" Brad yelled. "They'll think we did it! They'll put us in jail!"

"They'll know you didn't do it," Liz tried to explain, but Brad was having none of it.

"How?" he demanded. "They'll take one look at us and say, 'Get those goddamn losers!' and we'll be dead!"

"You wouldn't bring me to the body," Liz pointed out.

"We might." This was from Jesse. "If we were really demented."

"You're not really demented." Liz stared at him openly, reading him so easily he would have been offended if he knew. She'd counseled dozens of kids just like him. Boys who thought their *cool* made them appear like

men. Boys whose insides were so soft and insecure, their
outsides were even colder and crustier, a defense mecha-
nism that only worked half the time. "We'll go to the station and I'll explain—"

"No," Jesse cut her off harshly. "I'm not going."

"Me neither," Brad responded.

They both turned toward Tawny, who shuddered and
hunched inside her anorak. Aching inside, Liz strode
toward her. She wanted to hug her but wasn't sure Tawny
would accept her comfort in front of the boys. She knew
for certain she should have fought harder to keep her from
witnessing this body.

Blame it on the fact that I don't know how to be a mother,
she berated herself. *Blame it on the fact that I didn't really
believe Jesse's story of a dead body.*

"Then I'll go by myself," she stated to the teenagers in
general. "I'll report it."

"I'll go with you," Tawny whispered, swallowing hard.

Male pride surfaced in a gust of inhaled fury. "Oh,
hell!" Jesse grated. "All right, I'll go talk to them, but I
want to go alone." Brad looked relieved until Jesse added,
"Me and Brad'll report it."

"I think I should be there," Liz argued.

"'Cause you're an adult?" Jesse shot back. "'Cause
you'll take care of the stupid teenagers?"

"Look, you guys came to me—"

"Well, that was a mistake, wasn't it?" Jesse shook his
long hair, then ran a hand through it. His mouth hardened
in stubborn rebellion. "Brad and I'll do it."

She was being outmanipulated by a master. The very
personality type she encountered every day and saw
through like glass. Her first instinct was to tell him where
to get off; her second, the one she'd learned to listen to for
her job, was to graciously give in.

Besides, she could follow up later.

"Fine," she uttered tersely.

As they single-filed their way out of the woods, thoughts like guilty footsteps hurried through her skull. Someone should stay with the body, but that meant leaving Tawny because Liz was the only legal driver.

The hell with that, Liz thought with sudden resentment that this was her problem. *Let somebody else be a hero.*

Hawk pushed a toothpick from one side of his mouth to the other with his tongue. Weak sunlight filtered through deep, gray clouds and raindrops prismed into vibrant purple, orange, and red, then glittered from the drooping leaves of an oak that stood at the end of Anita Brindamoor's ruler-straight concrete driveway. The series of gaping holes that flanked either side of the drive were silent testimony to the thievery she'd so adamantly insisted had happened. Someone had gone to a lot of trouble to remove the trees. A lot of trouble. It had all the earmarks of a prank and yet they'd taken the whole lot of them.

Yew trees? Hawk thought in disbelief.

A dog was barking somewhere behind the house. Hawk hadn't paid it a lot of attention, but now he walked along the edge of the concrete toward the noise, examining each rain-sogged hole as he passed by.

A barn stood just past the house. Hawk could see inside the upper door, which was cracked open about three feet. It was on line with the second story of the house, just about the same distance the detached garage had been from Joey's bedroom window.

Joey . . . Dark, trusting eyes, scared but full of confidence that Hawk and his buddies would save the day. He'd been so young.

A familiar dryness filled Hawk's throat and mouth. Psychologists had faded in and out of his life offering all kinds of advice. *It's been less than two years, Mr. Hart . . . It takes a lot of time to get over this kind of trauma . . . You can't shoulder all the blame . . . It's not your fault . . . not your fault . . .*

Glancing down, Hawk was annoyed to find his hands were faintly trembling. He turned them over and looked at both the backs and palms, eyeing them like the traitorous strangers they were. Once, they'd been incredibly steady. So steady he'd sighted down a rifle barrel without so much as a lift in heartbeat. Detached. Just doing his job. Squeezing the trigger had been part of his daily routine, and he'd done it without so much as turning a hair.

And Joey had died.

The shaking in his hands was now matched by tremors in his thighs. Hawk stopped short, counting the painful beats of his heart. No detachment now, by golly. Every attack of conscience created physical fallout.

Shit.

"You need to see a good shrink," Perry had told him . . . again.

"I'm okay," he'd growled automatically.

"You're about as far from okay as you can be, but don't listen to me. Just go on being dark and morose and stupid."

Well, of course he hadn't listened. Perry knew about as much about Hawk's problems as he did about fine art, and considering he still had that picture of dogs playing poker and smoking cigars in his man cave, Hawk wasn't inclined to listen.

But that didn't mean Hawk was unaware that something was wrong. Fussing and digging and generally chipping through layers of self-preservation to find his core just wasn't the route he was willing to take. Time, that healer of all healers, *was* what he needed. Lots and lots of time. And work. The kind of work a man could immerse himself in with the passion and dedication of a lover.

And that's why he was checking out Anita Brindamoor's missing yew trees.

The good lady herself came out onto the porch, eyeing him with distrust and displeasure. A spark of recognition filled her eyes, but even that didn't loosen the clench of mouth muscles too long used to tightening a death grip alongside her mouth.

"So?" she demanded, her spine as straight as an iron rod.

"I don't believe it was a prank." Hawk stood, feet apart, waiting for the blast he knew was coming.

He wasn't disappointed.

"Protecting your own, huh?" she charged. "I saw the resemblance, don't think I didn't! That hooligan of yours deserves some time behind bars, don't you know! Too soft, today's youth. Too much time smoking that marijuana."

She pronounced every syllable so it sounded like *mary-ju-anna*. Irked, Hawk reminded himself that a verbal skirmish with Mrs. Brindamoor was a complete waste of time.

"This theft is specific to your yew trees. It's systematic and complete. No vandalism. Nothing else taken. Just a collection of trees."

"I'm missing a gun, too."

Hawk's ears pricked up. "What kind of gun?"

"My husband's hunting rifle."

This sounded more in the realm Hawk was used to dealing with, but somehow it didn't jibe with the yew trees. "Show me where it was kept."

This proved to throw Anita Brindamoor off. She waffled and hesitated and wasted time, until Hawk, whose patience had never been his strong suit, finally suggested, "Could you have misplaced it?"

Twin spots of color heightened her lined cheeks. "I don't misplace anything!" she declared, finally admitting him into her house.

The gun closet was made of oak with a glass front, rather crudely but beautifully hand-hewn. Though he could see through the glass, she opened the door and pointedly showed him how empty it was, apart from a few leftover cartridges on an upper shelf.

"Was it only one gun?" Hawk asked.

"Yes."

"Mind if I look around the house?"

"Why?" she asked cagily.

"Shouldn't we make certain nothing else has been taken?"

"Everything else is here."

"So, the thief stole your yew trees and a rifle?"

"Yes."

"You noticed the rifle was missing at the same time the trees disappeared."

"I noticed the rifle was missing."

Hawk studied her. Her chin was inched up belligerently. He would have bet his life savings she'd just thrown the missing rifle in for good measure, hoping more suspicion would land on Jesse and Brad because gun theft was more in keeping with a youth crime. She wanted it to be the boys. She wanted to be right.

"Does anyone have a grudge against you? A disgruntled neighbor or . . . anyone?"

"What are you implying?" Her back drew even straighter, if that were possible.

"I'm interested in finding the perpetrator."

"I'm going to ask that someone else be assigned to this

case!" she practically yelled. "You're incompetent . . . and biased!"

"That's certainly your prerogative, ma'am."

His complacency sent her blood pressure skyward. "You're a disgrace!"

For the first time in weeks, Hawk felt like grinning. His mouth twitched, which only added to her fury. She looked about to explode, so Hawk merely nodded at her and headed outside, forestalling what looked to be a hurricane of rage. He was met by the barks of the still wildly frenetic dog, detained somewhere outside his vision.

Hawk stopped short. "The dog didn't hear the thieves?" he asked as Anita Brindamoor was at his heels.

"What?"

"Was the dog barking two nights ago, when this happened?"

She blinked several times. "I—um—I didn't hear Hugo."

"Does Hugo always announce strangers?"

She was silent, cagey, worried somehow that this bit of information might spoil her theory. A line drew between her brows. "He wasn't feeling well," she said. "Kind of sluggish and tired."

"Was that the day of the theft or the day after?"

"I'm not sure . . ."

Yes, she was. She was entirely sure. And he'd bet money it was the day after. Someone had drugged Hugo, and that someone had had to sneak around the back of the house and deliver the dog some kind of doctored tidbit—probably hamburger with a dose of doggy tranquilizer inside. Then they'd ripped out the trees while Hugo was sleeping, and Hugo had spent the following day recovering, sluggish and tired. Whoever had taken the trees had been, as Hawk had said, yew tree specific. No prank. Someone had wanted those trees.

And Anita Brindamoor was damn lucky whoever it was hadn't decided to just poison her beloved Hugo and be done with it.

But telling her his theories would only irritate her because she'd already made up her mind about Jesse and Brad. "I'll tell Perry Dortner you want someone else on the case," was his bland response.

"Now, don't go getting your nose all out of joint," she called after him.

Hawk left without another comment, though several formed inside his head.

It went against every responsible fiber of her being, but Liz's own cowardice helped her drop Jesse and Brad in front of the police station without going in herself. The reason was one Hawthorne Hart. Past lover. Handsome male. Father of her child. She just couldn't face him yet. And when she finally could and demanded to see their son, she wanted Hawthorne's full attention. This unfortunate incident wasn't the introduction for that. Yet she did feel like she was abandoning her duty here somewhat.

"I want a full accounting of this report," she warned Brad, pointing at him as he unfolded his long legs from the cramped back of the Miata.

He nodded. "We'll come see you right after."

Liz wasn't entirely certain her home was the proper venue for a psychologist and one of her young charges, but Tawny's bright, "I'll be there," cinched the deal before she could protest. Besides, she consoled herself, so far everything had been handled properly, hadn't it?

Oh yeah? And what about that body out by the river?

The image returned. His fixed eyes and bullet-riddled body were enough to give her the heebie-jeebies all right.

Who was he, and why had someone felt compelled to gun him down?

Tawny, hunched in the seat beside her, said suddenly, "Can I stay with you tonight, Aunt Liz?"

Liz smiled at the endearment. She wasn't Tawny's aunt and she couldn't recall the last time Tawny had addressed her as such. It was another measure of how upset she was. "Sure thing, sweetie. But what about your mom?"

"I'll call her."

Liz wondered if Kristy should really be left alone, even if she did agree to let her daughter spend the night with Liz. But Tawny's reasons were easy to read: She was as disturbed and scared as Liz. Maybe more so. Liz could easily remember what it was like to be a teenager and she ached inside at all the emotional hurdles awaiting the impressionable girl beside her.

"Maybe your mom'll come over, too," Liz suggested without much real hope.

"Maybe," Tawny murmured and they headed to Liz's cottage.

Brad and Jesse appeared at dinnertime and Liz shepherded them in from the rain and fed them leftover pizza—Tawny's choice—while she waited for them to tell their tale. Tawny had been allowed to stay over, but it was because Kristy just wanted to be alone. It bothered Liz vaguely, but because there was no changing Kristy's mind, she let things stand as they were.

"We told Chief Dortner all about it," Brad revealed, looking to Jesse for corroboration. Jesse sat in a chair not far from Tawny, seeming more attuned to her than anything Brad had to say.

"What did you tell him?" Liz asked, relieved to hear Hawthorne wasn't around or involved in this case yet.

"That we found this dead guy in the woods by Hummingbird River."

"Did he ask you to show him where?"

"Um, no."

"Why not?" This was sounding fishy.

"He said he'd go look later."

"As soon as another officer returned," Jesse chimed in unexpectedly, glancing at Brad. He turned his blue eyes on Liz. "I don't think he believed us."

"I knew it! I should have gone in with you."

"They'll go look together. It's okay." Jesse shrugged.

"I don't like the idea of that body spending the night outside when I know about it."

"You're not going back there!" Tawny cried in alarm.

Liz had no intention of returning to the scene of the crime, but she was nettled—mostly at herself—for letting cowardice rule common sense. She should have gone in the station with the boys and insisted this was a real matter deserving immediate attention. "No, I'm not going back there," she assured Tawny. With the oak limbs dancing in the wind, rain splattering in rushing waves, and the sky black as pitch, Liz had no desire to trek through dark woods to rediscover a dead body.

"Maybe I should call the station," she said, thinking aloud, "and explain that I was with you."

"No!" Jesse leaped lithely to his feet. "God, it pisses me off that no one listens to us. Like we're morons or something!"

Brad gazed anxiously at Liz, expecting her to chastise him for his language. Before she could decide what to do, Jesse was at the door. "I'm leaving," he told Brad, slamming through the door.

"Don't worry. They'll find the body," Brad told Liz, following in Jesse's wake.

"Will they?" She met his troubled gaze.

"We did tell them. They'll go tonight."

Liz's, "Do you need a ride?" was lost in the bang of the door and the snatching fingers of the wind. Tawny, who'd climbed to her feet, sidled over to Liz, and they both stood silently at the window, watching the blackness outside as if there were ghosts lingering in the shadows.

Picking up the receiver, Liz placed a call to the station and asked for the chief of police. She learned Chief Perry Dortner was out on a case at the moment, which relieved Liz of the burden of retelling the saga of the bullet-riddled body in the woods. She hung up with a few vague words about calling back later, then turned to Tawny.

"Let's make coffee," she suggested, and by mutual consent neither one of them brought up Brad, Jesse, or the dead body again.

Chapter Five

Late in the evening, with Tawny snuggled asleep on the couch beneath Liz's afghan, Liz stood by the fireplace and gazed into stacked oak chunks, ready for an unseasonably cool July night. Touching a flame to the wood, she inhaled deeply of the burning scent, cognizant of time passing and her own paralysis when it came to her life.

She was disturbed by the male body lying lost in the leaves. Disturbed in the normal sense that a person felt when suddenly faced with the enormity of death. But she was disturbed by her own reluctance as well. It was like a kind of death, this tick, tick, tick of daily life that seemed to lead endlessly onward with no tangible end. She'd taken the first step, however; she'd moved to Woodside. But her feet were in concrete when it came to proceeding further. She knew Hawthorne worked at the police station. She'd had the opportunity today to walk in and see him—and she'd purposely squandered it.

She was way too cautious now. Once, she'd been headstrong and spontaneous, rushing pell-mell toward life, but she'd been burned.

Still . . . if she had to do it over again . . .

Liz paced the room, easing tension from her shoulders every few steps, closing her eyes and inhaling the fragrant, smoky scent of burning wood as the fire took hold. Though it wasn't cold, she hugged herself closely. Memories did that to her. Memories of a time that had altered the course of her life.

She'd been seventeen and full of vinegar when she met Hawthorne Hart. He was older, how much she hadn't been quite certain at the time, but it hadn't mattered. She herself looked and acted twenty and considered it quite a coup that he believed that to be her age without question. It was only later, when she looked back with the hindsight of misery, that she realized he'd been so immersed in his own pain that he'd been incapable of understanding she might actually have tricked him.

She'd just broken up with her boyfriend and she was restless. Not that Rich hadn't been cool. He was coolness personified. And she'd been lucky to have him, especially with him being voted the hottest senior guy. In fact, all the girls had wanted Rich. He was a football star with college aspirations. Cute, too, with a lock of hair forever falling over his forehead and a slow grin that brought girls to their knees.

Liz was the envy of all her friends and she'd milked it for all it was worth. It was a great self-esteem builder, especially because she'd been so paranoid and knock-kneed as a freshman. She would look in the mirror, smile at her reflection, and think, *I've got Rich. He's mine. All mine . . .*

There was only one problem: Rich was an intellectual zero. That didn't actually bother Liz that much. She wasn't looking for meaningful philosophical discussions over a greasy basket of fries. But sometimes she looked at his twenty-two-inch neck and wondered if having Rich was really all it was cracked up to be.

Still, it was a life. A life better than what waited for her at home. There she was treated in the same way the Havers' expensive champion-pedigreed golden retriever was: all for show and good manners. Any love doled out was earned by way of achievements: straight As; part of the varsity volleyball team; homecoming princess, etc. As Liz matured from a gawky freshman to a young lady, she was fairly adept at achieving these honors. Unfortunately, she began believing a bit of her own press, and it didn't do a damn thing for the fulfillment she so sorely longed for: unconditional love. Her parents just weren't great at providing for that need, something she understood and accepted now but had ached over during her teen years.

So, it was prom time. Just weeks before her eighteenth birthday. Rich had asked and Liz had dutifully accepted, but as the date neared, she was itching to be free. Every other girl might want Rich, but his fumbling attempts at "turning her on" had worn thin, and Liz, feeling unsettled and claustrophobic, spent most of that special day simply watching the hours pass with lukewarm enthusiasm.

Prom itself was as she'd expected. She would dance with Rich for all the slow songs and be subjected to hot breath and sweaty palms, then she would wait out the fast songs while her friends with less "cool" dates, but who obviously possessed more rhythm, danced around to cheerful laughter and shouts of glee. Rich couldn't bear to unbend for the festivities, so when it was time to go home, Liz was definitely ready to leave.

One problem: Rich wanted to park. By this time, Liz had come to the conclusion that "making out" was basically boring. At sixteen she'd had her share of kisses and fumbling sexual moves and even a moment or two when she'd felt an actual thrill. But the thrills came from the danger of being caught by a parent, and the truth was Liz really couldn't stand being manhandled at all.

So while Rich made his obligatory moves, a scary thought circled Liz's agile brain. Was it—could it be—oh, God, was she *frigid*?

No way. Not a chance. Uh-uh. She just wasn't a slut, that was all, and so she didn't really like all the bumping and grinding Rich seemed to pant over.

"C'mere, baby. C'mon, Lizzie. Please," he breathed in her ear, fingers gathering up the satiny folds of her royal blue dress and attempting to drag it up her thighs. The two of them were crushed into one bucket seat of his parents' Volvo sedan. Rich had managed to yank the lever of the seat release and Liz had been flung backward to where she could now count the tiny holes on the sedan's ceiling. Above her, Rich's body bounced and thumped and he started to make moaning noises even before he got his zipper down.

Liz began to feel murderously stubborn. She set her jaw, but Rich, not picking up on the signals, clasped her hand and drew it to the swell at his crotch, moving it up and down in rhythm to his increasing moans. She opened her mouth to protest and he thrust his tongue inside. Strangled, she was momentarily surprised into paralysis. For all his previous blundering, he hadn't been quite this determined, and it took her breath away. That, and his slimy tongue.

A second later he drew back, threw open the zipper, plunged her hand inside his pants, and came in hot spurts inside her palm, gasping, "Oh, oh, ohhh!"

Liz felt complete and utter revulsion. She thought about the little gift he'd left in her hand as Rich collapsed on her, and she had to fight the urge to wipe it on the back of his rented tux.

He was polite enough to hand her a handkerchief. Thank God for small favors. On the way home, he caressed her knee through the folds of her dress while Liz smoldered and despaired at the same time. Was this it? The big mystery of sex? When it came time for a good-bye kiss, she murmured something about it being late and fled up the steps to her house.

The following week at school, Rich was a rooster all fluffed up. On Thursday at lunch Liz finally heard the news. He'd told everyone they'd done "it." He'd gotten the prude to finally give in. Now, other guys eyed her with lust. God, they were disgusting. She had half a mind to announce the truth of the evening over the intercom, but chose instead to freeze anyone who mentioned Rich with a cold glare.

Rich, of course, was too dense to realize what he'd done. He not only believed he and Liz were still a couple, but was apparently convinced that because he'd prematurely announced their sexual relations they were now ready to do "it" without so much as a "please" anymore. On the porch at her parents' house the following Friday night, Liz hauled off and slapped his downy cheek with a wallop that brought hurt and disbelief to his beautiful brown eyes.

"What?" he demanded. "What?"

"Get away from me," she growled. "I don't want to touch you."

His jaw dropped. "Well, you—you sure wanted to the other night!"

Moron. Loser. Jackass. Liz wanted to weep aloud. High school boys! He was older than she was, yet she was eons wiser.

By Monday morning she was not only a slut, she was a bitch, too. *Well, la-di-da. Hurt me some more.* But it did give her pause when Rich started squiring around Sylvie Steerman, whose popularity was even more pronounced than Liz's.

There was no sympathy at home. All Mom and Dad could think about were SAT scores for their only child, and whether Liz should pick that private college or a prestigious out-of-state university. No Washington state school would be good enough for their cherished star, so it wasn't even offered as a choice.

Liz waded through this minor hell with rebellion growing like a hot beast inside her breast. She wanted to rage and scream, though she couldn't pinpoint exactly why. Unhappy to the point of depression, she walked home from school one afternoon rather than catching a ride with her girlfriends and kept right on walking until she'd reached the far side of town where the Elbow Room Tavern now stood, only then it had been a fairly quaint, quasi-respectable roadside stopover called the Candlewick Inn.

It was a warm spring night with flowers beginning to toss their heads in a rather brisk breeze. Azaleas, left to grow scraggly and wild, threw out brilliant clusters of rose red and lavender flowers. Liz stopped on the stone walk that led from the gravel parking lot to the front door of the Candlewick and fate dropped Hawthorne Hart in her path.

He was the most gorgeous thing she'd ever seen, or so she consoled herself later. Tall, dark, and handsome, with maturity eking out of every pore, he gazed at her through gray-blue eyes clouded with pain. But Liz didn't see that. What she saw was a serious, attractive hunk of male flesh. A hunk, moreover, who seemed light-years removed from the fumbling boys of Woodside High. He was a movie star, a hero, a mythological god. He was everything she'd ever wanted, and he was right in front of her.

"Are you—staying here?" Liz asked breathlessly as he paused on the walkway that wound to the front door.

He squinted toward the sky, surveying the area before glancing at the green-trimmed panes of the Candlewick's front windows. "They've got rooms?"

"A couple, I think. Attic lofts or something."

"No, I just drink here."

Had she been older and savvier, she would have realized he was dead drunk in the middle of the day and probably left him alone. But maybe not. He was just too perfect.

"I live over there," he added, sweeping one arm toward the section of land that dipped toward Hummingbird River.

"You live here? In Woodside?" Liz could scarcely believe her luck.

"I've lived here a long time," he said with a trace of irony Liz couldn't quite understand.

"What do you do?"

He half-closed his eyes, a small smile touching his lips. "I—don't do much—anymore. What do you do?"

She would rather burn in boiling oil than admit she was a high school student. "I teach," she improvised.

"Really?"

Liz nodded. "Preschool kids. I have to finish some courses before I'm a full-fledged teacher. I'm, umm, thinking of going back to school at U-Dub," she added for good measure, referring to the University of Washington in Seattle.

"So, you're not long for this town either?"

"I guess not."

"Want a drink? I'm buying."

Liz finally connected that her newfound friend might have already been tipping the bottle, but rebellion, recklessness, and physical attraction stifled the little warning voice inside her head. "Sure."

She followed him inside the Candlewick, which was decorated to resemble a Victorian sitting room with cabbage roses on the carpet and dark stained wood beams and paneling. The pub took up most of the first floor, the rooms accessed by a narrow stairway winding behind a central desk that was a half bar itself. Liz had never been inside, and though there was a lot to recommend the Candlewick, somehow it fell just short of the mark. It strove for a country inn, bed-and-breakfast feel, but she got the impression this was just a lot of eyewash to cover up the regulars, who got sotted every afternoon rather than go home to their miserable lives. The men seated at the bar looked as if their elbows had permanently adhered to the marred surface, and they eyed her with speculation as she followed Hawthorne to a secluded table tucked under the slant of the stairs.

"My friends call me Hawk," he told her when she asked him his name.

"I'm Liz."

"Well, Liz, what would you like to drink?"

She shrugged and smiled. "Whatever you're having."

His gray-blue eyes surveyed her carefully. She loved looking into them, enthralled by his physical appearance in a way she'd never known before. His face held character. He was still too young for lines, but his mouth seemed hard, almost cruel, although that small smile had started a quiver somewhere in her heart that was impossible to quell. His lashes were way too long and his nose was bent a bit, broken perhaps at one time. But the whole picture came together in a form that whispered *Adonis* to Liz.

She was in love before the barmaid brought their scotch on the rocks.

Liz had tasted champagne a few times. She'd even had half a bottle of beer with some friends one night before she'd decided it was the most disgusting beverage on the planet. But hard liquor was new to her, and she took her first sip with trepidation.

But Hawk never gave up his intense scrutiny of her face, so she fought to act naturally, and either she succeeded or failed miserably. In any case that soft smile returned as if he'd discovered something about her that he found sweet and distracting.

They talked about nothing. She was afraid to give away her true age and Hawk was lost in some self-absorption and alcohol numbness that kept him from revealing anything about himself. There were huge gaps in their conversation. Huge gaps where they just eyed each other with the silent interest of chemical attraction.

The afternoon wore on. The crowd increased. Liz began to worry someone might recognize her, but the men and women who showed up in twos and fours were younger than her parents and, from the looks of it, not nearly as well-connected and snobbish.

"I could get a room," he said.

The idea was more tempting than Liz would have credited. A week ago, she was worrying she was frigid; now she could feel the heat of desire like a living thing within her.

She couldn't answer him. She was afraid she would say yes; even more afraid she'd say no. Life was so full of small choices with huge consequences. Liz pressed her trembling fingers to the smooth facets of the old-fashioned glass and begged her heart to stop running rampant.

"I studied law enforcement," he said suddenly. "It seemed like a good idea."

"Wasn't it?"

"There are times when nothing matters at all. When every move you make only takes up energy. There's no productivity. But you think you're making a difference until *poof*." He snapped his fingers. "It's all bullshit."

Liz gazed at him with more adult eyes. "What happened to you?"

"I lost the only thing on this earth of any value."

"What was it?"

He shook his head. "Forget it. It's old news."

"No, what was it?"

For an answer his hand suddenly darted across the table, grabbing her forearm. Startled, Liz half-gasped, then gazed, mesmerized, at the fingers massaging her skin in a small circle. "I don't want to think anymore. You're beautiful, and I—want something beautiful."

His touch was hard and insistent, and the spreading warmth within her was enough to make her head spin. Trying to hang on to the rags of her sanity, Liz made a mewing sound of protest. Either Hawk read her wrong or didn't care, but either way his next move was bold and unnerving and devastating. He simply pulled her closer to him, leaned across the table, and kissed her for all he was worth with a scotch-scented mouth and a warm, persuasive tongue.

Devastation. Seduction. Complete destruction of her defenses.

She waited like a rag doll in the chair, limp and slightly inebriated, while Hawk got them an upstairs room. Liz sat in stupefaction, too full of unnamed wants and desires herself to recognize the danger of such self-destructive action.

And she wanted to know. *Know.* Other girls did it. With

jerk-off boys whom they thought were God's gift. They raved about it. What it was like to be in love. To be loved. To be made love to.

"I knew he loved me," one of the bolder girls at Woodside had moaned one afternoon in the girls' bathroom. She was sucking on a cigarette. "It just felt sooo goood!"

At the time, Liz had been highly skeptical that there was any hope she'd ever have an interest in sex herself, but that day, with the clock gently ticking and the slant of afternoon shadows touching the corners of the carpet, she determined she wanted to find out.

The upstairs room was tucked beneath the eaves, a faux Tudor with pink-flowered wallpaper and mahogany-stained slats. A double bed, wedged under the window and between the gabled roofline, was the only piece of furniture besides a rather beat-up dresser sporting a lace doily and a bowl and pitcher, as if the room's tenants might actually use these to wash up instead of the bathroom sink down the hall.

Liz took it in in a glance. Her heart beat a strange tattoo and her palms were moist with sweat. She was in over her head, but her head was spinning slightly anyway, a nice easing to an overly frustrated teenage mind. Rocking on her feet, she waited for a rush of romantic magic to decide her: should she stay or should she go?

Her "date" seemed to be having second thoughts, too. He stood to one side, brow furrowed, his gaze alternating between the bed and the window, where a distant glimmer of the green waters of Hummingbird River could be caught between the dense firs.

Silence spread through the room like a fog, enveloping them both. She felt choked by it. Shooting a nervous glance his way, she was disarmed to see his eyes were closed, the slant of his mouth full of unnamed misery. As if programmed from something beyond, Liz crossed the room and touched her fingertip to the curve of his lips. He swallowed and pulled her near, his forehead pressed to hers for a shining moment before he buried his face in the hollow of her neck, holding her like a drowning man, crushing her to him like he never wanted to let go.

It tore through her defenses like a hot knife through butter. Though she didn't understand his pain, she felt its searing emotion as if it traveled through his skin to hers. Comfort. That's what he needed. She wound her arms around his neck and kissed the side of his throat, smelling a tangy male scent that was like an aphrodisiac.

His first kiss was at the curve of her jawline. Liz's eyes fluttered closed. His second was at the corner of her mouth. His third crushed against her lips, full of tormented need. It was beautiful. Perfect. Too sweetly seductive to even think of resisting. Liz went limp, and Hawk's body gently pressed her down against the quilted coverlet on the brass bed.

Bedsprings protested, but it was music. A soft accompaniment to his ragged breaths and her trembling gasps. His body seemed huge as it joined her on the bed, and for a moment Liz felt true panic. But kisses rained upon her face, and the shuddering of his manly frame made her feel strong and womanly. She wanted to make love to him. Curiosity ran through her veins and desire awakened, hot and full of mystery. The heat of him was like a warm blanket. She wanted to wrap herself around him and shut out the world.

No words were spoken. His mouth found hers again, and when her lips parted he thrust his tongue between them.

She half-expected revulsion again. Her last experience with French kissing had been less than successful. But Hawk was not Rich, and after an initial exploration, he returned to soft, tender kisses accompanied by equally soft and tender touches, and Liz found herself dizzily waiting to feel his tongue's sweet invasion once more.

She didn't wait long. Sensing her growing interest and desire, he tasted her lips with his tongue until they parted willingly, eagerly. Then his tongue slipped inside to dance gently with her own. He lay beside her, then upon her, still fully clothed, but there was no question of his own desire as she felt the hard pressure of his manhood pushed against her flesh.

She'd never been quite this intimate. Rich's rumblings in the car had seemed annoying and comical, but now she felt the hot beat of her own desire so intently that all she could think about was the rubbing of his thighs against hers, his chest crushing her breasts, his tongue melting with hers.

"You're so good," he muttered, and she wasn't quite sure what he meant by that because she felt bad to the extreme.

Her clothes disappeared as if by some magical spell. Later, she couldn't honestly remember removing them or having them removed. She could, however, recall the soft jingle of his belt buckle, the gentle thud of it against the carpet as it slid off the bed, dragging his trousers with it. His own nudity intrigued her. Through desire-drugged, hooded eyes, she caught glimpses of his muscled back and hard buttocks. His tan line was blurred by the passing winter months but was still visible, and she delicately ran a finger across, stopping as he shivered when her touch reached the small of his back.

"I've missed you," he groaned, almost on a cry, and Liz briefly surfaced. Missed her? *Her?* He was thinking of someone else.

Before she could protest—before she could *move*—he

thrust himself inside her, not all the way but enough for Liz to feel some pain. Ripples of fear ran through her like a shock wave. Her hands gripped into fists. But his second thrust broke through the barrier of her virginity, and when she bucked backward and bit off a cry of pain, he went completely still.

"Laura?" he whispered in agony.

Liz's head whirled. She felt herself slipping, slipping, slipping into an endless, spinning void of blackness. It could have been moments; it felt like an eternity. Maybe it was.

But then she didn't have time to dwell on her misery because he began thrusting inside her, pushing forward in a rhythm as old as time. Pain lessened and Liz's body responded with a will of its own. She moved with him, riding the sensation, gasping her own pleasure and reveling in the pure joy of sexual love. It was wonderful. Fabulous. Better than anything she could imagine, and as Hawk climaxed with a sexy low moan, Liz teetered on the brink of her own intense pleasure, falling over the edge into a cataclysmic sensation that had her gasping and clutching him close.

When she opened her eyes again he was collapsed against her, sunk into a comalike slumber, the scent of musky scotch enveloping both of them.

And she remembered he'd called her Laura.

In those few seconds Liz grew up. She leapfrogged into an adulthood she'd only vaguely grasped, but because part of her was still a child, she made the only decision she could: she would make him hers. This Laura person was obviously out of the picture, at least temporarily, and though he was mourning the loss, he'd chosen Liz as the woman to help him put his life back together.

Looking back now, she could scarcely credit her warped

thinking, but at the time it had seemed utterly sane, utterly rational, brilliant.

She stroked his hair, felt his warm breath fanning her breasts, sensed the deep beating of his heart, and thought with utterly ridiculous, seventeen-year-old logic, *I love him!*

For the next two weeks, she came back again and again to the Candlewick Inn to meet with this slightly bemused hunk of a man who spent too much time seduced by alcohol and too little protesting his seduction by Liz. She was a Jezebel, a Siren, a man-eating female with one sole purpose: to have Hawthorne Hart if it were her last mission on earth.

And then, on her eighteenth birthday, she missed her period.

A day late. Two days late. Disaster. Fate. A touch of God's hands.

With a heart beating fast and furious, she ran home from school and to the Candlewick Inn. The desk manager gazed at her beaming face with a mixture of regret and sly knowingness. "Mr. Hart isn't here," he said. "Sorry."

"He's not?"

Her worried face only increased the man's ambivalence. He couldn't decide whether to be a friend or revel in the scandal.

"You know his address, miss? He lives here in town somewhere. Used to be a cop, you know."

I studied law enforcement . . . His words came back, and she realized at some level she'd thought of him as a student. Just a few years older than herself.

"Could you give me his address?"

Reluctantly, clearly torn, the manager eventually wrote it down. Liz stared at it long and hard, realizing Hawthorne lived in a moderately nice development. She'd forgotten Woodside was his home. The last two weeks there'd been only the Candlewick. If she thought about it at all, she pictured him living in some faraway and dreamlike place. A castle for her white knight. A lodge above a sparkling stream that glimmered like silver. A cozy cabin with smoke curling from a rock fireplace and blue chintz curtains in the windows. A houseboat rocking gently against barnacle-encrusted pilings with a cat curled on the upper deck.

"You go on now," the manager told her in a gentler voice. "You're young and pretty. He's chosen drink as his mistress and you're a distant second, honey."

She stumbled outside. An unusual spring heat had descended, dancing before her eyes, wilting the nodding azaleas, burning through her skin and scalding her soul. No, no, no! It wasn't true.

She could walk there. Everything in Woodside was within walking distance if you had the motivation.

Twenty-five minutes later she stood in front of Hawthorne Hart's house. It was a tract home. Natural gray cedar with a navy blue front door. With wide-eyed horror, she read the names painted on the mailbox in a woman's artistic scroll. Hawk and Laura Hart.

Laura!

Her name had fallen from his lips when he'd taken Liz's virginity. Her last name was the same as his. They were married. He had a *wife*!

With the instinct of a lemming charging to its death, she stumbled up the weed-choked walk, dimly noting the neglect and associating it with *her*, this devil woman who'd come between her and Hawk. She hated her, for she was a phantom witch who'd suddenly reappeared in a puff of evil smoke.

Never once did Liz consider that she, Liz, was the "other woman." Funny how the mind can rationalize anything.

Instead, she pressed a trembling finger against the bell and waited for Hawk, or Laura, to appear, and when neither did she camped out on the doorstep, placed her forehead on her bent knees, and bawled her eyes out in rage and anguish.

A day later she lay in bed at home, lost in her own world of misery. He was married. The word rang through her head like a death knell. *Married, married, married!*

She devised scenarios in her head. This Laura was a hag. An ugly, dried-up crone of at least thirty-five. Maybe forty. She made his life such hell that he drank his afternoons away. He needed someone to rescue him. Someone like her.

But all her scenarios couldn't lift the weight from her heart, and as the week trudged by, Liz came to the very unpalatable conclusion that she'd been a mere dalliance to one Hawthorne Hart.

Bastard. *Fucking* bastard.

But Liz couldn't quite forget her own part in that attic bedroom. Covering her face in her hands, she wept until her face was red and swollen, then wept some more.

With dead eyes, she examined her reflection in the mirror, feeding on self-hate. Her mother, ever acute, watched the signs of depression and apathy in her daughter and threw open Liz's bedroom door one afternoon and announced in her imperious way, "You're pregnant, aren't you? God, I knew it! Well, don't worry, I've already made an appointment to take care of it."

So Liz saw a doctor in nearby Willoughby, a sleepy

hamlet compared to bustling Woodside but equipped with one very wizened Dr. Raines, whose lined face and doleful expression said he'd seen it all and then some. He recommended a young doctor in Seattle who ran a women's clinic. Liz was whisked into a modern office building sporting metal chairs with ice-blue seats and efficient young female personnel with plastic smiles.

The abortion would be quick, relatively painless, relatively cheap, and performed with perfect discretion. The date was scheduled two days before Liz's graduation from the faux-brick walls of Woodside High.

One tiny glitch. It turned out one of the plastic smiles that worked at the clinic was originally from Woodside, and she'd recognized Liz's mother as "someone to know" in town. Against all rules, she mentioned the source of Mrs. Havers's embarrassment to her own husband, who was also a Woodside High grad. Word trickled through town and hit a junior member of the police department and a personal friend of Detective Hawthorne Hart's, who was currently on leave.

This friend, in turn, just happened to mention Mrs. Havers's daughter's problem one afternoon while he and Hawk were having a beer together. He brought the subject up as a means to point out that other people besides Hawk had problems, too. That fate was unkind sometimes, and there was nothing really to do but pick up the pieces and move on.

He started an avalanche.

Hawthorne Hart awoke from his alcohol-induced sleep and threw the Havers's home into complete turmoil. He wanted his child. He didn't give a damn about Liz or the Haverses' position in town or anything else. If Liz had an abortion he would make her life a living hell. He would create a scandal the likes of which Woodside had never seen. He wanted the baby, and if it took legal action on his part, or public humiliation of the Haverses, or whatever, he *would* have his child.

He scared Liz. She shook from head to toe as the handsome man of her dreams stood, legs apart, head thrust forward a bit, glaring down at both Liz's mother and father, who sat side by side, chins up, hoping to bluff. But no one could bluff Hawk.

Liz stared openmouthed at a stranger—an intimate stranger—who would have his way come hell or high water.

Of the two, it looked like hell was fast approaching.

Liz's parents held hands and tried to present a united front. Hawk's condemning gaze moved from them to Liz who cowered a bit. Her parents flicked her a look. More condemnation. And fury that she'd put them in such a delicate situation.

Hope raced through Liz's heart. He wanted their child. He *did* care! She hadn't wanted the abortion either, but just hadn't been able to stop the freight train of her parents' will. She threw him a tremulous smile, but his eyes were cold as the North Sea.

"The baby's yours," Liz's father suddenly declared to Hawk as he rose from his chair with dignity. "Liz will have it and give it up."

Her mother gaped in horror, a vista of grandmotherhood opening up before her stricken eyes. A moment later she clamped her jaw shut, then decreed to Liz, "You will go to Aunt Emily's."

And so she did. Graduation was a fog, the summer a quiet, dullish memory in San Francisco sharing an apartment with Aunt Emily, whose nose was clearly out of joint at this forced babysitting of her niece. Hawk was gone and all hope had departed with him.

Liz's little boy was born in the dead of winter. She got one glance and he was whisked away forever. By that time, she felt nothing. No pain, no relief, no nothing. She started college in the spring term and threw herself into school like never before. No friends, no fun apart from her relationship with Kristy Smith, whose own love affair with Guy Fielding and subsequent marriage, was Liz's only connection to romance, and Woodside, at all.

Now, thinking back, Liz alternately cringed at and sympathized with her naïve, ego-involved younger self. She'd been so young, so inexperienced, and so short-sighted. However, she believed now that her youthful mistakes were what kept her from being too judgmental as an adult. When she recalled how virulently she'd hated Laura Hart, it reminded her to tread carefully when dealing with teen emotions. What others considered puppy love Liz knew from personal experience could be as deep, passionate, and destructive as any mature emotion. At seventeen, Liz had been so immersed in her own world, she hadn't realized that Hawk's melancholia was because of the death of his wife. She'd only looked at one side—her side. She'd wanted him so much she'd blocked out reality.

In the end, though, Hawthorne Hart had done her a giant favor: he'd saved their child. Liz suspected she would never marry, never have another baby. The son she shared with Hawk was all she had.

Her son. Now sixteen years old . . .

"Tomorrow," she whispered aloud. She would face Hawk tomorrow.

Staring at the glowing red embers of the fire, she shook from head to toe. The cold breath of reality had blown into her soul, and there was no amount of self-delusion that could protect her from its wintry power. And even that couldn't rival the freeze that would come when she met up with Hawk again.

Any way you cut it, Liz was looking at the next Ice Age.

Chapter Six

Barney Turgate's plastic-shrouded body lay on a stretcher beside a small army of emergency vehicles. A carnival of red and white flashing lights illuminated the rain-sloshed grass roadway and surrounding area. Barney'd had to be carried out of the woods about a quarter of a mile by two muscle-bound paramedics before his remains reached the roadway. Now, as the paramedics hefted the stretcher into the van, they both panted as if they'd sprinted a lap around the track in record time.

"Hey, Chief," a young officer said as he spat onto the ground. "What do you think?"

Perry wrinkled his nose, and his normally good-natured face pulled into a scowl. He glanced at Hawk, who'd arrived on the scene late, having learned of the corpse after his trek to Anita Brindamoor's.

"I think Barney Turgate took at least four bullets," Perry replied.

"You know the victim?" Hawk asked in surprise.

"So do you, probably, once you get a good look at him. Barney hung around the Elbow Room and any other watering hole that tickled his fancy. He's just—a Woodside tradition, if you know what I mean."

"Nobody hated him," the young officer said. His name was Bill Smith, but everyone called him B. S. for reasons that were painfully obvious as one got to know him.

Rain ran in a small stream off the bill of Perry's hat. "Doubt it's a crime of passion. Barn just didn't stir up those kinds of feelings." Perry snorted in regret. "Though he had a string of old girlfriends, or at least acted like he did."

Perry and B. S. laughed softly, more in tribute than condemnation.

"Maybe he just stepped into something he shouldn't have," Hawk guessed.

"He did that all the time," Perry said with a shrug. "Never got him killed before."

Hawthorne threw a glance at the body. "Somebody meant business."

They stood, a silent trio, as the van doors slammed and vehicles began pulling out.

"Meet me at the station; there's something I want to talk about," Perry said, climbing into his car. B. S. joined him in the passenger side.

"Sure," Hawk responded, mystified.

Thirty minutes later, Hawthorne slouched into the chair opposite Perry's desk, stretching out the kinks in his back. Perry seemed unusually thoughtful, he noted, so he waited with a certain amount of anticipation for his boss to deliver the news, whatever it was.

But Perry was taking his own sweet time: fiddling with a paper clip, rummaging for a toothpick through each and every desk drawer, shuffling and reshuffling the papers on his desk, which Hawthorne knew for a certainty he never looked at anyway.

"Java?" Perry asked him. "Coffeepot's on the fritz, but I could send B. S. to the Spot."

"No, thanks."

"So how's our friend Mrs. Brindamoor?"

Hawk related what he knew of the yew theft, the missing gun, and his suspicion that Hugo, the dog, had been drugged. Surprisingly, this didn't seem to interest Perry in the least.

"That gun's been missing for years. I think her husband sold it before he died, but she won't believe it," Hawk finished.

"That's a lady who doesn't like hearing she's wrong."

"Amen. She's likely to call and ask for someone else. She practically accused me of protecting my son."

Perry snorted, but his mind was elsewhere. "Stolen trees don't make that pressing of a case, do they? Especially when you consider that Barney Turgate's a corpse now."

"So, what did you want to talk to me about?" Hawk asked, growing impatient.

"You know how I told you an anonymous caller tipped us off to Turgate's body? Well, that was a bit of a lie. Actually, Jesse and his friend, Brad Barlow, stumbled over the corpse."

"What?"

"Apparently, they were out in the woods and there he was. They came in and reported it to me."

So, that's what Jesse's earlier visit had been about. The connection sizzled in Hawk's brain, and his first reaction was fury. Why couldn't Jesse have just spit it out? What blockage was there that prevented him from talking to his own father about something so shocking as a dead body?

"I figured you'd be upset, so I thought we'd get the work done first, then I'd tell you."

"You're a pal."

Perry shrugged. "Always have been."

Hawthorne threw him an ironic glance. Perry had been a junior officer for the Woodside Police Department at the same time Hawthorne was. They'd fraternized a bit, though Hawk's star had risen faster and higher—until Laura's death. He'd taken a leave of absence then; more like a drunken binge. Perry had then continued on at Woodside while Hawk had stumbled into a sordid little drunken affair that had miraculously produced Jesse.

Now, while Perry gazed at him with an expression of empathy, Hawthorne reflected on the events that had led to his son's birth. Rarely did he think back on it; too much emotional garbage. Jesse's birth, about a year after Laura's death, would have caused a certain amount of speculation, but Hawthorne had left Woodside for good—or so he'd believed at the time—as soon as he learned he'd impregnated a girl on the verge of high school graduation. Worse, she'd only been seventeen and from a wealthy Woodside family. Worse yet, he barely knew her name because their affair was a dim, dim memory even while it took place because he'd been wallowing in self-pity and grief.

It was Perry, unwittingly, who'd given him the information about young Elizabeth Havers's pregnancy. Whether he knew now that Hawk was the father, Hawk very much doubted. Nobody paid much attention to dates, or if they did, they didn't ask, and when Hawk returned to Woodside with his sixteen-year-old son, Perry assumed Jesse was Laura's son. He either wasn't doing the math or he just didn't think about it—probably the latter. As well as he'd known Hawk in those days, Hawk could have had an infant son. What the hell. Who cared anyway?

Hawk was just damn lucky he'd stopped Liz from getting an abortion, which had been the family's plan to save face. In those days, the Haverses were used to getting what they wanted.

The intervening years may not have been so kind, however, as he understood them; family's financial resources had significantly dwindled and old man Havers and his missus had moved to warmer climes. Arizona, maybe. Or New Mexico. Hell, they might even be dead. As grandparents, they'd shown zero interest in their bastard grandson, and for that Hawk was glad. Liz, too, was a phantom, just the way he wanted it. He'd heard once that she'd gone on to school—something in the medical profession. Probably was a famous heart surgeon now, or something. If she ever came back, she'd undoubtedly think he'd screwed up as a parent big-time.

If she ever came back . . .

A frisson of premonition slid down his back. Hawk shook it off. Ridiculous.

Perry heaved a sigh. "I don't think there's any chance either of those boys knows anything about the murder. They seemed spooked enough just telling about it."

"I'll talk to Jesse," Hawk muttered, lost in his own private thoughts.

"Use a little tact, will ya?" Perry suggested.

"I'm the model of tact."

A horsey snort was Chief Perry Dortner's answer to that.

Tomorrow came a little too fast for Liz. She awakened with a start, her neck squinched painfully. With a groan, she realized she'd fallen asleep in the chair next to the sofa where Tawny was blissfully sawing logs. Liz unfolded her legs and massaged the side of her neck. Squinting an eye at the clock, she stumbled down the hall to the bathroom.

Twenty minutes later, after a bracing shower and

popping some ibuprofen for the ache in her neck, Liz emerged feeling almost human. Her ubiquitous jeans and a white, ribbed, sleeveless shirt from Old Navy were today's uniform.

Rubbing steam from the mirror in the bathroom, she gazed at her solemn expression, recognized the anxiety in her eyes, and was pissed. She wanted courage and she wanted it now. Sixteen years was too long to wait. It was high time she faced Hawthorne Hart. High time she stepped into that long-awaited role of motherhood.

Motherhood. She'd spent so few moments with her child that it felt like someone else's dream. Her mental picture of her son was dim: all pink skin and wiggling limbs and a hoarse cry, the memory of which could still cause her skin to break out in gooseflesh.

Brushing her teeth with more fervor than finesse, she ran the scene in the hospital delivery room over in her head—like she had a billion times before. She'd refused anesthesia of any kind, but the body had a way of doping itself. Everything seemed hazy and surreal, and when they'd pulled her son from her and whisked him away, she couldn't summon a squeak of protest. The hospital staff was adept at keeping him hidden, too. All she remembered were green surgical robes, a tiny flash of rosy baby flesh, several bleating cries, and he was gone.

Okay, you've gone through the guilt again. Try something more constructive.

She would go and see Kristy. Maybe drive her to the doctor and await the final verdict. Something.

Anything but face what she'd promised to do today.

"My mom wants me to get a job," Brad complained, a wad of dip stuck in the side of his cheek making his words sound like he was talking underwater. With that, he spat a stream of brown stuff onto the ground near Jesse's feet.

Now Jesse wasn't grossed out by much. Sure, the dead guy's body had given him a scare, but thinking back on it just turned on the curiosity machine. All those little black holes. And the guy's eyes had been kinda puffed out, like the explosion from the bullet had practically blown them from his head.

He was definitely going to have to ask about that.

But Brad's new addiction bugged him to no end. In disgust, he watched Brad mangle the dip around in his mouth, spit once more, dribbling some down his chin.

"That stuff gives you mouth cancer. Huge sores inside your lips."

Brad swiped the back of his hand across his mouth. "Yeah, well, you smoke, butthead. Wha'd'ya think that does to your lungs?"

"I've given up smoking."

Brad broke into laughter, little black bits of dip sticking to his teeth. "Since when?"

"Since we ran from the dead body, that's when! Thought I'd die myself. Jesus, I can't get it outta my head."

"Think they found it yet?"

"Yeah."

Jesse had no doubt. With as little fanfare as possible, he and Brad had relayed the information to Chief Perry Dortner. Thank God Dad hadn't been there. He'd tried to mention it earlier but just couldn't bring himself to do it. His father was looking for a reason to be pissed at him—or worse—and Jesse knew finding a dead body would qualify. So, it had been a relief when Dortner had been there by himself. Jesse had dropped the particulars on the police chief, who'd stared him down as if he were an alien with three green horns sticking out of his head and an attitude to match. No matter. The deed was done and the body had probably already been tagged and bagged.

As Brad pinched out another wad of dip and shoved it in his cheek, Jesse asked, "What kind of job does she want you to get?"

He shrugged. "Something that pays good and keeps me out of trouble."

"Yeah right. Find one of those in Woodside."

"Thought I might check at Lannie's."

Lannie's was the local gas station and minimarket. It was also a great place to buy cigarettes because nobody gave a good goddamn what age you were.

"That'll keep you out of trouble all right," Jesse said sardonically.

"Better than cleaning out Uncle Roy's houses," Brad muttered. This was the job he'd had the year before: sweeping up and hauling debris from the homes Brad's uncle built. It wasn't actually that bad a job, but Brad and his uncle were constantly at loggerheads. Brad was naturally slow in his movements and he hadn't appreciated it when Uncle Roy nicknamed him Sloth. Though Jesse was pretty sure Brad didn't know what it meant, he was quick enough to understand it most likely wasn't complimentary.

"Just don't light up while you're pumping gas," Jesse suggested.

"That's why I took up chewing."

"I didn't figure it was for your health."

"What's bugging you?" Brad demanded.

Jesse couldn't answer. He wasn't entirely sure. He wanted to know more about the dead body, but he didn't want to talk to his dad. "C'mon," he said after a moment. "Let's go see your shrink and find out if she knows anything more."

"Think Tawny's still with her?" Brad asked, grinning

like a devil. He knew Jesse's weaknesses and loved to nail him.

"Shut up," Jesse answered good-naturedly.

He certainly hoped so.

Late afternoon and nothing happening. Liz sat in her office and toyed with a pencil, knowing she should head home. She'd called Kristy and had learned surgery was scheduled for tomorrow, so Kristy was busy getting prepared. That left Liz unsettled and with time on her hands, so she'd decided to stop by after work. But there were no appointments scheduled, so when her thoughts weren't on Kristy and Tawny, they were on the task she'd set for herself. She was scared spitless and she knew why. She was terrified her son would reject her.

And why shouldn't he? she asked herself, playing devil's advocate. You abandoned him. You've never tried to contact him. You nearly aborted him. Why should he want to see you? Come up with one solid reason. He doesn't want you. You weren't there for the first sixteen years; he won't thank you for trying to be part of the next fifty or so.

Liz paced the room like a caged animal, frustrated and anxious. She had no appointments for this afternoon. She'd only come to work to avoid the whole issue.

But it was time for action.

Snatching up her hobo purse, Liz slung it over her shoulder. She would go to the police station and address Hawk face-to-face, then, depending on what his reaction was, she would take further steps.

Such as?

"I don't know," she whispered aloud.

Determined footsteps sounded in the outside hallway. Liz half-turned, then jumped.

Bang! Bang! Bang!

Someone sure knew how to pound their fist on a door.

"Come on in," Liz said, fighting a certain amount of reluctance. An unscheduled caller with that kind of frustrated energy didn't sound encouraging.

The door flew open as if jet-propelled. In the doorway stood a young girl wearing a snarl. Carrie Lister. The same young girl Liz had seen the day before. Yesterday's two o'clock appointment.

"Hey, Carrie," Liz greeted her, as if her sudden appearance were as common as summer rain in Washington.

"I gotta see you ten billion more times, so I thought I might as well get it over with." Carrie strolled into Liz's office and plopped into a chair. She crossed her ankles on top of the desk, caught Liz's eye, shrugged, and dropped her feet to the floor.

"I thought we determined you'd come in next Thursday." Liz sank back into her own chair. She'd been given a reprieve.

"Why wait?"

Carrie had been in some minor trouble with the law that had resulted in ten hours of counseling with Liz and thirty-five hours of community service. She was currently "employed" at the senior center, sweeping floors and cleaning restrooms, and everyone at that establishment couldn't wait to be done with her. Carrie's attitude stank. A perpetual scowl tightened her brow, and Liz had yet to scare a smile from those dark burgundy-painted lips.

"So, basically, you're interested in expediency over results," Liz suggested, her mouth curving upward.

"Huh?"

"Never mind. Remember yesterday, when I asked you about school this fall? Any more thoughts on that?"

"I hate school."

"You said you might go back, though."

"Are you deaf? I told you, I can't stand bein' home! Sarah's an insane bitch."

Sarah Lister was Carrie's mother, and Liz privately felt half of Carrie's problems stemmed from their relationship. A secretary for a local government agency, Sarah spent her leisure hours with a lover whom Carrie had tagged the asshole and quality time with her daughter appeared nonexistent. Not that Carrie was a dream companion by any stretch of the imagination, but Liz generally met with both Sarah and Carrie and suspected blame could be evenly divided.

As if her thoughts had conjured up the woman, Sarah strode into Liz's office at that moment, her face a thundercloud. "Carrie!" she bellowed. "I don't have time to chase you all over the goddamn place. My boss is screaming at me, and you're just leaving messages like I should jump when you snap your fingers. Next time you come by yourself. The doc there can just mark me absent. I don't give a shit."

Carrie rolled her eyes. Liz, seeking control, said, "Unless there's an emergency, it would be better if we could all stick to an appointment schedule."

"This *is* an emergency," Carrie declared. "I need to divorce my mother."

Sarah swore under her breath. Her mouth tightened. Unhappiness surrounded them both like a dark cloud.

"That old lady down the street accused you of stealing her trees," Sarah said to her daughter.

Carrie snorted and scratched her arm. Liz noted a series of bruises running from shoulder to elbow. She'd seen some before, but Carrie had assured her on more than one occasion that bruises were the price one paid for sneaking

out the back window and carousing with friends at night.
Liz wondered.

"Trees?" Carrie repeated.

"Mrs. Brindamoor's trees. She's been bitching about
them. Told me you were probably involved."

"I ain't involved."

Something about the way Carrie denied that perked
up Liz's ears. She might not be involved, but she knew
who was.

"What about the trees?" Liz asked Carrie.

"She had trees linin' her driveway and somebody took
'em all. There were quite a few, too."

"You mean someone felled the trees and actually took
them away?" Liz asked.

"Um . . . yeah, I guess." Carrie shrugged.

"Then it wasn't straight vandalism, or else why would
anyone bother?" Liz pointed out. When Sarah stared her
down, Liz elaborated, "They must have taken them for a
purpose."

Now it was Carrie's turn to stare. "Yeah, you're right. It
ain't vandalism at all. So stop thinkin' what you're thinkin',"
she ordered her mother. "None of my friends were anywhere near that old bitch's trees."

"Watch your mouth," Sarah said distractedly.

Liz glanced from one to the other. Something was going
on here and it had nothing to do with Carrie's truancy and
sometimes criminal behavior. Both mother and daughter
were suddenly rather subdued and lost in thought—
characteristics Liz had seen in neither of them to date.

Before either of them could explain further, Brad and
his friend, Jesse, appeared in the doorway. Spying Sarah
and Carrie, Jesse looked about to bolt, but Carrie suddenly leaped up and threw him a brilliant smile—her first
ever in Liz's presence.

"Hey there!" Carrie cried. "What's up?"

"Oh, nothing," Jesse murmured, his expression Sphinx-like, almost stern. Something piqued Liz's spook button. That was twice now that he'd reminded her of something or someone she couldn't quite name.

"We just dropped by," Brad put in.

Like hell. The Brads and Jesses of the world didn't just drop by.

"So did we," Carrie said pertly. "My mother thinks I'm a tree thief." She rolled her eyes.

Jesse's head turned swiftly. "Tree thief?"

"Oh, it's dumb. That old lady with the long driveway." Carrie waved it aside. "Someone stole 'em all."

"She thinks I did it," Jesse said, sliding a glance to Liz to check her reaction.

"She thinks *I* did it." Carrie laughed. "What would I do with a bunch of old trees? And how would I get 'em out of there? Like I drive a truck!"

"She thinks every kid who ain't on the honor roll at Woodside High did it." Brad snorted. "That old bag's been screamin' at kids on the street. She nailed Josh Martin pretty good yesterday."

Liz thought of how Deanne Martin must have liked that. She would probably hear about it when, and if, Josh, and therefore Deanne, made another appointment.

"She's crazy," Carrie said, circling a finger beside her ear to indicate Anita Brindamoor's mental state.

"Somebody probably took the trees to see if they could send her over the edge," Jesse said with a shrug.

"A lot of work to go to just to be ornery," Liz pointed out.

"Carrie, I've got to get back to work," Sarah broke in sharply. Liz glanced her way. With the new arrivals, she'd almost forgotten about Carrie's mom. Still with that same distracted air, Sarah left the office, snapping her fingers for Carrie to follow. Carrie, however, was in no mood now that the two boys had appeared. It didn't take a rocket scientist, or even a fairly good psychologist, to figure out Carrie had a major thing for Jesse.

"Carrie!" Sarah screamed from the hallway.

"Did you want to talk?" Liz asked Brad.

"Nah . . ." He hesitated.

"You're gonna mark me down, aren't you?" Carrie demanded. "I came and saw you."

"I'll mark you down," Liz assured her dryly.

When she still didn't leave, Liz pointedly held open the door. "Next Thursday," she told Carrie, who lingered beside Jesse long enough to make everyone feel impatient.

When she was finally gone, Jesse and Brad both sighed as if they'd been holding their breath on purpose. "Did you find out anything about the dead guy?" Jesse asked Liz.

"Not yet."

"Yeah? I figured you went to the station after we did."

Liz inwardly winced. That's what she should have done. "I was thinking of going today."

"Is Tawny staying with you?" Brad asked.

Jesse shot him a lethal look, which Liz translated to mean, *I don't want to be that obvious, you jerk.*

"I think she's home right now, but she'll probably be staying with me for a couple days starting tomorrow. Her mom's going into the hospital," she added for Jesse's information.

Now those blue eyes turned her way. He *knew* she'd seen his interest in Tawny, but she couldn't tell what he thought of the whole thing. Liz carefully schooled her features to keep from giving too much away.

"Well, if you hear anything," Jesse muttered.

"I'll be sure and let you know. Stop by and see Tawny and I'll update you," she suggested.

"Yeah . . . well . . ."

"We will," Brad told her.

At the office door, Brad turned around and, with the guilelessness of youth, warned, "That Carrie's a big pain in the butt. She's a liar. I wouldn't listen to her."

"I'll keep that in mind," Liz said, fighting a smile.

"No, I mean it. She needs professional help."

And with that, he and Jesse disappeared around her corner and Liz listened to their retreating footsteps. She considered facing Hawk, but cowardice ruled once more. Next week, she told herself, and this time the resonance of fate sounded around her.

She would do it.

Hawthorne munched on a greasy burger and even greasier fries from the Elbow Room. What the place lacked in charm it lacked in everything else as well. Once upon a time it had been several rungs up the ladder from where it was now, but those days were long gone. A dump by even the most forgiving standards, it had one redeeming quality that put it at the top of the list: It was the only game in town.

Everybody knew Barn and everybody expressed shock about his untimely death.

And then everybody said they pretty much expected it to happen.

"He'd finally struck it rich," a half-in-the-bag three-hundred-pound ex-lumberjack informed Hawthorne. "Braggin', braggin', braggin'. Bought the place a round last Friday."

"Bullshit," the barkeep said around a toothpick. "He bought a couple drinks when you stuck it to him. Old Barn was cheap," he said in an aside to Hawthorne.

"This time he had money. It was in the bag. Barney was a real estate guy, but he was no good. Something else came along. He was flyin' high."

Hawthorne looked from the lumberjack to the barkeep, who seemed to concur on this at least. "Practically giddy," the man said. "Try to imagine that. Did you know Barn?" Hawthorne shook his head. "Well, he was this big football star in high school. Never got over it. Women seemed to go for him, though."

Lumberjack snorted. "Only the losers."

"Like you'd know the difference."

For a moment, it looked like Lumberjack might take offense, but then he shrugged and he and the barkeep guffawed.

"Any woman in particular?" Hawthorne asked.

Lumberjack considered. "Well, Barn was married once. Had a kid right away, but that lasted less than a year or two. She took off back East with the kid and married some hoity-toity guy in a suit. Barn used to brag that he didn't pay nothin' but nickels in child support."

"Anyone more recent?" Hawk asked.

Barkeep sighed. "There's always Lora Lee."

"Well, yeah." Lumberjack nodded.

"Lora Lee Evans," Barkeep illuminated. "She's been after Barn for years. Kinda pathetic," he added with a trace of humanity. "She broke down when we heard the news. Was sitting right over there by the window. Started crying and crying. I drove her home." He drew a sympathetic breath. "Her car's still out front."

"Do you know where she lives?"

"Little house in that development south of town. You know the one?"

"Yes," Hawthorne said somewhat tersely.

"You can't miss her place. It's the one with the pink door."

He hadn't expected this investigation to be a trip down memory lane, but Hawthorne knew the development well: He and Laura had shared their first and only home there,

"Want to take her car to her, Detective?" Barkeep asked. "I've got the keys."

"Sure," Hawk said. This was the kind of task expected of the police department in Woodside, Washington.

He drove Lora Lee's blue Subaru through the streets of Herrington Heights, the lofty name given the sprawling development. It had expanded in the sixteen years since Hawk had lived there, and now dead ends connected to more housing. Trees, skinny and small, had grown into deciduous monsters in the intervening years and Hawthorne almost drove past his old house without seeing it.

Almost.

He glanced at it quickly, as if too much sight might actually wound his eyes. No more gray cedar. No more navy door. It had been painted a dull brown and trimmed in white. He was inordinately *glad*. His gaze touched the mailbox. Solid gray with stick-on letters that spelled Johnson. No more flowers. No first names. The wave of sadness he'd braced himself for didn't materialize, and he drove past with only a hint of memory tagging him.

Lora Lee's house was on a newer street. It was small and tidy and bounded by a chain-link fence. A sluggish-looking mixed breed shepherd lifted one brow as Hawthorne headed to the front door but showed no other interest.

The bells chimed in cheery, tinny trills. Hawthorne threw a glance at the sky. Slate gray but breaking up. Maybe they were finally in for a spate of decent weather.

The door creaked open. A woman of perhaps forty peered out. Her face was lined and right now devoid of cosmetics. Weariness emanated from her, as if it were a physical force. Her eyes were faded blue and full of some inner torment or sadness.

"Lora Lee Evans? I'm Detective Hawthorne Hart from the Woodside Police Department, and I'm here to—"

He didn't finish. Her blue eyes watered with sudden tears and she hiccupped against a sob. The weariness was sorrow, he realized belatedly, and the cause was plainly the death of one Barney Turgate.

"Come in," she invited.

Her house was furnished in early garage sale, but she'd done a nice job of it anyway. The chair she gestured for him to take was a burgundy plush with discreet embroidered arm protectors. It was comfortable and clean. He handed her her car keys and she gazed at them for several moments, as if committing them to memory. Apparently, she hadn't missed her vehicle much.

"Someone murdered him, didn't they?" she asked, swallowing.

"Barney Turgate was shot several times," Hawthorne agreed.

"How many times?" Her voice was small.

"Five, ma'am."

She winced and turned her head. She wasn't beautiful by any stretch of the imagination and probably never had been, but she was the kind of woman who epitomized solid loyalty and responsibility. Good wife material. Not someone to have an affair with. But by all accounts, Lora Lee and Barney had conducted an on-again-off-again affair for twenty years. "She waited for that ring," the barkeep had told Hawthorne. Tess Trueheart to Barn's Dick Tracy.

"He finally struck it rich," she said bitterly, repeating what the barkeep had said. "All that talk and he finally did it, and it killed him." More tears, falling unheeded to the hands clasped rigidly in her lap.

"How did he strike it rich?"

"I don't know. He wouldn't say." She lifted a trembling chin and stared to the side, anywhere but at Hawthorne. "You could check with Manny Belding."

Manny's name was on a list the barkeep at the Elbow Room had supplied Hawthorne, but in the interest of discovering more information, he asked, "Who's Manny Belding?"

Her lip curled. "A lowlife. He was thick with Barney lately. I never saw him anymore because of Manny. I called him, but he was too busy setting the 'deal.'"

"You have no idea what this deal was?"

"Who cares?" Lora Lee gazed directly at him. "Barney's gone. Who cares?" she repeated deliberately.

"Do you happen to know how I could get in touch with Manny Belding?"

"Hang out at any tavern in town and follow the smell. That'll be Manny."

Hawthorne considered, feeling empathy toward this unhappy woman. "Can you think of any other reason someone might want to kill Barney?"

"What?"

"Another motive? Other than this big deal he was involved in."

"Like what?"

"Personal problems. Financial trouble. Passion?"

Her lips quivered. "What do you mean?"

"Did anyone hate him enough to kill him?" Hawthorne asked, feeling foolish. He suspected Barn's number-one fan was sitting right in front of him.

"Nobody hated Barney." Fresh tears welled. "He had his faults, but he was good."

Hawthorne nodded. He'd gotten about all the information he was going to get.

"I loved him," she added, as if that truth weren't painfully obvious already. "I can't believe he's gone."

Awkwardly, Hawthorne waited as she bent her head and cried and cried. "I'm sorry, ma'am," he said softly.

She nodded, silent tears mourning the death of the man she loved.

The sun had nearly set by the time Hawthorne returned to his house, a small log cabin down a long, wooded drive. There were two bedrooms and a loft. Hawthorne checked both his and Jesse's bedroom and then the loft, but Jesse was nowhere to be found. No note either. For some reason this pissed Hawthorne off more than usual, and in a fit of restlessness, he climbed back in his Jeep and went in search of his errant son.

He wasn't at Brad's, but Mrs. Barlow gave him the name and address of one Tawny Fielding, the object, apparently, of his son's affections. This was news to Hawthorne. He couldn't decide whether it was a positive sign or not. An interest in girls could be bad or good, depending on who the girl was and what the circumstances were. He hoped with little hope that this Tawny person would be a good influence on Jesse, but the likelihood was that she was just one more headache to add to the growing list.

The Fieldings lived in a modest ranch-style home about a half mile from Hummingbird River, accessed down a curving driveway. Pulling his Jeep up behind a black Miata convertible, ragtop closed against the threatening rain, he suddenly gasped when the Miata's backup lights flashed on and the damn driver threw it into reverse without looking.

"Hey!" Hawk yelled, laying on the horn.

The loud blast caught the driver's attention and the Miata screeched to a jerking halt. Muttering beneath his breath, Hawk jumped from the car. The driver of the Miata did the same, and Hawk watched one denim-clad leg—definitely female—slide out of the car. *Tawny?* he thought dimly. But no, this brownish-blond woman was closer to thirty.

And then he looked at her face and his jaw slackened. He stared. "Shit," he muttered in shock.

Those aqua eyes. That uncompromising stare. Those pink lips.

Liz Havers.

Jesse's mom.

"Shit."

Chapter Seven

Liz was in a vortex. Down, down, down to a distant, ever-smaller core where she would be squeezed into separate atoms and flung into a distant galaxy.

Hawthorne Hart.

Her stomach flipped. Her heart thundered. A rushing in her ears deafened her. Looking at him made her eyes hurt.

He was poleaxed. He stared. The only word passing his lips was "shit." She was so numb this seemed the height of conversation. Absurd. Ridiculous.

"I'm going to throw up," a voice said from far away. Her voice. She staggered two steps, rested a shaking hand on the hood of the Miata, and lost her lunch in deep, retching spasms.

Hawthorne was beside her in an instant. A cool hand on the back of her neck. Humiliating. Deeply, deeply humiliating.

She couldn't do anything but vomit.

"Relax," he told her. The voice was too familiar. But strained. He was suffering, too.

Relax, she thought half hysterically. *Relax!*

It felt like an eternity before she could lift her head.

Wiping her mouth with the back of her hand, she wanted to cry with embarrassment. She couldn't turn around and face him. Jesus. Hawthorne Hart. God Almighty. She'd known it would be bad but hadn't expected to feel so completely annihilated.

"Are you all right?" he asked.

Liz inhaled and exhaled several times, screwing up her courage. With a monumental effort, she managed to twist enough to meet his eyes. Their blue-gray depths seemed to swirl with unspoken accusations. She couldn't stand it. She just couldn't stand it.

"What are you doing here?" she demanded.

"Are you Mrs. Fielding?" he asked.

"What?"

"Is this your house?"

"Oh." Liz laughed half hysterically again. For a moment, she'd thought he didn't recognize her, but of course he did. He simply thought she was the owner of the house. It made perfect sense. "No, I'm . . ." What was she? Liz shook her head. "You're here to see Kristy." For some reason, Liz found this incomprehensible. "She just got out of the hospital. Major surgery. What do you want?"

He shook his head, as if the conversation was moving too fast. Small wonder. It *was* moving too fast. Liz felt slammed back in time. Hawthorne looked older, yet at the same time he appeared exactly the same. Even the underlying pain that had been so evident then—a result, she now knew, of his wife's death—was still there at some level. And his magnetic attraction, she realized unwillingly, was as powerful as ever as well.

"What are you doing here?" he asked.

"I'm a friend."

"I didn't know you were in Woodside."

"I moved here this summer."

"Moved here?" He seemed to shake himself from his reverie. His gaze sharpened on her face, and suddenly Liz felt naked. She saw herself through his eyes: jeans, blue cotton shirt, white sneakers, no socks, no makeup. Thirty-four years old with less sense of style than when she'd been a teenager.

Tough.

"You're living in Woodside?" he demanded, as if he could scarcely believe it.

"I'm the resident school psychologist."

He swore bitterly beneath his breath. "Like hell."

That did it. "I want to meet my son," she told him baldly. "Hawthorne Hart, Jr.," she added with a trace of bitterness. "I know you work with the department and I've been planning to make an appointment with you."

"You wanted to abort him."

Liz sucked in a shocked breath. How unfair! It wasn't true. She hadn't wanted the abortion. She never would have gone through with it. She'd just been swept along the crest of her parents' tidal wave.

But to bring it up *now.* As if that were the only thing that mattered sixteen years after the fact. Bastard. Did he have no soul? No concept of what it had been like for her?

No. He just didn't care, that's all.

"I don't give a damn what you think," she told him heatedly. "I'm going to meet my son, and hopefully have some kind of relationship with him, and there's not a damn thing you can do about it!"

"Oh no?"

His soft threat only strengthened Liz's courage. "No," she whispered, meeting his gaze. To hell with attraction. She hated him. Lots of attractive people were worth hating. Hawthorne Hart was one.

"You think he's going to really want to know you?" Hawthorne posed.

He was hitting all her worst fears. She could imagine how she'd been portrayed; how *he* had portrayed her. She was the vile, wicked killer of offspring, the nastiest villain of all. No fairy-tale monster could compete with her pure evilness.

"Yes, he's going to want to know me," she told him in a remarkably controlled voice. Remarkable when you considered how her insides were gooey mush.

Hawthorne's lips twisted. "You don't have any idea," he said softly.

"When can I see him?"

It was as if she brought a new question to his mind, His eyes widened a bit and he threw a sharp glance toward the Fielding house. Liz's gaze followed his. *What?* she wondered vaguely.

As if on cue, the front door suddenly opened and Jesse and Brad sauntered out, Tawny shadowing them. The three teenagers stood on the porch for a moment; then Jesse, as if his radar had suddenly switched on, jerked around to regard Liz and Hawthorne. His posture changed to instant insolence. He narrowed his gaze, flipped his hair, then separated from the pack, slowly ambling to where Liz and Hawthorne stood by the Miata.

Liz shifted her gaze to Hawthorne, perplexed. Did Jesse think she'd gone to the police? Hawthorne didn't wear a uniform, but maybe they'd connected when he and Brad had gone to see Chief Dortner.

"Looking for me?" Jesse asked belligerently.

Liz opened her mouth to respond, then was stunned when Hawthorne answered, "I heard you were here."

"Who told you?"

Liz stared. The build. Those eyes. The quicksilver

déjà vu that passed over her every time she saw him again. Her breath tore into her lungs. Now she really was going to pass out. Jesse? Jesse was *Hawthorne Hart, Jr.*?

"So, you've already met," Hawthorne uttered bitterly.

"Who?" Jesse stared at his father in bafflement. He glanced around, his gaze touching on Liz. "Oh. Yeah."

"It's all a big secret, isn't it?" Hawthorne added, throwing a cold look Liz's way. "You could have told me."

"No, I—" she began, realizing he thought she and Jesse had already learned each other's identity. But Jesse cut her off.

"She was the one who talked me into reporting the body, okay? Don't be pissed off at her. She's Brad's shrink," he added by way of belated introduction. "He just wanted to talk to her first, so we—wouldn't get in trouble."

Silence pooled around them. Jesse, picking up the vibes, merely kept frowning, as if there were undercurrents here he'd been missing, which indeed there were. Hawthorne stood in utter silence and immobility, as if movement would somehow give him away. Liz, reeling from information overload, simply waited like a convicted murderer for the death sentence to be read.

It was a bitch all the way around.

"Hey . . ." Jesse murmured.

She stared at him. Her son. Her *son*! The familiarity she'd felt was really the connection of mother to child. *Flesh of my flesh. My God.* She couldn't take it in. Knees buckling, she sank against the car.

"Hey," Jesse said again, reaching a hand out to steady her. His fingers closed around her upper arm as Hawthorne swept in a sharp breath. "Are you okay?"

Liz nodded.

"Jesse," Brad called. He and Tawny were walking their way.

Jesse swiveled around, long hair swinging. He kept a hand burning into her arm, steadying her. *My son. Jesse is my son.*

"We're going to my house," Brad yelled.

"You and Tawny?"

"Yeah, just for a while. You coming?"

Jesse nodded, then gazed searchingly at Liz. The color of his eyes was a shade or two off from Hawthorne's, closer to Liz's own greenish-blue shade. And his nose was more like hers, but that lantern jaw was all Hawthorne Hart. "What the hell's going on here?" he asked.

"Nothing," Hawk bit out.

"Are you harassing a citizen?" Jesse asked his father with a touch of humor.

"Come *on*!" Brad waved at him to join them.

"I'll be fine," Liz told him, and with a last puzzled look he released his grip on her arm and fell in line with Brad.

"See ya later," Tawny told Liz, then she swiveled back to get a good look at her. "You sure you're all right?"

"Yeah." Liz's voice was squeaky.

"Nothing's wrong?"

"No. Is your mom still—resting?" she struggled out.

Tawny nodded, throwing a wary glance Hawthorne's way. "I'm just going for a few minutes," she warned, as if Hawk might think less of her for leaving. "I'm coming right back."

"I'll stay." Liz swallowed hard. "Take your time."

"Maybe I shouldn't go," Tawny said, glancing, and then glancing away, at the remains of Liz's lunch lying on the ground.

"What?" Brad and Jesse demanded in unison.

"Go," Liz urged. With an effort, she reached out and touched Tawny's shoulder. She managed a quavering smile. "I'm just—tired."

Tawny's concerned gaze traveled from Liz to Hawthorne, who'd remained remarkably silent up to that point. As if her look started his engine, he flicked a glance at his son and said, "What's the chance of finding some time to talk to you?"

"What do you mean?" Jesse was cautious.

Liz drew a breath.

"I mean, I came looking for you to bring you home. There're a couple things I'd like to talk about, one of them being Barney Turgate's death."

"You think I'm involved?" Jesse was indignant.

"No."

Jesse gazed at him through narrowed lashes. "I'll be back later," he said abruptly, then took off in long, ground-devouring strides up the crooked lane to the road to Brad's. Tawny and Brad followed.

And Hawthorne and Liz were alone.

"I want to talk about this later," Hawthorne said tautly.

"Fine." Rotely, Liz opened the door of the Miata and pulled a card from her purse.

With a snort, Hawthorne accepted the tiny white card. "Elizabeth Havers, teen shrink."

"Yep."

"Is this a way to ask me to stop by your office?"

She shook her head. She'd only given him the card as a means to buy time. "There's a little coffee place, The Coffee Spot."

"I know it."

"We could meet there after you see—Jesse," she pointed out, diffidently saying his name. He'd always been Hawthorne Hart, Jr. to her. And he'd always been an infant in her mind, even though she'd known he'd grown up. Now she had to face that he was a flesh-and-blood boy—no, *man*—and it made her feel strange and incredibly used up. "It stays open 'til nine."

"I'll be there at eight," he told her flatly and turned to leave.

"Fine." It irked her that he never seemed to answer any of her questions. Passive-aggressive type, she decided with an inner snort.

She didn't like him at all.

"What the hell was that all about?" Brad wondered as he opened the back door and let Tawny and Jesse inside. His mother and siblings were at a movie, so the teens had the place to themselves.

"He's mad 'cause we told the shrink lady first." Jesse flopped down on the couch in front of the TV.

Out of the corner of his eye, he watched Tawny slide into the chair next to the foot of the sofa. She was in his line of sight but yards away. It might as well have been miles.

It was a minor miracle she was here at all. He couldn't read her. She seemed content to hang out with him and Brad, but God, it was like she had a force field around her. There was just no getting in.

In a kind of masochistic agony, Jesse watched her slide her feet out of her sandals and tuck her legs in the chair, pink toenails peeking from the frayed hem of her jeans.

"He's mad 'cause you don't come home," Brad said.

"I go home," Jesse protested.

"Oh, sure. Like you don't sneak out. Like we don't go scare the Ryerson twins."

Tawny tilted her head and looked Jesse's way. Her

brown-blond mane swung gently against her shoulders. "You're the ones throwing stuff at their house?"

"No!" Jesse wanted to throttle Brad. "We just scared 'em once."

"I threw an apple, okay? A Gravenstein. It was just little. They don't get ripe 'til August." Brad was unrepentant.

"It broke their window," Tawny said.

"Brad, you asshole," Jesse muttered. He hated looking bad in Tawny's eyes, though she wasn't shaking her finger at them and clucking her tongue like the Ryerson twins would. "Why don't you go call that Texas girl?"

"I don't like her anymore." A moment of silence followed and Brad lifted his palms, "Okay, I'm sorry about the window, all right? So shoot me."

Tawny hunched her shoulders at that, and Jesse had to force himself not to jump up and strangle his best friend.

Desperate to move on, Jesse said, "I want to know what the deal is with that dead guy."

"Barney Turgate," Tawny supplied.

"Yeah. Why'd he get shot? Who would do that in Woodside?"

"Lots of guys have guns," Brad said with little interest. He picked up the remote and started switching channels on TV.

"Yeah, but they don't just go blow somebody away. That guy didn't have a chance. Whoever did it wanted to be sure he was dead."

"You sound like a detective," Brad said, then went off on his Joe Friday imitation from *Dragnet*. Normally, Jesse found this the height of humor, but he snatched up a pillow and hurled it at Brad, causing him to drop the remote.

"Hey!" Brad complained.

"Stop being such a jerk."

"Who's the jerk?" Brad demanded.

"I think they hated him," Tawny said. "They just kept shooting him. They couldn't stop."

Jesse and Brad both stared at her. Girls were weird, Jesse determined, but that didn't mean they were all bad. "Nah, it's gotta be something else," he said. "They wanted something from him. Or he'd ratted 'em out about some big deal."

"Or he stole from the mob and they came and took him out," Brad suggested, holding an imaginary Uzi and wiping out everyone in the room.

"He let them shoot him," Tawny said. "He looked right at them, so he knew them. Otherwise he would have run."

"Oh, sure. They come up on him and blast the hell out of him. He had a lot of time to turn and run." Brad rolled his eyes.

Jesse said evenly, "We don't know what happened. But I'm going to find out. I'm going to go home and talk to my dad."

"He won't tell you anything," Brad complained.

"Yeah, well, he might."

"You're leaving now?" Tawny asked, unfolding her legs. She looked about ready to bolt.

Jesse hesitated. "Well, not quite yet."

She relaxed back in the chair, and Jesse obsessed on what this meant for the rest of the evening. It seemed like she wanted to be with *him.* She was ready to leave if he wasn't staying. A quickening of his heart. Shift of attention. Sexual thoughts. His body reacted against his will.

Shit. He was fighting back a serious woody here. Grabbing another pillow, he hurled it at Brad, who took up the fight and unknowingly helped ease Jesse through the moment.

* * *

The Coffee Spot was empty. Mostly a drive-through, it managed to squeeze four tables in an anteroom decorated with smiling coffee cups painted on the walls. Corny, but okay. Liz sat in a chair in the corner and sipped another latte.

She still hadn't recovered from seeing Hawthorne. All those years and then *wham*! She felt like she'd been run over by a freight train.

Nothing could warm her. No latte. No thoughts of her son. Nothing. She didn't know which was the harder kick: realizing Jesse was her son or coming face-to-face with Hawthorne again.

She couldn't bear the thought of seeing Hawk again. She wished he would just—evaporate. She wanted to know Jesse and she didn't want Hawthorne involved. She supposed that was the way it was in divorce when there were children involved.

She thought back on those afternoons at the Candlewick Inn. Soft, slanting sunlight. Physical pleasure. A sense of the world stopping for some monumental occurrence that only she and Hawk could share.

But the Candlewick was now the Elbow Room. Fitting, she thought bitterly. The romantic love nest was now the peanut-munching, beer-swilling domain of the Barney Turgates of the world. Not that Hawk hadn't done his share of drinking inside those walls.

Lord, she'd been *dumb*.

But it had given her Jesse. And miracle of miracles, she and Jesse already had a relationship, a rapport, a history together. Hawthorne would try to destroy it; she knew that already.

She had to think of a way to stop him.

The door swung inward with a little *ding*: a small brass bell hung above the jamb that tinkled whenever the door opened or closed. Liz's spine straightened as Hawk strode inside. If he took note of his surroundings she couldn't tell. He seemed to stare her down from the moment he crossed the threshold.

He purchased a plain coffee. Black. Somehow, she wasn't surprised, and as he came her way she braced herself for the confrontation destined to happen. The wheels had been set in motion some sixteen years earlier.

"Ms. Havers," he said carefully as he pulled out a chair across from hers.

This struck her as funny, though what in fact he should say after all these years and the strange circumstances of their first encounters was, after all, going to sound off no matter what.

"Mr. Hart," she responded just as carefully, but he must have seen the twinkle in her eyes because the flat line of his mouth relaxed just a little.

"I don't want Jesse to know who you are—just yet," he said.

"I thought his name was Hawthorne Hart, Jr."

"Yeah, well, that's probably what the birth certificate says."

"Don't you know?" Liz asked.

He gave her a long look. It was almost more than she could bear, those eyes turned on her so closely. "I didn't pay a lot of attention at the time. I just wanted my son. I believe his legal name is Hawthorne Jesse Hart. No junior. I don't have a middle name."

"Oh."

"He's a typical sixteen-year-old, as you probably noticed. I didn't realize you'd met."

"I didn't realize we'd met either," she admitted, "I only knew him as Brad's friend, 'Jesse.'"

Hawthorne nodded. Some of his antagonism lessened,

but his fingers moved restlessly on his coffee cup though he didn't take one swallow.

There seemed so little to say when, in fact, there was way too much. Liz was unusually tongue-tied herself. She couldn't seem to find one conversation starter.

After several uncomfortable moments, Hawk said, "Jesse came home tonight with a lot of questions about Barney Turgate."

"What did you tell him?"

"Nothing much. There's nothing to tell yet, and I couldn't trust information with Jesse anyway. He said they found Turgate's body and came to you with the information."

Liz could see that bothered him a bit. "Brad comes to see me on a regular basis. He's a good kid. A little troubled, but who isn't these days? He trusts me, I think, and he and Jesse were really bothered when they stumbled on the body."

"They could have come to me," Hawthorne pointed out. He grimaced, looked away, then admitted, "Actually, Jesse stopped by the station, but we didn't—communicate."

"Mmm." Liz was noncommittal. Her ploy didn't work, however; he gave her another sharp glance, his lips twisting in self-deprecation.

"I'm his father, not his friend," Hawthorne said.

"And you're a detective with the police department."

"We have a few difficulties, but it's generally okay."

Liz nodded.

"Don't think I don't realize what's going on," he said softly. "You've got an inside track and you're going to exploit it for all it's worth."

"I don't know what you mean."

"Bullshit."

Liz forced herself not to slide her gaze away from the accusations in his. He was right. She *was* on the inside track with Jesse. Fate had stepped in and shown her the route. And she *was* going to exploit it for all it was worth.

"I want to know my son."

"You sure took your time coming to that conclusion."

"You think this idea just struck me? Like I woke up one day and thought, 'Oh, gosh. That's right. I have a son. Maybe I'll go see what he's like now that he's a teenager.'"

He shrugged that away, as if her reasons were nothing. "If you tell him the truth, you'll lose him."

"So, I'm not the only psychologist in the room."

"I'm asking you what your plans are."

His directness wasn't something she remembered. He'd been so foggy and fuzzy, undoubtedly the result of drink. But he wasn't that way now, and though she still sensed the basic sadness and unhappiness inside him that she now associated with his character, she realized he possessed the straightforward, no-nonsense bluntness of a police interrogator. Which, she realized, he was.

"I won't tell him who I am. I'm not going to slit my own throat."

"I want you to stay away from him for now."

"No can do, Mr. Hart. He's my *son*," she reminded him.

"He's *my* son. He's someone you gave birth to."

"There is no distinction."

"The hell there isn't."

That she understood how he felt only made things worse. Their forced civility strained. It crawled under her skin. She was bugged. Irritated. At him, mostly, but at herself as well for even *caring* what he thought of her.

And she did care. She could feel it. That small stirring in her blood. She'd experienced it before—with him—and therefore recognized it for the danger it was. It made her positively ill to think she was still attracted to him. Half of her wanted to spit in his eye, the other half . . . well . . .

She couldn't think about it.

"I'm not going to disappear," she told him from her heart. "I'm not going to go away. I'm his mother and I don't give a damn that you think I'm a poor excuse for one. I don't care. I've got a chance to know him and I will know him. You can't stop me. I—won't—let you," she added quietly.

"As soon as he learns who you are, it's over."

"Fine. I'll deal with it." She could well imagine all the terrible denouncements of her Hawthorne had uttered over the years.

"He's not an easy kid," Hawthorne said, more reflectively. "He's been in trouble with the law. I'm not talking about with me. I mean, he's been arrested."

This didn't surprise Liz; he was, after all, Brad's best buddy. But it was a knife to her heart, and it took her several moments to recover and come up with a response. "What's he done?"

"The worst was grand theft auto. He and a friend went joyriding in a car when he was fifteen. That's why he hasn't got a license yet."

"I like him," Liz said simply.

"You don't even know him," Hawk admonished harshly.

"Doesn't matter. I'm a good judge of character." This time she didn't add, *And he's my son.*

Hawthorne just shook his head.

"What have you told him about me?" Liz dared to ask.

He drew a deep breath. She could see him thinking that one over, which didn't bode well. Unconsciously, she braced herself for what was to come.

"He knows you were young and your family wanted you to give him up."

Did you tell him they wanted to abort him? Did you tell him I wanted to abort him?

Liz said carefully, "Despite what you think, I always wanted to keep him. I couldn't, of course. I was so immature. My family did have a lot of influence over me."

"The Havers family," he said softly.

"They're both gone now. Died within six months of each other." She didn't add that she'd never quite reconciled with her parents after Jesse's birth. The subject was taboo. That episode of her life wiped out. But it was something Liz thought about every day; sometimes nearly every moment, sometimes with a jolt when a sound or smell or feeling reminded her.

He had the courage not to say *I'm sorry*. That, she knew, would have been a lie. But he looked thoughtful, almost grim, as if the changes affected him more than he'd like to admit.

"Does he ever ask about me?" Liz asked.

"No."

She bowed her head. What had she expected?

Long moments passed, an eternity in a handful of seconds. Hawk stirred and rose to his feet. Liz stared at him askance. Apparently, their meeting was about to end and she still had so many things to say.

But she kept her mouth closed. Her head clamored with unvoiced queries.

He walked several paces, hesitated, half-turned. She waited, her eyes begging for more. Pain etched long brackets on either side of his mouth. She longed to reach out and erase those marks. She longed to be near. To hold. To touch.

"He's a lot like you at the same age . . ." Hawk managed to force out, and then he left quickly, as if the admission might start an avalanche that would bury him if he stayed in one place too long.

Liz gazed after him after the door *dinged* shut behind him. By the time she got to her own feet she'd battened down the hatches on her own bursting emotions.

Tomorrow, as they said, was another day.

Kristy Fielding lay propped against some pillows on the couch, smiling faintly at all the fussing Liz and Tawny were wont to do. "Stop that," she told them without heat. "Stop that right now."

"Do you want your feet up?" Tawny asked, concerned

"How about some juice? Are you thirsty?" Liz chimed in.

Kristy waved them both away, then tiredly rested her cheek on one of the chocolate velveteen throw pillows. It was two weeks since the surgery and Guy, her ex-husband, had called her every day. Liz wasn't sure if that pleased her or not. The good news was the surgery looked to be successful and her doctors were adopting a wait-and-see policy—the usual medical bullshit, as far as Liz was concerned. Meanwhile, she was taking Taxol, a drug specifically targeted against ovarian cancer. Whether it staved off another cancerous attack or actually worked on the cancer itself, Liz wasn't sure. It hardly mattered. Either way, it was the best answer there was.

"Just speak up if you need anything," Liz told her.

"Don't worry. I will."

"Mom?" Tawny asked. "Is it okay if I go out with a friend for a while?"

Kristy's eyes closed and she sighed. "Ask your aunt Liz," she suggested.

Aunt Liz threw Tawny a sideways look. "Would this friend be Jesse Hart?"

"And probably Brad," Tawny agreed. "We just wanted to go get some ice cream."

"Uh-huh. What mode of transportation?"

"Walking," Tawny admitted. "Unless you'd care to drop us off downtown . . . ?"

Tawny, wily young thing that she was, had quickly figured out that Liz actually enjoyed being with Brad and Jesse. Liz was afraid to ask her what she thought, but because Tawny seemed to accept, and sometimes use, the information, the subject hadn't needed to be addressed.

"Get in the car," Liz said with a grin. Her pulse quickened at the thought of seeing Jesse again. They'd had a few encounters since the day she'd learned the truth, but Liz ached for more. As the summer waxed on, she struggled for ways to be near him and had luckily stumbled upon the fact that Jesse was very interested in Barney Turgate's death and harbored a secret desire to solve it before the police. Liz fed that interest with questions and insights of her own, so a natural rapport had sprung up between them. Brad was bored with the whole thing, but Tawny seemed also to be infected by the "detective" bug.

As far as Hawthorne went, the less she saw of him the better, Liz figured. She was fairly certain he didn't know of her ways of seeing Jesse. And she was just as certain Jesse didn't tell him. Hawthorne's son could be as closed off as his father when he felt like it, and where Hawk was concerned, Jesse felt like it darn near all the time.

Which only worked to Liz's advantage.

"My dad wants me to come live with him in Seattle," Tawny said as they headed down the winding driveway.

"What?" This was the first Liz had heard of it.

"Mom's sick and he thinks it would be better if I was with him."

"Oh, come on!" Liz sputtered emphatically. "Better for whom? Certainly not your mother."

"You don't think so?" Tawny gazed gravely at Liz.

"Your mom needs you now, Tawny."

Tawny chewed on her lower lip. "You don't think I'm a bother to her, then?"

Liz's fingers tightened around the steering wheel. *Damn Guy Fielding,* she thought viciously. Another man might actually believe those excuses, but she knew Guy and Kristy's relationship too intimately to buy into that. Guy wanted everything. And if he was making noise about having Tawny live with him, then that meant he'd decided—belatedly—that he wanted the daughter from his first marriage. And calling Kristy every day to inquire on her welfare was just a blasted cover-up.

"Babe, you're not a bother to anyone," Liz told her. "Don't let anyone say you are."

"Anyone—like my father?" There was a touch of sardonic humor in her tone. Liz had originally tried to hide her aversion to Guy Fielding, but Tawny was too astute for that. Because she was only too aware of her father's personality type, Tawny didn't hold it against Liz.

"All I'm saying is your mom needs you now. Your dad should know that, but maybe he doesn't."

"If I can't get through to him, would you talk to him?"

Liz pictured that conversation. "Yes," she said resignedly, to which Tawny actually chuckled. The kid was fifteen going on fifty.

It turned out Jesse was at Brad's, which made Liz sigh with relief. Not that she couldn't pick him up at the log cabin he shared with his father. It was, after all, the middle of the afternoon and she was unlikely to meet Hawk during a weekday. But she naturally preferred to avoid a scene—and a scene it would be if, and when, Hawk realized she was seeing Jesse on the sly.

"We're catching a lift?" Brad asked, jumping in the back of the Miata. His long legs knocked against his chin.

"I'll probably get a ticket for no seat belts," Liz complained as Jesse climbed in beside Brad. The two boys were a massive wall behind them, their bodies contorted to fit the small confines of the backseat.

"It's only a couple miles," Jesse pointed out. "If we see the police, we'll run for the border."

"Yeah right." Liz knew she was piling on another transgression.

The ride was uneventful and she cruised along Woodside's main street until they found the ice cream shop, which was also a small café. As Tawny, Jesse, and Brad jumped out, Tawny glanced back at Liz and invited, "Would you like to join us?"

"Thanks, but I'm okay."

To her amazement and secret joy, Jesse suddenly swung around, straight hair flying and said, "Yeah, c'mon," to which Brad gave him a look that said *You're a total nutcase.*

Liz didn't question the fates. With a shrug, she cut the engine and joined the three teenagers inside. Tawny and Jesse had accepted her at a different level than "adult" or "shrink," and she was eternally grateful. Brad couldn't get over the fact that she was his psychologist and therefore felt differently. She couldn't blame him. But because he put up with this strange arrangement without much fuss, Liz continually took advantage of it.

Three steps into the café, Liz stopped short and inwardly groaned. Ahead of them in line was Deanne Martin. No sign of Josh. He stayed as far away from his mother as possible unless he was forced to be with her—that much had been obvious from the start.

Liz half-hoped Deanne would get her ice cream and leave without seeing Liz or, barring that, just smile in acknowledgment and head on her merry way.

No such luck. As soon as Deanne turned around and her gaze touched on Liz, she bee-lined toward her, chocolate mousse nut ice cream nearly melting in the wind created by her sudden speed. She was completely unaware that Liz was with Tawny, Brad, and Jesse.

"Josh is with his father," she said. "He wants to stay with his father! Robert's getting married and he wants Josh!"

Liz wasn't certain how to respond. It was difficult to see which way Deanne felt.

Her hesitancy went unnoticed. "Josh has been hanging around with some juvenile delinquents," Deanne continued. "He got in some trouble last week—nothing serious— and then Robert just came in and swooped him up. I'm taking him to court. He's not going to get away with it."

Deanne belatedly became aware that Tawny, Brad, and Jesse were all staring at her. Collecting herself, she glanced around and focused on Jesse's long hair. "It's not like Josh is really bad, like a lot of kids. *He* didn't take those yew trees," she added pointedly.

"Yew trees?" Liz questioned. "You mean, Mrs. Brindamoor's trees?"

"Well, we didn't take them either," Brad declared, puffing up with indignation.

Jesse stared Deanne down, his blue eyes simmering with repressed anger. Liz said quickly, "Mrs. Brindamoor's tree theft doesn't sound like teen vandalism."

Tears brimmed in Deanne's eyes. "I'm going to kill

Robert in court," she declared. "He's an unfit father, and I'm going to make sure everybody knows it."

"Josh is a decent guy," Jesse stated flatly.

"How the hell would you know?" She whirled on him. "You're a *thief*!"

"Deanne," Liz protested.

Jesse moved a step closer, threatening with his size. Deanne, tough lady that she was, didn't budge, though she did flinch at his cold tone. "I didn't take those trees."

"Hey." Liz sidled between them, unconsciously preparing for a fight.

"Anita Brindamoor saw you and your friends digging them up. She said so. Vandals! You should be ashamed of yourselves!"

"She said the same about Josh," Brad put in.

"Let's not make accusations," Liz intervened firmly, but Brad couldn't help muttering something under his breath, which sounded suspiciously like *stupid cow*.

Jesse just continued to glare at Deanne in that awful way young men can use to intimidate. It eventually worked, too, because Deanne lost a bit of her confidence and headed for the door. She stopped, one hand on the exit bar, seemed to want to say something, then pushed into the late afternoon sunshine, chocolate mousse nut ice cream speckling her navy double-breasted dress.

"She's unhappy," Liz said into the uncomfortable silence.

"Friend of yours?" Jesse asked.

"More like an acquaintance."

"She's a bitch."

"Do you think Josh wants to live with his father?" Tawny asked, sounding worried.

Liz didn't know. She hadn't seen Josh enough to have

an opinion. "She'd sure like to blame the theft of those trees on you," she told Jesse.

In a way that could make Liz's heart squeeze because he resembled his father so much, Jesse sent her a sardonic smile. "I'm a bad boy."

"Not as bad as me," The Brad Influence chimed in.

"Worse. My dad's a detective, and he can't control his own son. I went out in the dead of night, dug up twenty-two yew trees, and sold 'em for timber."

"Nobody wants yew trees for timber." Brad stuck out his tongue and rolled his eyes.

Something twitched inside Liz's brain. Something she almost knew. She thought about it long and hard while the three teenagers picked out ice cream flavors, but nothing gelled. Maybe later it would come to her.

Tawny, Brad, and Jesse decided to walk home together. Liz climbed back in her car. She was turning the ignition when Jesse suddenly leaned his arms on the door of the Miata. Sunlight slanted across his young face. She saw, vaguely, a resemblance to herself and it took her breath away.

"We really didn't take those trees," he said.

"I know."

"That's more than a prank. That's a damn lot of work."

Liz barely heard what he said. Something about the timbre of his voice picked at her memories of Hawthorne, and she couldn't really pay attention to anything besides the quality of those low, rumbly tones.

But later, when she was alone in her house, brushing her hair at the bathroom mirror and gazing at her own reflection and the slight tan she'd achieved over the last week and a half of much-anticipated sunshine, Liz considered Jesse's words.

Why would someone steal twenty-some trees that weren't worth much in timber?

And then the little prickling memory swam to the surface of her memory. Yews. Yew bark.

Grabbing the phone, she placed a call to Tawny and accidentally wakened Kristy, who sounded groggy and disoriented.

"I'm sorry," Liz apologized, realizing it was late. "Is Tawny there?"

"She's in her room. The music's loud." Kristy yawned.

"Kristy, do you remember when we were at the hospital and the doctor was talking to you about Taxol, the medicine you were prescribed?"

"Yes . . ."

"Where did he say it came from?"

"Oh, I remember that. It was weird. He said it came from the bark of yew trees. He said it took tons of bark to squeeze out the derivative for Taxol." She paused. "Is that what you wanted to know?"

"Yeah." Liz was thoughtful. "That's what I wanted to know."

"You want me to have Tawny call you?"

"No, that's okay. Take care, all right?"

Liz hung up. She thought about Mrs. Brindamoor's trees and wondered if she'd stumbled on the reason for the theft. If so, the culprit might be more easily caught and the heat would be off Jesse.

Drumming her fingers on the receiver, she considered calling Hawthorne and explaining her theory.

Do you just want to make contact?

No, she didn't want Hawthorne. Criminy, the guy had treated her abysmally sixteen years ago and she was still licking her wounds. She couldn't still have feelings. She *didn't* want contact.

Still, the memory of his blue-gray eyes and low voice and strong muscles did strange things to the cool detachment she prided herself on. With just the slightest trick of memory, she could recall sharp images from when his body and hers made magic: hair-roughened limbs, smooth sheets, slanting sunlight, trembling gasps, warm skin, and alcohol-laced breath.

She went to bed early that night, covering her head with blankets, listening to her heartbeat. *Don't think, don't think, don't think*, she admonished herself until way past the witching hour and into the empty hours of early morning.

Chapter Eight

The sun beat down with gleeful vengeance, as if laughing at the poor, foolish Washingtonians who'd prayed for deliverance from the rain mere weeks earlier. Hawthorne slipped Barney Turgate's key into the lock on his apartment door, meeting stale, sweltering air head-on. The rent was paid up for three months and no one had come to claim Barney's things. His ex-wife and daughter apparently didn't care in the least. Upon learning of her father's death, the daughter merely said, "How sad," in a bored tone that left Hawk feeling strange all day.

Barney had left no will; he'd thought he would live forever, according to those who knew him. Hawk stretched his shoulders and glanced around without much interest. Someday the landlord might actually manage to box up his belongings and turn them over to the state, but for now they remained in limbo, having been combed through time and again by the police as if his meager pile of worldly goods could hold some clue.

So far the only lead in the Turgate case was Manny Belding, and Hawthorne had had a hell of a time catching up with him.

The guy was a phantom. Everyone had seen him—ten minutes ago. The barkeep at the Elbow Room, whose first name was Lars, had made the mistake of relaying to Manny that Detective Hart was looking for him. Manny, assuming the worst, was now acting like a fugitive. Apparently, he believed if the cops wanted to talk to you, make yourself invisible.

Except he hadn't left Woodside, at least according to the landlady who rented him a garage apartment sadly in need of some TLC, paint, and indoor plumbing. She explained that he was around in a kind of vague way that reminded Hawk of those hazy, alcohol-numbed weeks after Laura's death. Yep, she was a tippler. But she was adamant that Manny was around.

Hawk had spent the last few weeks alternately working on the Turgate murder and fending off renewed bile from Mrs. Anita Brindamoor. Not enough was being done. No one had any gumption. Teenagers were running rampant. The Woodside Police Department was manned by fools and incompetents. She was going to the F.B.I.

Consequently, no one, including Chief of Police Dortner, had any burning desire to help her. Any sympathy once felt by Woodside's finest had been eradicated by furious remarks from an extremely sharp tongue.

One of the junior officers who'd been particularly scorned by Mrs. Brindamoor, based on his youthful appearance apparently, had even had the audacity to pin a newspaper picture of an elderly woman celebrating her one-hundredth birthday, label it "Our Friend Anita," and throw the first dart. Perry had been forced to remove it from the storeroom wall, but it kept making reappearances. Hawk was pretty sure he'd seen it there this morning.

So, Hawk had been following after Manny Belding and gleaning more information on Barney Turgate's small-town life. Turgate was as unremarkable as gray stone, yet people seemed to get a kick out of him. There was always a Barney somewhere. But any speculation on who'd killed him or why it had happened was offered with a shrug and a shake of the head.

He just didn't inspire that kind of fury, and he didn't have anything anybody really wanted.

"Maybe he was in the wrong place at the wrong time," one of the regulars holding up the Elbow Room bar suggested. "It happens."

Hawk pointed out that it was a very removed "wrong place" and it looked like Barney Turgate had been instrumental in setting up the time, be it wrong or otherwise. It turned out that the very property where he was killed was the site of one of old Barn's failed real estate deals. This had intrigued Hawk for a while. Maybe there were bad feelings over money. People had died for a lot less. But no, the property had been fought over by a couple of corporations that'd wanted to develop it. Any fight was with the city of Woodside, whose council wasn't interested in commercial development of any kind. Barney's failure as a real estate man was in thinking he could fight city hall. The corporations backed out and that was that.

So, now, he stood inside Barney's abode for the second time that week. It was a four-plex unit along the trendier side of Woodside's South End. Barn had recently made a few rungs up the economic ladder, enough to change his address and buy himself a newer model pickup that stood out front baking in the sun. Hawk had searched it a few days before. Nothing. He'd told the daughter about it, and she'd told him to sell it and send her the check.

Offspring. Ya gotta love 'em.

Inhaling the stale scent of small, hot rooms and forgotten belongings, Hawk couldn't help thinking about Jesse, who'd been remarkably "good" these past few weeks. His friend Brad had gotten a job at Lannie's and Jesse was showing interest in the work as well. Hawk hadn't suggested he find employment this summer because Jesse's irresponsibility had gotten him fired several times before. The kid just couldn't take orders. But now there was new hope.

So, Jesse hadn't been the headache he was earlier, and the investigation was proceeding at the rate of molasses in January, which left Hawk with time on his hands.

It gave him way too much time to think about Liz Havers.

"Damn," he muttered without heat. He should have known she would show up sometime. The fact that she'd been out of the picture until now meant little. She was Jesse's biological mother, and no matter how hard he wanted to believe—and have others believe—Laura had been Jesse's mother, it simply wasn't true.

He grimaced. He'd almost forgotten about Liz. She was a fuzzy memory from that grief-stricken, hellish period after Laura's death. She meant nothing to him. She'd been a panacea, and a damn poor one at that.

He would have felt guilt about using her; he would have worried about her feelings. But she'd almost destroyed the child he'd wanted so desperately to have with Laura, a child clearly never meant to be.

But then Jesse had come along, and he wasn't about to let anyone—especially the bluenose Havers family—take the boy away from him. Liz had given him Jesse, but that was as far as their relationship went—then and now.

Hawk shook his head, still startled by how beautiful Liz had become. Up until a few weeks ago, he wouldn't have been able to say what she looked like; he'd spent too many years crushing her memory. But when he'd suddenly seen her, he'd known immediately who she was. And it had hit him soul-deep.

And now she wanted to be part of Jesse's life, and she couldn't have come at a worse time. He was frightened Jesse might be susceptible to her, though he would never admit it. Though they'd been close during all those years alone together, he and Jesse had entered a pretty rough stretch. Who knew what could happen now?

Hawk had learned the hard way how to care for a baby. He'd been a single parent with a tough, demanding career to balance as well. It had been okay. They'd made out, somehow, until Joey's death and Jesse's subsequent dive into adolescence.

It was partly his own fault. He'd pulled away from Jesse at a time when his son had really needed him. He'd been unable to do anything else. If Laura still had been living and there to help, the transition might have been easier and Jesse might be on a more stable path.

Except Laura wasn't Jesse's mother. Liz Havers was.

"God . . ." Hawk murmured, shaking off the past and turning to the job. Here he was again. Looking for something. Anything. It was annoying to admit, but his investigations in Los Angeles had always followed predictable paths into drugs, sex, money, and power, and criminals invariably messed up. But here in his bucolic hometown, Hawthorne couldn't come up with one logical explanation to Barney Turgate's untimely death.

The guy just wasn't that interesting.

Hawk glanced around the living room of Barney's two-bedroom unit. Newspapers were stacked in piles all along the periphery. Old Barn loved the sports page; it was on the top of each pile and sometimes the rest of the paper beneath appeared to be untouched. His furniture looked like a cross between Grandma's hand-me-downs and bachelor chic: smoked-glass shelves and chrome tubular black-leather slingback chairs cheek by jowl with claw-footed, overstuffed armchairs sporting tattered lace doilies.

In his bedroom, Barney had several posters of big-breasted women bursting out of bikinis. Barn's appetites clearly hadn't matured over the years. Hawk lifted the blind and discovered a picture of Barn and Lora Lee on the windowsill. The fancy brass filigree frame suggested Lora Lee had bestowed the gift on her favorite guy. It looked to be a fairly recent photo, but Barney's expression seemed merely patient, while Lora Lee fairly glowed.

Poor, poor thing. Hawk, who generally refused to acknowledge or tap into deep emotions, couldn't help feeling sorry for Lora Lee Evans. He'd lost someone he loved to death. Its finality could be paralyzing.

He hoped Lora Lee would pull herself together and recover more quickly than he had.

Wandering aimlessly around the apartment, Hawk rotely catalogued the same information in his head he had his first time through: the same chip in the wall, the same hum of the refrigerator, the newspapers, the furniture, the pile of wood bits on the counter, the scent of dog urine that never quite faded.

The missing dog had been a mystery until the landlady, directly beneath Barn's unit, admitted that she'd taken the animal in when she'd learned of Barn's death. It was a tongue-lolling mutt who seemed as brain dead as the public declared Old Barn to have been. It certainly hadn't learned good toilet habits, or maybe Barney hadn't cared.

Hadn't cared . . .

Hawk understood about not caring, about giving up, about sinking into subterranean levels known only to the deeply depressed and mentally ill. He'd been there twice: once after Laura's death, though alcohol had been a twenty-four-hour friend that time; and once after Joey's. Jesse's impending birth had shocked him out of his first slide; this second one was more difficult to shake because no matter what Perry said, it was his fault.

He thought about that now, but surprisingly, its power had abated somewhat. Searching through his brain, he slammed smack dab into the cause: Liz Havers. Seeing her had pushed aside his misery like nothing else. She was bad news. She wanted to know Jesse. She was here to steal him away.

How weird. Hawk jerked as if physically struck. It had been Liz both times who'd brought him back from the brink.

So, what was she doing now? Plotting some way to infiltrate Jesse's life? Planning some scheme to win her son's affections after she'd abandoned him? Hoping to play mother now that it was eons too late?

For a moment Hawk thought serious, dark thoughts; then he suddenly threw back his head and laughed. Was he crazy? He must be.

She'd be lucky Hawthorne Jesse Hart didn't steal her goddamn black Miata and burn the interior with one of his cigarettes!

His heart lifted a little. One could only hope . . .

Liz pulled her car to a stop at the end of a field of small trees. Sprinklers were working overtime to keep their slender stalks from frying in the now ultrahot August sun. Climbing from the convertible, Liz leaned down and examined the nearest group of trees. Yew trees. Pacific yews, to be specific. Of the variety known to produce the drug Taxol, derived from the yew's bark.

Yep. She'd done a bit of research through the Forest Service.

And they'd suggested she meet with one tree farmer, Mr. Avery Francis, who lived about five miles outside of Woodside and whose main interest was the growing of Pacific yews for the production of their bark for Taxol.

Now, as she climbed back in the Miata and put it in gear, Liz wondered what the hell she expected to learn. She was no investigator, for Pete's sake, and she sure as heck didn't want to tell her theories to one Hawthorne Hart.

Or did she . . . ?

Speeding up the dirt pathway that bisected the yew tree fields, Liz left a plume of dust behind the Miata that could be seen for miles. By the time she reached the rather dilapidated farmhouse stuck in the middle of the fields, it was clear the occupant, Avery Francis, was already aware of her presence.

Expecting to meet some crusty old farmer, Liz was amazed when the man who walked onto the front porch was in his midthirties and wore a white shirt and holey blue jeans. Brown hair and eyes assessed her carefully and the suspicious look that had marred his features evaporated and he broke into a welcoming smile.

"I generally don't get such pretty company," he said, holding open the screen door. "Come in."

"I talked to some people at the Forest Service and they suggested I meet you," she said, although they'd already covered these particulars on the telephone.

"You said your friend's taking Taxol?"

"She was diagnosed with ovarian cancer and has had both ovaries removed, but she's taking Taxol, too."

"It's darn near a miracle drug," Avery said with a smile. "Taxol appears to be effective in combating breast, lung, and rectal cancers. An amazing discovery." He gestured toward the living room of the farmhouse, done in warm tones of fir and oak. "I'm a bachelor," he said, his gaze falling on the sparse and fairly unremarkable furniture tossed around the area. "Don't know a thing about decorating. Let me get you a chair."

It was an oak dining chair, a cheaply made rip-off of a classic style Liz had also invested in. She smiled. "You don't have to apologize to me. If it works, it's perfect."

"Could I get you something to drink? Coffee, soda, lemonade?"

She glanced outside to the back porch. A rusted double swing with a flowered cushion hung from the rafters. The thought of lemonade on a dusty summer afternoon, gently rocking in a swing, brought a smile to Liz's lips. Avery's gaze followed hers and he answered himself, "Two lemonades. I'll meet you out there."

He returned a few moments later with two tall glasses of lemonade—from a powder, not fresh squeezed. He was, after all, a bachelor. But it was heaven anyway, and while Liz touched a toe to the porch floorboards and sent her swing swaying softly, Avery sat on a rocker made of twisted tree limbs, which he explained had come with the house.

"I'm new at farming," he admitted. "Just got the bug and went into the yew bark business. It'll be a few years before I can harvest, though, so I've got some other things going, too."

Liz glanced at the little trees, valiantly reaching upward to a terribly hot sun. "How old do they have to be before you can harvest the bark?"

"Three to five years or so." He shrugged. "It takes long-term planning and a lot of prayer. If we get an Arcticlike freeze, they could be wiped out."

Liz made a sympathetic sound. "Did you know a lady

in Woodside lost all the yews lining her driveway? Someone took over twenty of them. Just ripped them out of the ground."

"What? Ugh."

"Do you think it could be for their bark?"

"Probably. Poachers are out there. It takes about nine thousand pounds of dry bark to produce a pound of Taxol. And Taxol sells for over twenty-five thousand dollars an ounce."

Liz grimaced. "So that's why Kristy's medicine costs an arm and a leg."

"And a few more limbs besides," Avery agreed. "That's why I'm growing the stuff."

"So, in your mind there's no doubt the trees were taken for their bark."

He spread his palms expansively. "If it looks like a duck, walks like a duck, and quacks like a duck, it's probably a duck. Besides, yew bark is collected only in the summer, when the sap's warm." He paused. "I think it's a duck."

Liz smiled. "The lady whose property was robbed thinks it was juvenile vandalism."

"I bet the police don't believe that."

"I don't know," Liz answered truthfully. "I haven't talked to them."

"You're just interested because of your friend?"

That sounded as lame as it was. "And I have teenage friends who're tired of being blamed."

"Ah . . ." He gazed at her with open appreciation. "What do you do, Ms. Liz Havers?"

"I'm a psychologist specializing in young adult problems. I've been hired by the Woodside school district, but I see patients on my own as well."

"Some of your patients have been on Anita Brindamoor's hit list, I take it."

"You know Mrs. Brindamoor?"

"I'd heard about her trees already," he admitted.

"Any idea who might have taken them?" Liz asked.

"Anybody who could be talked into doing a little midnight raiding for a quick buck or two."

"That could be quite a list," Liz realized.

"Well, they'd have to have the equipment to fell twenty-some trees, but there are a lot of ex-lumberjacks in this state, and some have been out of work for years."

Liz found she'd run out of questions. What was it to her anyway? This wasn't exactly her area of expertise, and a part of her knew she only cared because she wanted to free Jesse of suspicion and because she wanted to somehow show up Hawk with the information. Childish, yes. Fruitless, undoubtedly. But she was as human as the next person, and the thought of beating Hawk at his own game and scoring a few points warmed the cockles of her heart.

"Thanks so much for everything," she told Avery as she helped him take the glasses into the kitchen.

"My pleasure. And now I want something in return."

Liz's antenna went on alert.

"A return engagement. You have to promise this won't be the last time we see each other."

"You've got it," Liz said. She gave him a friendly glance. Why not? She'd been alone a long, long time, and Avery Francis was an interesting man.

What about Hawthorne Hart?

Liz snorted to herself. What about him? She and Hawthorne were as compatible as fire and ice, and she didn't give a goddamn about him anyway.

And there was absolutely no truth in that old axiom that she doth protest too much.

* * *

Splat! Brad shot a stream of tobacco juice somewhere near Jesse's feet. Examining the pool of brown liquid, Jesse stated tautly, "Watch it. Your aim sucks."

"I wasn't aiming for you."

"I *know* you weren't, but you damn near got me anyway."

"Sorr-eee. Jeez, you're touchy."

Jesse didn't answer. As far as he was concerned, he had a lot of things to be touchy about. Tawny and he were to-gether—kind of—but she was all wrapped up in her mother's illness and her dad's noise about moving her to Seattle. To top it off, she had some dance thing coming up the last day of August that was all she could talk about.

What the hell was he supposed to do now?

"Hey, c'mon," Brad said, quickening his pace. They'd been walking along the railroad tracks east of town and had reached an older neighborhood surrounded by fir trees. It seemed like half the houses used rusted car parts and trucks up on blocks as part of the landscaping.

Brad was in hog heaven. "We could steal some parts and sell 'em on the side at Lannie's."

"Oh, sure."

"Lannie's never there. We just do it all our way. It's great."

Brad's stab at employment wasn't exactly improving his character. Privately, Jesse felt he should have taken the job cleaning houses under construction for his uncle Roy. He, Jesse, had helped Brad out a time or two so he wouldn't get fired.

"What's the matter with you?" Brad demanded when Jesse lagged behind.

I'm sick of it, he thought. Sick of passing time and trying to think up another criminal prank.

"Shit," Jesse muttered aloud, wondering if he were growing up and thoroughly embarrassed at the idea.

"C'mon, there's the Listers'," Brad encouraged, jogging down the road to another ramshackle home choked with dry, brittle weeds. No car parts here. Just an overall sense of too little time invested in home, hearth, and real estate.

Jesse slowed to a walk behind Brad. "You want to see Carrie?"

"Yeah, why not? She's a good time."

Jesse wasn't so sure. Whether Brad knew it or not, or whether he cared if he did, Jesse remembered how Carrie had turned it on for him at Liz's office that day. If he'd given her half a glance, she would have been all over him. Jesse, who was still a virgin by choice, had experienced enough to know certain girls would get on you if you looked even marginally interested—sometimes if you didn't at all.

And that wasn't the kind of girl he wanted.

"Maybe you should start using the phone again and call up your Texas girl," Jesse suggested.

"I prefer 'em in the same state."

"Brad . . ."

"What?" Brad swiped back his hair, which had grown really shaggy and unkempt. Jesse thought of his own wild strands and wondered if it was time for a trim.

"Never mind."

Carrie spied them coming and ran out the front door and down the cracked concrete steps. Her black hair was pulled into a braid that made her look younger and more appealing, but her matching black lips didn't do it for him. Just imagining kissing her made the priesthood look inviting. And he wasn't even Catholic.

"Hey, guys," she greeted them with a grin. In a ragged pair of denim cutoffs and a navy tank top, her slim body was tough and athletic. A tattoo peeked from beneath one shoulder strap.

"So, what are you doing here?" she asked, her gaze all over Jesse.

Brad didn't appear to notice. "Just hangin'. Want to do something?"

"Sure. What?"

"The Ryerson twins are back from vacation . . ." He spread his palms open.

"We'll scare the shit out of 'em!" Carrie enthused.

"I'm out," Jesse stated flatly.

Carrie was crestfallen. "Why?"

"I don't give a damn about the Ryerson twins. Let's move on, for Christ's sake."

"All he can think about is that dead body we found," Brad declared, to which Carrie naturally asked a thousand questions because she hadn't heard who'd discovered Barney Turgate's body. Brad expounded upon the whole saga. Jesse remained silent. To hell with it all.

"Were you scared?" Carrie asked, sidling close to Jesse. She gazed up at him raptly.

"Nah."

"Yes, he was!" Brad crowed. "Ran like a rabbit!"

"So did you, asshole," Jesse reminded him angrily.

"Now he wants to solve the crime, just like his old man," Brad continued, desperately working to turn Carrie's attention his way and discredit Jesse. More power to him. Jesse wanted nothing to do with her.

"Yeah, well, I know one crime that's solved: that old bitch's missing trees."

"Who did it?" Jesse asked, dropping all pretense.

She gazed at him, assessing how much she should reveal. Her eagerness to gossip overcame her inclination to reel in Jesse by his interest in crime and she blurted out, "My mother's boyfriend. The dumbass and some buddies actually took down those trees all in one night. Had to drug the dog to do it."

"Why?" Jesse asked.

"Just being assholes, I guess." Carrie shrugged.

"How do you know this?"

Called upon for serious information, Carrie grew cagey. "I heard the asshole braggin' about it."

"I'm surprised the old lady didn't wake up," Jesse murmured. "I can't believe anybody could think we could do it."

"She's old and stupid," Brad declared, uninterested.

"And deaf as a post—to quote my mother," Carrie said, lips forming a sneer.

"Nobody's that deaf," Jesse was sure.

"Oh yeah? You taken a look at her? Double hearing aids—when she feels like wearin' 'em. And she doesn't ever wear 'em around the house, because I was there once with my mom. That lady don't hear nothin', believe me."

"But twenty-two trees? I mean, *trees*!"

Carrie shook her head. "That's what I'm sayin'. She can't hear, period. She goes into town bitchin' and moanin' about us juvenile cases, but she can't hear a bunch of assholes rippin' her trees out of the ground. She doesn't know jack shit."

"Maybe somebody put somethin' in her drink, like they drugged the dog," Brad suggested.

"Oh sure. Like you're going to have a drink with someone like her." Jesse snorted his annoyance.

"Maybe he walked into her house and put somethin' in her drink." Brad stuck out his chin belligerently, refusing to be wrong.

"The asshole did that once. Spiked the jar of iced tea we keep in the fridge. He said he wanted to get me drunk." She shrugged. "We were all wasted that night. Mom thought it was her wine, but I was flyin' high, too."

"Great guy," Jesse muttered.

She nodded. "He's a bastard."

"You didn't like getting drunk? Oh, come on." Brad laughed aloud.

"I don't like *him*," she clarified.

"Brad, I'm heading back," Jesse said, itching to get motoring away from Carrie Lister and all this talk. It bothered him at some level he couldn't assess.

"Go on, then," Brad dismissed him.

"No, don't go," Carrie whined.

Jesse paid no attention. Breaking into a jog, he headed back toward what passed as civilization in this rural hell-hole. But the thought of facing his father—whom he shared grunts with over what his daily itinerary might be—turned his feet in the direction of Tawny's.

Kristy sat just inside her back porch on a rattan lounge, her feet tucked within a blue and green afghan. She sipped iced tea, courtesy of Liz, and listened as Liz and Tawny wrangled good-naturedly on the patio about whether Tawny should invite her father to the dance recital.

"I don't want him to come," Tawny said, showing an unusual obstinacy.

"It'll do more good than harm," Liz argued. "If he sees how locked in you are to the community, he'll—"

"He won't care. He's obsessed."

"—understand how much you want to stay."

"Wanna bet?" Tawny raked her fingers through her hair. "My recital's the thirty-first. He'll make me leave with him. School starts the next week."

"He won't just take you away. He can't."

Kristy cleared her throat, and both Tawny and Liz glanced her way. "He's looking for an excuse. Just don't give him one and everything'll be fine. Tawny, you've got to ask him to your recital."

"You promise I don't have to go with him?"

"I promise," Kristy said solemnly.

"I don't even know him that well," Tawny whispered, turning to Liz.

"Hey, babe, I know."

"I won't leave with him."

Teen rebellion brewing big-time. Liz recognized it and, upon meeting Kristy's eyes, realized Tawny's mother did, too.

The doorbell rang and Tawny raced through the house to admit Jesse. Liz slowly walked into the family room and took a chair next to Kristy's. Kristy watched her daughter react animatedly to Jesse and her gaze shifted to Liz. They shared a look.

Kristy was the only person besides Hawthorne and herself who knew the whole story—at least from Liz's end.

"We'll be back in a while. We're just going for a walk," Tawny sang out moments before the front door closed behind them and they were gone.

When Kristy didn't immediately remark on the situation,

Liz took the initiative. "I don't know how long I can remain silent."

"Have you talked to his father recently?"

"No."

"You said you were going to tell him your theory on the yew trees."

"I've said a lot of things," Liz murmured a trifle bitterly. "I know I should try to forge a relationship. I know it would ease my way with Jesse. But it's *so hard.*"

"You want me to talk to him? I mean, his son is seeing my daughter." Kristy smiled.

Liz smiled in return. She felt like a heel, absorbed in her own problems when Kristy's were a million times worse. "How're you feeling?"

"The same as when you asked me twenty minutes ago. Fine. Tired. Surgery's a bitch, isn't it? But things are going well so far. Remission, though it's really too early to tell, I guess."

"Are you worried about Guy?"

"No. I mean, come on. I'm doing pretty well, and Tawny's damn near perfect. I've let him have visitation rights, which he's ignored until now. No judge would grant him custody." She set down her glass and stretched her arms over her head like a contented cat. She'd been through the fire. She was safe.

"Tawny would have to suddenly turn criminal before anyone could find fault with her upbringing. Guy's the loser," Liz agreed. Still . . . Guy Fielding had a lot of money and even more determination. Like a hungry lawyer desperate for any case, he wouldn't go away until he'd gotten his way. "All right, you've shamed me into it. I'll go see Hawthorne."

"He might be impressed with your theories."

Liz's laughter echoed through the house. Kissing Kristy on the cheek, she murmured, "When did hell freeze over, and why didn't someone tell me?" With that, she took a deep breath, examined the mettle of her courage, and headed for the Woodside Police Station.

Chapter Nine

Doodling on a notepad, Hawk made a face and thought over his latest conversation with the Manny Belding sighters. One of Manny's buds, who favored a dim bar sandwiched between an old clapboard building that housed a perpetual flea market and a less-than-squeaky-clean laundromat to the relative spiffiness of the Elbow Room, had insisted Hawk have a drink with him—a serious scotch and water, mind you—before he would talk. Because Hawk had basically given up booze after his collapse into its soothing depths once before, he'd declined. But Manny's pal, Ed McEwan, wouldn't hear of it, and Hawk had nursed a drink while Ed loosened his jaw.

Two things happened: Hawk recognized the dangers of alcohol again by waking up dead drunk three hours later and Ed told him that Manny Belding and Barney Turgate were business partners.

"Business partners?" Hawk had asked with the beginnings of alcohol's sweet numbness softening all the edges.

"Big money, Barn said. Big, big money." Envy loomed in Ed's booze-reddened eyes. "I been workin' my butt off for years runnin' my daddy's farm. Never worth a penny except for the land, and taxes eat that up anyway. Some inheritance, huh? The old man was a bastard, but it sure didn't help when he died."

This little speech slurred and jerked along, but Hawthorne picked up the gist of it. "Do you know what they were into?"

Ed snorted. "Farming! Can ya beat that? Barney was in real estate, y'know, but that turned to shit. And Manny was always scroungin' off some rich relative back East who finally gave him a stupid-ass job bein' a goddamn rep for a bullshit company he owned. Good way to pass somebody a few bucks, huh? We should all be so lucky." Ed burped at this juncture, forgot what he was saying, then came back madder and meaner. "They're both fuckin' assholes. One's dead now, and I don't give a fuck."

"Where's Manny?" Hawk had managed to insert before Ed tore off on a further f-word rampage—something he was wont to do, as Hawthorne had learned.

"Fuck . . ."

And that was the end of Ed's enlightening tale. Now, Hawk wondered if making another pilgrimage to Manny's garage apartment was worth the effort. Nothing had come of his trip to Barney's.

Still . . .

The station's front buzzer announced a visitor. Hawk was seated in the back, at the desk reserved for whoever needed one. He'd recently appropriated it, at Perry's eager suggestion, and now felt as if he did indeed belong here. For too long he'd been living in limbo. Time to heal.

"Hello, Hawk," a cool, familiar voice greeted him.

He glanced up swiftly, surprised. Liz Havers stood before him, crisp and collected in a pair of khaki shorts and a white sleeveless blouse. Her tan limbs glowed with good health and her hair, light brown and shining, swung gently, just brushing her shoulders. But it was Liz's eyes that arrested him. A shade of blue-green close to turquoise. Lighter, though. And so brilliant he could still remember seeing his reflection in them all those years ago.

Dim memories. The result of liquor. He fervently thanked the fates that had saved him from a life of alcoholism, and this latest falling off the wagon had just reconfirmed the intensity of his resolve.

"Liz," he returned stiffly.

"I have a police matter I'd like to discuss—with you."

Her hesitancy rang out even while her voice held an edge of belligerency. "Chief Dortner is out right now. You can wait or I can have him call you." To hell with it. She didn't really want to talk to him, and he certainly didn't need the aggravation.

"I said, I'd like to discuss it with you."

He eyed her blandly. *What you really said was you'd rather fight the fires of hell than be anywhere near me.* "Does this have something to do with Barney Turgate's murder?"

"No."

"What is it?"

She seemed to want to look anywhere but in his direction. Her gaze moved restlessly over his desk to the front of the building to Dortner's cluttered mess and back. "I've heard a lot about Mrs. Brindamoor's missing trees."

Hawk's brows lifted. "From Jesse?"

"Well, partly."

"Go ahead."

"I think I might know why they were taken." She gave him a look. He could read triumph in her eyes. Irked, he said, "So, you're involved in Mr. Turgate's murder and also you've found out about the missing yews. You're in the wrong profession."

She lowered her lashes, stung. That bothered him, too. He hadn't meant to be nasty, but Lord, she brought out the worst in him.

"I think they were taken for their bark."

In front of his eyes, she dropped her bravado and transformed into a beautiful woman who'd clearly puzzled out an answer—one that could very well be correct, he realized. He wished he weren't so distracted by her.

"Take a seat," he said gruffly, watching obliquely as she crossed her legs and settled into a chair. "Why do you think the trees were taken for their bark?"

"I met with a man named Avery Francis, who's a yew bark farmer." Carefully, meticulously, she explained the nature of Taxol, the cancer-fighting drug that was, coincidentally, one that her friend, Mrs. Fielding, was taking. While she talked, Hawk returned to doodling, way too cognizant of the soft, fresh scent of her perfume and the rise and fall of her voice.

"So . . . what do you think?" she asked at length.

He realized he was scratching out a series of evergreen trees, a tiny forest. The connections sizzled, and Hawk found himself admiring her.

Which pissed him to no end.

"So, you think poachers felled Anita Brindamoor's twenty-two yew trees to sell the bark to profiteers?"

"To someone," she agreed.

"Like a drug company?"

"I don't know." A bit of doubt crept into her voice.

Hawk considered all she'd said. She was waiting. Feeling foolish now, as she realized she hadn't thought it completely through. But Hawk was impressed despite himself.

"It sure makes more sense than to believe a couple of

teenagers spent a night yanking out twenty-two trees just because they felt like it."

Her lips parted in surprise. She hadn't expected him to believe her in the least. "That's what I thought."

"Mrs. Brindamoor's can't be the only yew trees stolen, then," Hawk added thoughtfully.

"Apparently, there's a lot of money in it," Liz added.

Big money. Big, big money . . .

Ed's words came back to haunt him. Hawk wondered if Barney could somehow be involved with this deal. Liz had said Taxol cost about twenty-five thousand dollars an ounce.

Big money.

Hawthorne stared into Liz's eyes. For a moment, he was thrown back in time to when she'd sat across the table from him at the inn where the Elbow Room now stood. It startled him to realize that even though that period of his life was hazy, certain aspects, perfect moments, remained in his brain with awesome clarity.

He remembered what she'd worn that first day. A pair of slim-fitting denim jeans and a short-sleeved, peach-colored blouse with an open collar. He'd noticed the smoothness of her throat, and over the intervening years, nothing much had changed. The khaki shorts she wore today were casual and sent him a view of slim, muscular limbs, and the sleeveless blouse once again seemed to heighten attention to her long throat.

In a distant corner of his mind, Hawthorne admitted how beautiful she was. And he could see a resemblance to Jesse in the quirk of her brow, the turn of her head, the shade of her hair.

With a certain amount of horror, he realized he was still attracted to her. Very attracted.

And she was the last female on earth he wanted to be attracted to.

"I hope she quits blaming every teenager in town for the deed," Liz said, raking a hand unconsciously through her hair. Strands slipped through her fingers. Honey gold. Satin threads. She gave him a quick look. "Think she'll get off that?"

"No," Hawk admitted. "She wants it to be Jesse and Brad."

"But if you told her this theory . . . ?"

"She's already threatened to have me removed from the case for bias. Unfortunately, Chief Dortner insists I stay on it." He inhaled deeply. "Although it's looking more interesting than I thought."

Liz smiled, clearly pleased. Hawthorne felt his muscles tighten. Expectation. Anticipation. The old male-hormone thing responding to an enticing female.

"Thanks," he said briefly. "Was there anything else?"

"Um . . . no."

"Have you seen much of Jesse?"

"What do you mean?"

"I mean, I know he's seeing that friend of your's daughter. I'm sure you're right there."

His cold tone penetrated. She half-winced. Good. He didn't want to like her, therefore she couldn't like him.

"I've seen him a few times."

"He doesn't know yet, does he?"

"I said I wouldn't tell him, and I won't. It is my job, you know, to have some understanding about teens and how to deal with them. He should be told soon, but unfortunately, that decision is really yours."

"How noble." Hawk sent her a faint smile.

"It just makes sense."

"Who are you kidding? You're going to tell him when

you feel like it and there's not a damn thing I can do about it—except try to keep the two of you apart."

"What are you so afraid of?" Liz demanded, her cheeks flushing.

"Damn near everything."

"Liar," she whispered, her gaze dueling with his. It wasn't often Hawk met a woman willing—no, *eager*—to do battle, but Liz Havers had clearly been waiting a long, long time. "I'm not going to apologize for wanting to know my son."

"You say anything to him, he'll turn on you like nothing you've ever seen in your sheltered life."

"You don't have to scare me. I know what to do."

"Neither of us knows what to do," he retorted tautly. A pulse beat somewhere inside his head. Anger, or desire? He didn't want to know.

She jumped to her feet. "Forget I ever came in here. From now on, I'm handling things my way."

"You step in where you shouldn't, I'll cut you down."

"Strong words, Detective Hart."

"I've got stronger ones."

Bull's-eye. A direct hit. A flash of indecision and pain in those eyes. Her skin paled beneath her new tan, and a twinge of regret twisted Hawk's conscience.

"Good-bye," she bit out.

"Think hard about what you plan to do," he added as a final warning.

"Yeah, yeah . . ." She walked out the door, back straight, hair swinging, strides filled with repressed fury. Through the window, he watched her cross the street to her little black car.

As soon as she was out of sight, he sank back into his chair and swallowed hard. Her scent lingered. Images danced behind his eyes from that time long, long ago. Taut, muscular limbs wrapped around him. Soft sighs and rapid heartbeats. Warm, lazy afternoons when he'd locked grief in a distant part of his brain and the rest of him belonged to Liz Havers.

He'd had years to get over her. Hell, he hadn't even *thought* about her. How could it be that after all this time she was the first woman to stir his blood, when she should be the last?

"Damn it," he muttered to the world in general. The last thing he needed was another complication.

Brad drew hard on the tip of his cigarette and exhaled like he'd been smoking for years. Which, if Jesse thought about it, was very likely. When Jesse had first arrived in Woodside he'd hooked up with Brad because they were birds of a feather. Brad's happy-go-lucky nature, coupled with his total lack of inhibitions and a general desire to raise hell, had been a magnet for Jesse. They were two halves of a whole. Young, wild, and looking for trouble.

Except Brad was really beginning to get on his nerves.

Thunking his finger against the round can visible through the pocket of Brad's T-shirt, Jesse asked, "After you're done smoking, you plan to have a dip?"

"Yeah. Maybe. Why?"

Jesse couldn't answer. He was irked. Pissed, really, that Brad was so *the same.*

"You'll be dead before you're thirty."

"What are you, my mother?"

He didn't know what the hell was wrong with him. "Just don't make a sound. Remember what we're trying to do here."

Brad snorted and took another drag. The cigarette tip glowed red in the deepening twilight. They were outside Carrie Lister's house, waiting for a glimpse of her mother's boyfriend. Jesse wanted to know who this guy was. Carrie thought he had stolen Old Lady Brindamoor's trees, and it dug at Jesse's curiosity. When he'd been younger, he might have taken the information to his father; he'd really liked that whole Boy Scout thing once.

From faraway, a dog barked. Then it howled. A lonely, eerie sound that was echoed by another dog, and yet another. Brad cocked his head, and Jesse shivered a little. He was glad he'd talked Tawny out of coming.

Faintly, he smiled, remembering their argument. "I want to be there," she'd declared.

"No way. We'll come back and tell you all about it."

"What if he catches you?"

"What if he does?" Jesse asked. "We're not doing anything."

"Trespassing," Tawny pointed out stubbornly.

"That's why you can't go."

His roundabout logic drove her crazy. She set her jaw, looked down at her toes, then glanced up at him in that sideways way that got to him. "I want to be there with you," she said softly.

He'd almost caved. Boy, had he ever wanted to. But the truth was, he didn't know what the hell would come down. Any boyfriend of Carrie's mother was bound to be trouble; the Listers were just made that way. And if the asshole really had stolen over twenty trees for their bark . . . well . . .

"We'll be back," he'd answered just as softly, and because he'd felt like it, he'd dragged her close and kissed her forehead—a bold move he still couldn't believe he'd made, but it had felt so right.

He feared he was in love.

"Shhh . . ." Brad stepped back into the shadows of the laurel hedge as a pickup swerved into the driveway. Jesse pressed himself against thick green leaves, his shoulder touching Brad's.

Moonlight fell across a patch of gravel right at the nose of the truck as it cruised to a stop. The newcomer cut the engine and it hiccupped a couple of times before it shook violently and died. A man climbed out, eased the small of his back, then stumbled forward, as if he'd had a few too many drinks. He staggered on the stairs, swore, grabbed the rail, half-hung on it a second, then struggled the rest of the way up the front steps. With a hammy fist, he pounded on the front door. Carrie's mom opened the door and immediately they had words. A sharp, angry fight broke out to which Brad and Jesse heard a smack and then wild crying.

The boys exchanged silent looks in the darkness. The newcomer had hit Carrie's mom.

"Fucker," Brad whispered.

"Who is he?" Jesse asked.

"Don't know. I've seen him around, though."

"I want to know who he is."

"Why don't we just ask Carrie, dumbass?" Brad suggested.

Jesse thought about the scene he'd just witnessed. He shook his head and Brad, showing more intuitiveness than usual, silently agreed. Stealthily, the two boys headed for the road, and as soon as they were out of sight of the house, they ran like wild dogs.

It was evening. Hot and sultry. Unusually so for Woodside, even in August. Liz wore a full-length, tan sundress that snapped up the front. The snaps were undone to just above her knee, so that she could move freely, and she currently was striding along the boardwalk that circled Woodside's largest park where, tonight, there was an outdoor barbecue, a fund-raiser for Woodside High's fall sports. Liz had met several of the teachers and coaches who were helping the kids organize the event, so she'd thought she'd stop in and offer her services. She could flip a burger with the best of them.

A slice of Americana. If there were a traveling carnival pitched down the road with a Ferris wheel . . . nirvana.

Which reminded her of Jesse and his favorite band.

She'd had a conversation with him about it, briefly, one afternoon. He'd been at the Fieldings', waiting for Tawny. Liz was there, waiting for him, though of course he didn't know it. Tawny, immersed in a phone call to her father, wasn't immediately available, so Liz had enjoyed a few extra moments with her son.

It wasn't that Jesse objected to being with her. As far as adults went, she was about as cool as they got; she could read that clear enough. It was that teenagers didn't see adults. Their world was so closed that anyone over the age of nineteen was damn near invisible.

Yet Jesse could recite Kurt Cobain's life story as if he were going to be tested on it. Liz realized her son was merely going through the motions of living in Woodside, Washington. His fantasy life was clearer, closer to him. He wasn't so different from other teenagers, but his passion, at least currently, happened to be the long-dead lead singer of Nirvana, who was a suicide victim to boot.

It could scare a mother to the depths of her soul.

Still . . . being a good listener was worth its weight in gold. She, too, now knew more about Kurt Cobain than most of the rest of the world.

The most interesting bit of information she'd gleaned was one Jesse didn't even deem important: Cobain had grown up in Aberdeen, Washington, not so very far from

Woodside. He'd found his way to the Seattle alternative rock scene, and then fame hit him like a freight train— something he apparently never really wanted. To Cobain, music was everything. That and heroin. But when an overdose didn't do the trick, Cobain shot himself with a shotgun . . .

A frisson slid down Liz's back. The stuff nightmares were made of. Yet most kids managed to find their way through the maze of adolescence without getting lost completely. Jesse might have a fascination with Cobain, but that didn't necessarily mean he had the same fascination with suicide.

She had to keep reminding herself of that.

And truthfully, though she knew she was probably being overly optimistic, she sensed Jesse was out of danger. Since she'd first met him, he seemed brighter, more focused, yet a little detached, too. As if none of it really mattered as much as people liked to believe.

Lord, she hoped she was right.

Liz turned onto another boardwalk that angled toward the center of the park. Japanese lanterns hung from a wire, casting mellow pools of pastel colors onto the ground. To one side were three propane-powered barbecues going gangbusters, while two administrators and one coach hawked burgers good-naturedly to a generally chatty crowd.

The scent of broiled beef and onions and spicy mustard wafted through the air. The *plink, plink, plink* of a soft rock quartet, tuning guitars, vied with the screech of jerry-rigged microphones as voices tested the sound system.

Liz smiled and soaked in the sensation. All those years ago of dying to get out of Woodside—what a waste. It was love at second sight. It was coming home.

"Hey, there, stranger," a male voice said warmly. Liz

turned. Avery Francis, in tan Dockers and a white Polo shirt, pointed a finger at her. "What does it take to get you to call me?"

"The phone works both ways," Liz pointed out lightly.

"Yeah, well, I guess I like this in-person stuff better anyway."

Liz just kept smiling. She wasn't sure what to do with Avery. Flirting was long over for her. She was too rusty, and she'd never liked it much in the first place. Besides, she hadn't made up her mind whether she was really in the mood to date someone. A date sounded so innocuous. One date. But invariably, it led to another, and then decisions needed to be made.

Or worse, you really liked the guy and after one date, *poof,* he disappeared.

That didn't, however, appear to be the problem with Avery.

"Could I interest you in a burger?" he asked, lightly touching her elbow and guiding her in the direction of the barbecue.

It seemed easier to acquiesce than demur, which was what she really felt like doing. She and Avery jostled through the line, filled paper plates with hamburgers, chips, a cookie, and picked up a soft drink at the end. They sat next to each other at a picnic table, which Liz found difficult because she had to keep half-turning to talk to him.

And what was there to talk about? She knew next to nothing about him except for the yew trees.

Which was as good a place to start as any.

"How long did you say it would be before you could harvest?" Liz asked, biting into her hamburger. It was rather dry and the bun could have been fresher, but hey, what did one expect from an outdoor barbecue fund-raiser?

"Three to five years, and this is my first season. Wish

I'd gotten onto this scheme faster. It's good money, but you've still got to be patient."

Remembering Hawk's questions at the station, Liz asked, "Who actually buys the yew bark?"

Avery was eager to talk. "Pharmaceutical companies that want to produce Taxol. One company's currently got an exclusive contract with the National Cancer Institute to bring the drug to market, so you've got to get with them—although that'll probably change."

"And all of this Taxol comes only from Pacific yews?"

"Well, no. You can also get it from the needles and twigs of the more common Himalayan yew, which actually produces a chemical precursor of the drug that can then be transformed into Taxol. But Pacific yew bark's still the most direct route."

"Interesting."

He smiled the smile of someone counting money in the bank. "All I really have to do now is prove myself."

"Prove yourself?"

Avery nodded. "The big wood products companies have millions of trees planted to produce Taxol. They're in like Flynn with the pharmaceutical companies connected with the National Cancer Institute. It's like the in crowd, y'know? You've got to be in."

"How do you get in?"

"There are always ways, otherwise the poachers wouldn't be doing such a bang-up business." He shoved his plate aside and rested his forearms on the table, as if he were settling in for a long yarn. "There's so little Taxol available that the black market's huge. And most of the mature Pacific yews are on Forest Service land, so poachers head onto all that acreage and just take, take, take. Of course, if you get caught—" He dragged a finger across his neck. "Penalties are stiff."

"How hard is it to catch a poacher?"

Avery thought about that for a moment. "Environmentalists are all over this thing because Pacific yews grow in old-growth areas. And the tree huggers can't bear to have them cut down."

Liz wasn't certain she agreed with his sardonic tone. "Well, there are limited old-growth trees. It takes years and years. I can see why people would want to preserve them."

He sniffed. "You sound like a Californian. Tell the truth, you fell in love with those pictures of the poor spotted owl."

Avery was referring to the owl that had gained national attention because it only made its nests in old-growth timber. Harvesting old growth had displaced the owls and limited their nesting area, hence the creatures were diminishing rapidly and possibly facing extinction. Ads with cute little baby spotted owls looking forlorn and helpless had aided environmentalists in acquiring donations to help save them. Timber companies were the enemy, but timber was used for housing and old growth was the best.

There were no easy answers.

"I grew up in Woodside," Liz informed Avery a trifle coolly. "And yes, I'd like to save the spotted owl, but I know we need timber, too."

"Well, there're a lot of people out there who'd do anything to stop tree harvesting. They go out in the woods and form circles with their friends. Sing and chant and make a goddamn nuisance of themselves. Drives everybody crazy. But once in a while they catch a poacher in action; then they're vicious. Like to cut the guy's balls off, if they could." He paused, then added, "You can't trust fanatics."

Liz silently agreed, but a part of her brain had ceased listening. Avery Francis was a bit of a one-note song, and though his interest in yew tree farming was what had brought her to him in the first place, it also appeared to be the only thing they had in common.

As if reading her thoughts, his hand suddenly stole sideways to cover hers. Liz's first instinct was to recoil, but she refrained. She just couldn't help her reaction. Would it be this way with any man? she wondered. Or was this aversion to Avery Francis specific?

"How would you like to—" He cut himself off with a sharp intake of breath.

Liz glanced around. Spying the reason Avery had cut off so abruptly, her heart started pounding. She slid a sideways glance at her "date." Hawthorne Hart was on the boardwalk, headed straight their way.

Chapter Ten

"You know him?" Avery asked under his breath, his gaze on Hawk.

"We've met," Liz said carefully.

"He's a hotshot detective from L.A. who's moonlighting here with the local police department. A first-class asshole, from all accounts."

"Really." Liz hid her expression inside her paper cup, nearly choking on her soda.

To her dismay, Hawk walked straight to their table and seated himself across from her and Avery. This disconcerted Avery to no end, and it didn't do much for Liz either.

"Detective Hart?" Avery asked, holding out his hand. "Avery Francis."

Hawk gave him a long look, but he shook his hand. "The yew tree farmer," he said, and Liz was impressed that he remembered so quickly.

"That's right," Avery said, clearly trying to figure out how, or why, Hawk knew so much about him.

Liz jumped in. "Avery was just telling me more about the yew tree business."

"Ms. Havers said you agreed that poachers may have taken Mrs. Brindamoor's trees," Hawk said smoothly. "That right?"

"Mm-hmm."

"So, there's quite a bit of money in it?"

"Can be," Avery agreed.

"I've been doing a little research," Hawk put in conversationally, but Liz's radar went on alert. A little research? Hawthorne Hart never did anything without an express purpose.

With a jolt, she realized how well she knew him for how little time they'd actually been around each other. Food for thought, she told herself, not liking it one bit.

"Most of the Pacific yews around here are on Forest Service land—about eighty percent—and you have to have a permit to cut the trees. But only certain people can get a permit, and those are determined by the Forest Service." Hawk let that sink in, then said, "Apparently, that's the Forest Service's way of making sure trees aren't being wasted."

"Makes sense," Avery agreed. He, too, could see how intense Hawk was, and he was trying hard not to squirm.

"I talked to a guy named Rob over there who said poachers have been showing phony permits. Even some of the people issued real permits have been turning in large amounts of yew bark from a very small number of trees." Hawthorne's smile didn't quite reach his eyes. "You find a crook every time you lift a rock."

"I hope the Forest Service is cracking down on those permits," Avery said.

Hawk nodded. "It'd be a shame to let some of the opportunists out there slip through the cracks. I'd hate to see the undeserving make some quick money."

Liz had the distinct feeling she was missing a whole lot

of subtext. Clearly, Hawthorne was sending Avery some message she was meant to only guess at.

"Ain't that the truth," Avery said, his smile a little forced.

Hawk turned to Liz. She swept in a breath, way, way too susceptible to the shock of his blue eyes. He had no right to look so good.

"Jesse's missing," he said, bringing her to earth with a bang.

"What? Did you try the Fieldings?" Liz was supremely conscious of Avery's listening ears. If Hawk wanted to keep their relationship secret, he was doing a damn poor job of it.

"Someone stole a couple of four-packs of wine coolers from Lannie's. An employee. Brad's name came up."

"But that doesn't mean Jesse's involved."

Hawk lifted a brow, silently saying how naïve she was.

"Who's Jesse?" Avery asked.

"A friend of mine," Liz answered. "I told you, I'm the school psychologist."

"Ahh." Avery frowned, clearly not getting it.

She lifted a brow to Hawk in response, silently querying him on whether he wanted their relationship to be Woodside's newest gossip.

His mouth tightened into a knife-blade line. The answer was pretty clear.

"Could I talk to you a moment?" Hawk asked, an edge to his voice.

"Sure." Liz picked up her paper plate and cup and dumped them in the designated trash can.

"I'll call you," Avery said vaguely as Liz walked away with Hawthorne. He watched them as they headed along the boardwalk that bisected the park.

"Did I interrupt a date?" Hawk asked when they were out of earshot. He sounded so much like a spurned lover who was trying hard to be cool that Liz smothered a smile. "What's so funny?" he demanded, watching her.

"Nothing. We just accidentally bumped into each other."

"Avery Francis doesn't seem like the kind of man to accidentally do anything."

"You don't like him much, do you?"

Her directness derailed Hawk momentarily. At a loss for words, he merely kept pace with her. Liz took the opportunity to walk past the festivities to the end of the boardwalk, where a small creek bubbled westward, away from the hubbub. Here the gurgle of water and whisper of leaves seemed remote, as if they were a long, long way from civilization with all its traps and trappings.

"You really think Jesse's involved in this theft?" Liz asked.

"It wouldn't be the first time."

Liz wanted to argue but quelled the urge. She knew. Better than most. "Will the store press charges?"

Hawk nodded, his face gaunt in the shifting shadows of moonlight. Illumination from the Japanese lanterns was far away. "It's their policy. It tends to keep their employees more honest."

"Oh, Brad." Liz sighed, more resigned than upset.

"I thought they'd be at the barbecue, but I guess not."

"Are you sure it couldn't be someone else?"

"It could be anybody who works there, but they all fingered Brad."

"He's their newest employee. Maybe they used him as a scapegoat."

She expected him to laugh at her, but he merely frowned in a way that she'd come to recognize as his expression when he rolled something over in his mind. "Maybe," he said at length. "They were pretty solid on it being Brad, which isn't the way things usually go down. Mostly they protect one another."

This lightened Liz's heart. "That's right."

"Maybe they're protecting themselves and to hell with the new guy on the block." He rubbed a hand over his jaw, a curiously sensual gesture. "I wish Jesse would materialize."

"Maybe he's already home."

"That would be a long shot."

They stood in silence for several moments. The breeze tugged at Liz's hem, undulating the tan folds around her knees. She felt overdressed, yet that was ridiculous. Hawthorne wore a white shirt, sleeves rolled to just below the elbows, and a pair of jeans. His pants rode low on his hips and were worn around the edges in a very attractive way, the image seemingly imprinted on Liz's retinas.

So much for worrying she wouldn't be attracted to another man. Criminy. This man was the worst choice of all.

"So, what was that all about with Avery?" she asked lightly, more as a means to steer the conversation to something neutral than for any burning desire to know.

"What do you mean?"

"You acted as if he were a poacher." She hesitated. "Is he?"

Hawthorne stretched his shoulders and shrugged. "All I know about Avery Francis is that he suddenly turned up in Woodside, asked a lot of questions, tried to be a little too friendly to some of the locals, who're suspicious of everyone, and then decided to grow Pacific yews."

"Something wrong with that?"

Hawk looked at her. *Big, big money . . .* "I don't know yet."

A softball thunked down their way, passing between them. A boy of about twelve loped after it, dark hair flopping. At the same instant, Liz heard a loud pop: a car backfiring. Before she could turn her head, she was slammed to the ground, along with the boy, who screamed and flailed his arms.

She could feel Hawk's body pressing down against hers, quivering all over.

"Hey! Hey! *Let go!*" the kid yelled. He squirmed away from Hawk's grasp, jumped to his feet, and ran like hell.

"Hawk?" Liz whispered, scared.

"Joey . . . ?"

Confused, Liz said, "He's all right."

He didn't answer. Unwillingly, she noticed how the contours of his body meshed with hers, matching perfectly. The slightest movement would be described as sensual, so she stayed still.

Distantly, she recognized the trembling. Some kind of trauma going on here, Liz realized through her own needs and desires. With a strange feeling of déjà vu, she wrapped her arms around him and simply waited. Like old times at the Candlewick Inn. Hawk locked inside his own private hell and Liz providing comfort.

Slowly, he drew a shattered breath, lifting his head. Those inner demons danced in the depths of his eyes. It took him a long time to focus on her and when he did, he immediately rolled off her onto his back.

"Who's Joey?" she finally asked, having come to the conclusion that it wasn't the boy with the softball.

Hawk didn't answer. Liz sat up, dusting herself off. Footsteps warned of approaching visitors and Hawk climbed to his feet, silently offering Liz a hand.

The footsteps stopped short. A woman with a scowl on her face and the twelve-year-old boy by one hand glared at Hawk. "What the hell do you think you were doing? I could have you arrested for assault!"

"Oh, no," Liz began, but the woman swept on, her fury escalating with each syllable.

"My son says you threw him to the ground and held him down. I've sent someone for the police. Don't leave. They'll find you. What kind of sick bastard are you?" She shook with fear and anger.

Hawk, still dealing with his own torment, couldn't seem to think of an answer. Liz came to his rescue.

"Detective Hart is a police officer," she told the woman. "He heard the backfire and pushed both your son and me to the ground to protect us. He thought it was a gunshot."

Her mouth dropped open. She blinked rapidly. She was so upset she couldn't shift gears that fast. "Well, he shouldn't have!" she declared in outrage. "He shouldn't have!"

"I'm sorry, ma'am," Hawk put in. "You're absolutely right. I should have given some warning to your son at the same moment, so he'd know."

"You scared us," she cried, then burst into tears.

A crowd surged around them, everyone staring at Hawk as if he were a child molester—everyone except those who knew he was a police officer. They wanted to know where the pedophile had raced off to.

Liz explained the mistake, quietly, calmly, and in a way that minimized embarrassment. The woman finally pulled herself together and half-laughed at the mishap, squeezing her son close until he looked as frightened of her as he'd been of Hawk.

Fifteen minutes passed before Liz was alone with Hawthorne again, and by that time he was completely in control. "I'm going back to the house to see if Jesse's there," he told her, and Liz said, "I'm going with you."

It was bold, and another time he would have laughed her out of the park, but this was now, and after regarding her intensely in the half-light he merely nodded and led her to his Jeep. She climbed inside and let her hair blow from the wind of the open window. A thick strand found its way toward Hawk and lay across his shoulder long enough for him to flick a look its way.

His log cabin was lit from the inside, a warm yellow glow that struck some chord within Liz's heart. Gravel crunched beneath her sandals as she followed him up the steps to a porch very similar to Avery Francis's.

Hawthorne pushed open the door and hollered, "Jesse?" to no immediate answer. "I'll check," he told her, leaving her just inside the threshold to examine his rather bare living quarters.

Like herself, he was a fairly recent returnee to Woodside. This was evidenced in the row of neat boxes still standing to one side of the hearth. The fireplace was made of river rock with a pine mantel. On the mantel was a picture of Jesse, taken several years earlier, in which he was grinning and holding up a good-sized salmon.

Her heart somersaulted painfully. She'd missed so much. So very much. Yet here was a chance. After all, she was inside Hawk's house—with his permission—and drawing closer to her son. Mentally, she crossed her fingers as she walked to the hearth to get a closer look.

Hawk returned a few moments later. In the light, she noticed the grass stains on his shirt. "He's not here."

Though disappointed, Liz nodded, hoping Hawk wouldn't suddenly return to himself and order her to leave or something worse. "Tell me about Joey," she suggested, leaning a shoulder against the fireplace.

Hawk exhaled a frustrated breath, his old self returning. He shook his head.

"Does it have anything to do with Jesse?"

"No."

"Truly?"

"Yes." Raking a hand through his hair, he ground his teeth together.

"Tell me," she urged softly.

* * *

"No," Hawk said. He was struggling not to yell at her. Talking about Joey was too difficult. He couldn't do it. But everything about Liz Havers invited confidence. He'd let down with her before. He wanted to now.

And he hated himself for it.

But after his ridiculous behavior this evening, she deserved to know. He was so damn weak he wanted to kick himself senseless. She was waiting, and he wanted to toss her out, but what the hell would that accomplish? Nothing. It would only invite more questions. He struggled with himself for several moments, then heaved a sigh. "Joey was a kid who got taken hostage," he said carefully. "We sent in a SWAT team, but he died in the crossfire."

"You sent the team?" Liz asked gently.

"I fired the bullet."

Silence fell around them like a blanket. Hawk stared at her, raw. He shouldn't have said it. Shouldn't have shown the truth of his failing. It was his fault. His. No one else's. There was nothing to do now but wait for the ax to fall.

Liz swallowed against a dry throat. Holy Mother of God. Her head pounded. Her own heartbeat deafening her. She understood. Really understood. Remorse consumed her. Guilt for all the awful things she'd thought about him.

"I'm sorry," she murmured, stumbling toward him, her legs woolly, her heart full.

She'd never been known for offering physical comfort. Except with Hawk, and no one knew about that. She dispensed advice and direction and reality checks for her patients who were lost and confused. She rarely hugged or touched unless the patient practically threw themselves at her.

But with Hawk it had always been different and that hadn't changed. She walked straight to him, stopping in front of the well-loved couch with pine arms and feet. Acting on impulse, she laid a palm against his cheek, felt the beginnings of stubble and caressed his skin empathetically.

It seemed as natural as sunlight to kiss him. Her gaze fastened on his mouth, the urge irresistible. But she didn't have a chance for he took it from her. One moment he was standing in front of her, the next his mouth was hard against hers, slanting, demanding, eager for her own special brand of comfort.

Sixteen years receded like mist. She was seventeen and in love. She lusted naïvely yet passionately.

"God, Liz," he murmured, all burning need and emotion.

It was soul-breaking. Undeniable. Impossible. His hands swept down her back spasmodically, one palm searching for her breast, molding it within strong fingers aching with need.

She was liquid. Nothing. Limp. Willing. Only his strength kept her on her feet. She clung for support, her head lolling back as his lips searched and found the arch of her throat, the beat of her heart at the hollow between her clavicles. Chest heaving, she longed for him to lower her to the floor. To equilibrium. To the chance to have his hard body pushing against her yielding one.

Sixteen years was an instant. A crystal moment. Forgotten beneath desire. Hawk's body pushed against hers. He was hard and she was soft. But there was space behind

her, not solid ground. Her knees bent. She wanted down—
and she wanted him with her.

He groaned. His hands on her buttocks held her tight
against his throbbing need. What was the delay? she asked
herself in frustration, her thoughts distant, drugged, cap-
tured beneath her own demanding ardor.

"Liz . . ." he whispered.

She kissed his mouth, shutting those lips. But not
quite. They were parted and his tongue reached forward
to touch its tip to hers. It broke apart her last objection—
had there even been one?—and she tugged him toward
her, moving downward so he couldn't miss the message
she was sending.

That did it. One instant they were on their feet, the next
Liz's back was against the couch's cushions and Hawk's
body was on hers. A minute of restless hands and grinding
hips was all they could stand.

He reached beneath her dress, yanking the snaps. She
saw the scalloped edge of her bikini panties a second
before his fingers slipped beneath and his hand found her
moist heat. She gasped. It was so quick. So hot. She
couldn't wait. She, who had abstained from sexual trysts
and wild affairs, wanted to be possessed so badly she was
actually moaning and thrashing around.

Her panties were dispensed with. A muscular twist and
he was out of his trousers, falling upon her as if they'd or-
chestrated this from the beginning. He tore off his shirt
and the remaining snaps of her dress, those last sentinels,
broke away.

And then his body was on hers and there was only the
sound of breathing, gasping mouths, and twisting bodies.

"Liz . . ."

She moaned a response. He was poised at the entrance,
ready to plunge into her. She wanted him to. She squirmed

to urge him on. But he hesitated that one heartbeat too long, and reality fought its way inside her head.

This is how you created Jesse.

Jesse.

Her son. Who could appear at any moment.

Hawthorne's head was cocked. He was listening. Panic surged over Liz, and she hissed through her teeth, "No! Oh, God. What if he comes home!"

Hawk pulled away from her as if she'd burned his skin. Scrambling, Liz grabbed for her panties, snapping her dress with trembling fingers. Hawk dressed quickly, too, but his shirttails still hung loose as Liz, re-clothed and standing ten feet away, stared him down in horror.

She couldn't speak. Neither, apparently, could he. At least for a moment. When he finally did open his mouth, she winced at his words.

"You always appear when I'm at my weakest. I don't know who to blame, me or you. Probably me." He was sardonic. "It won't happen again."

Liz struggled. How could she have believed, even for an instant, that he was someone special? Because she had believed it. She'd desperately wanted to believe it. But he'd spoiled it. He told the truth. And she hated him—and herself—a little for it.

"No, it won't," she agreed tightly.

"You don't have to feel sorry for me."

That was it? He thought this was because she felt sorry for him? Pissed, she said, "I don't. I'm just naturally sexual. I can't help myself."

His eyes narrowed. He almost believed her, which pissed her off some more. But then his gaze fastened on her still quivering lips—those damn betrayers—and she knew he sensed she wasn't as bold as she pretended.

Liz tore her eyes from his. She was still fighting to

get her breath under control and so was he. He finished
tucking in his shirttails.

"I'll take you back to your car," he said.

"Thank you."

She sat stiffly beside him. They traveled silently through
the warm August night, the air feeling thick and enveloping. At her car, she slid out of the Jeep, but some latent
chivalry brought him outside the vehicle and he closed her
door behind her as she climbed into the Miata.

The top was down. His hands rested on the edge of the
door. She looked straight ahead and said, "Let me know
about Jesse."

A moment.

"All right," he told her, then headed toward his Jeep,
climbed back in, and drove away.

Liz laid her head against the headrest and fought a sting
in her sinuses that had come out of nowhere.

Chapter Eleven

Slipping back inside the old homestead unnoticed was no easy task, but Jesse had years of experience. It was quiet, only an occasional cricket sending out its own music. His window was cracked open, although you wouldn't be able to tell unless you went right up to it—something he'd banked on his dad not bothering to do. And it was greased. Thank you, WD-40. Sliding it upward was soundless and effortless. With animal grace, Jesse hoisted himself inside and, managing only the faintest of rustlings, stripped naked and slid between his sheets.

He fell asleep instantly and dreamed of Tawny.

She was crying. She didn't want to leave. He didn't want her to leave, and he was trying to tell her as much but was distracted by a major woody. While he struggled with this embarrassment, she just kept on crying. He was glad all over that she couldn't see, but he wanted to help.

Maybe if he touched her . . .

Someone was shaking him. Violently. His teeth rattled. Holy shit! Her father! He'd been about to make love to her when Guy Fielding—with Arnold Schwarzenegger's body and teeth like a grizzly—grabbed him around the throat and started bellowing at him.

"Wake up. Damn it all! Do I have to yank you out of bed?"

Jesse's eyes flew open. His dad was yanking on one arm. He jerked it back and yelled, "Let go of me!"

"Why'd you come in through the back? Afraid to face me?"

Slowly, Jesse recognized that his dad was livid. "What's eating you?" he demanded, to which Hawthorne Hart swore pungently and dropped Jesse's arm as if it burned.

"Brad's been stealing from Lannie's and you're implicated."

"Bullshit!" Jesse sat straight up. "Who told you that? They're lying. Those jerk-offs set Brad up. They took the goddamned beer and they're—"

"Stop swearing."

"—covering their asses! Go ask 'em. I'm sick of being the only delinquent around here. They'd all sell their own mothers for a dip or a cigarette. They'd murder for a beer! Goddammit," he added, belatedly responding to his father's request to stop swearing.

"Is that right?"

"Yeah, that's right," Jesse rejoined heatedly. "God, I'm sick of this. You go ask them. Be a lawman. Go ahead." He was suddenly slammed back into the bed by one strong palm. "Hey . . ."

"Let's get one thing straight," Hawthorne said through his teeth. "I'm on your side. So get over that attitude."

Jesse didn't respond. His dad reeked of hostility, so who was the one with attitude here? Wisely, he kept that thought to himself and simply nodded in the semidark. It wasn't often that Dad lost his cool. Oh, sure, that kid being wiped out with the sniper had definitely done a number on him, but you had to expect that, being a cop and all. Jesse was a little unsure about why his dad had taken it so hard. Blamed himself. Like, what? Hawthorne Hart, ace shot and dead-calm aim, could take out an innocent victim? That was a total joke!

But he had to admit his dad felt differently about the whole thing, so Jesse kept his thoughts to himself. And he'd heard he'd once had a drinking problem, so he supposed Hawk was a little sensitive on the stolen beer issue.

But it wasn't his or Brad's fault. "Those guys at Lannie's really did steal the beer and blame it on Brad," Jesse said seriously.

His dad slowly pulled away, standing beside Jesse's bed, thinking hard. That's what he always did. Think hard. The guy didn't know how to lighten up.

"Something wrong?" Jesse guessed.

"No."

It wasn't often they conversed. Jesse just didn't have time and Hawk's authority got in the way. But Jesse was intuitive enough to sense a change and he mentally groped for a cause. "Did you have something to drink?"

"No," he snapped.

"Okay, okay."

"It was wine coolers that were stolen, not beer," he said at length.

Jesse tried to read his father's mind. "So, okay, it was wine coolers."

"Doesn't sound like you did it if you didn't even know what it was," Hawk pointed out.

"Well, yeah, that's right." Jesse shook off his nightmare-haunted sleep and clicked his brain into gear. "That's right!"

He debated whether he should be incensed that his father thought the worst of him but, given his own personal history, that might be pushing things too far. Instead, he waited for Hawk to say something more, but silence was the only response.

Conscious of his father's darker outline in the dimness, Jesse asked, "How's the murder investigation going?"

"It's going." His bitten-off answers didn't invite questions.

"Any idea who killed the guy?"

"Nothing concrete."

Because he felt a strange connection tonight, Jesse offered, "A girl I know thinks her mom's boyfriend stole that old lady's trees."

Hawk's interest sharpened; Jesse could feel it. "Who?"

"Carrie Lister's mom's boyfriend. I don't know his name, but he's at the Listers' a lot." He paused, thinking. "Carrie goes to see Brad's shrink, Mrs. Havers, too."

"Ms. Havers," Hawk corrected,

Jesse smiled in the darkness. Oh, ho. "'*Miz* Havers,'" Jesse drawled.

"Why does Carrie think he took the trees?"

"Money," Jesse responded.

His father jerked visibly.

"What?" Jesse asked.

"I'll talk to her," Hawthorne said, heading for the bedroom door.

Jesse lay awake in bed for quite a while, his hands cradling the back of his head. A general feeling of dissatisfaction crept over him as he reviewed the events of the day. He was so pissed at Brad. Here they were, in trouble again, and it wasn't their fault. And Brad, the dumbass, acted like it was no big deal. In fact, he'd been really annoying. Jesse'd wanted to hit him.

"Did you get on her yet?" Brad had asked, referring to Tawny. They were on the run from Lannie's, having realized they'd been set up by the older guys.

"No!" Jesse's fist had balled. If he'd ever wanted to hit Brad it was right then. At least he hadn't said, "Did you do her yet?" Tawny wasn't like that. Jesse doubted she'd French kissed a guy yet, and although he'd never admit it to a living soul, he was fairly limited in experience himself.

But, Jeezus, Brad's timing and crassness pissed him to no end.

"She's a prude," Brad guessed with a disparaging snort.

"You're a dumb shit."

"You're an asshole."

"Asshole," Jesse repeated right back.

"Dumb shit."

That established, they'd kept on running, letting the argument simmer. Now, however, Jesse's blood boiled all over again. He simply couldn't hear anything bad about Tawny.

His lips twisted. He sure as hell hoped he'd get back to his dream—minus the crying. He might not be able to get on Tawny, but it didn't spoil the fantasy.

Which reminded him of his dad's reaction to *Miz* Havers. Whoa, wouldn't that be something?

Jesse chuckled, loving the irony. Dad falling for the shrink. What a joke! He hoped to hell it was true because he liked the lady. She was cool. And God knew his father needed to get laid.

If Hawthorne Hart had to do his life over again, he would change two things: Laura's and Joey's deaths. But he wouldn't, he realized with a sense of awakening, change the time he'd spent with Liz Havers—and not just because of Jesse, like he'd always told himself.

His Jeep bumping over the rutted track that rimmed

this section of federal Forest Service land, Hawk couldn't quit reflecting on Liz. No . . . that experience had been character building. He'd needed it to snap him out of his alcoholic misery, and he'd needed it to realize that life went on.

If only she'd been there after Joey's execution, he thought, his lips twisting grimly in memory. Just his thoughts touching on that time brought back the shakes. Internal this time. His hands were steady; it was the steering wheel that was jumping. That very instant the front bumper yawed downward, the Jeep slammed forward, nearly jerking Hawk's arms from their sockets.

He swore softly through clenched teeth. The track ahead zigzagged through stands of firs and pines, forcing his full attention on driving.

Finally, he came to a small clearing and stopped the vehicle, listening to the engine tick and ping as it cooled. Stepping from the Jeep, he stretched his back until it popped, his mind still on Liz instead of the task at hand.

Liz Havers. He could almost smell her on his skin. He'd wanted to make love to her something fierce and to hell with the consequences.

He still felt that way.

"Damn," he muttered, closing his eyes and fighting the feeling. Too long without a woman; that's what it was. Way too long. He should have been looking before this happened.

He felt spent. Used up. He wished he were more involved in this case than just going through the motions, but he knew his heart was somewhere else. With Liz? God. Maybe. He hated to think. But also, he was distanced from Barney Turgate and deadly bullets and stolen yew bark. He just didn't care that much.

Memory stirred. He ignored it. Wanted to slap it away

like an irritating gnat. He kept telling himself he wanted to forget Liz, but it was really all he wanted to think about. He didn't want to stop to examine this buzzing memory, but it was too insistent to ignore. Shoving thoughts of Liz aside, he concentrated on what was bothering him.

Barney Turgate . . . yew bark . . . Manny Belding.

Hawk snorted in disgust. No mystery there. He was finally getting to meet the ever-missing Mr. Belding, although the scenario was rather interesting. Apparently, Manny shared the same affinity as Barney when it came to rendezvous sites: he liked the forest. Either that or both men shared the same paranoia.

Probably a bit of both.

It didn't matter either way to Hawk who'd taken Manny's breathless, panicked call with a measure of amusement. Manny was sure someone was after him. The same killer who'd wasted his good buddy, Barn. Could Manny tell Hawk what it was all about? Hawk had wanted to know. *No!* Absolutely *not!* But he could meet him if Hawk would be at the Elbow Room in ten minutes and wait for Manny's call.

Sure, why not? If Manny Belding believed his life was in danger, and he wanted to resort to clandestine meetings and secret codes, hey, Hawk could do that.

So, here he was, following Manny's telephone instructions and feeling like a bit of a fool. Still, it gave him time to ruminate on his attraction to Liz Havers and wonder what the hell he should do next

Yew bark.

Hawk frowned. He'd stopped by Sarah Lister's, but there was no boyfriend in sight. She'd been mighty reluctant to talk about him, too, but Hawk thought it was something a little closer to home than being a yew bark poacher. He wasn't sure, but before he could follow up Manny had stepped into the picture.

Memory swirled like a storm, then abruptly cleared. In his mind's eye he saw the pieces of wood on the counter of Barney Turgate's apartment. It had been bark, he realized now, the significance registering. Pacific yew bark, he would bet.

So, Barney Turgate's big deal had to do with yew bark? Was he a poacher? Highly likely, based on what Hawk knew of his character.

Hawk's interest sharpened. Suddenly, he couldn't wait for Manny to provide some answers. Maybe the guy's life was in danger after all. Money had a tendency to put unnatural spins on things. Big money, that was.

With growing impatience, Hawk walked around the Jeep, searching the shadows of the forest beyond the clearing for some sign of the mysterious Mr. Belding. He wished now that Manny had been more specific.

The hairs on his nape lifted. He jerked around, heart racing. There. On the edge of the brushy woods. A flash of color.

While Hawk narrowed his gaze, a man slowly half-rose from a crouched position. Skittish as a deer, he motioned to Hawk to come closer. As soon as Hawk started moving, he vanished into the thicket, and it was only after Hawk had traversed the clearing and was fifty feet into the trees did Manny address him.

"Over here" came the whisper.

Following the sound, Hawk moved deeper into the forest. He'd brought a handgun, but it gave him no comfort. His passion for guns had ended with Joey.

Suddenly, Hawk was upon Manny. One moment he was breaking his way through underbrush and low fir limbs, the next he was stumbling over a stone-rimmed fire pit and sleeping bag.

"I been livin' here," Manny told him.

He was seated on a stump, newly made, Hawthorne suspected, as a small fir was cut into neat hunks and obviously used for firewood. A spit stood over the fire pit with the remains of what looked like a charred rabbit sticking from the wooden skewer.

Hawk might have pointed out the danger of a forest fire, but given Manny Belding's appearance, Smokey the Bear was the furthest thing from the man's mind. Manny was scared shitless. Petrified with fear. He periodically shook all over, his small, wiry frame thrumming like a tuning fork. His hair was matted and dirty, and God knew the last time he'd seen running water. His eyes were a sharp blue in a dirty, lined face. He could have been thirty or a hundred. Impossible to tell.

"I been scared to talk to anyone. Heard you were lookin' for me, though. Hate to involve cops, but I'm a dead man."

"Why?"

"Don't you know?" Manny gave a soft whoop of laughter.

"Yew bark?"

He blinked several times, taken aback. Another whoop. "Guess you do. That's what killed Barn, y'know. All that money."

"Barney Turgate was a poacher."

"What? No!" Manny shrugged. "Maybe a little on the side, y'know. But not since the permits and all."

"Permits to harvest yew bark off Forest Service land?" Hawk asked, surprised. To Manny's nod, he added, "Barney had permits? I heard those were hard to come by."

"Oh, they are. Real hard. You gotta have connections. But we do, and that's why Vandeway got upset."

"Vandeway?" Hawk inserted, but Manny was still going.

"He's the one that murdered Barn. Mean as crabgrass, y'know. Didn't like it that me and Barn had the permits and were legit. You check him out, Detective. Fuckin' bastard killer."

Hawk rubbed his nose, thinking hard. "Your name came up as a possible suspect in Turgate's murder," he pointed out softly.

Manny was incensed. "Who the hell would say that? Barney was my friend. We were partners."

"Partners sometimes have a difference of opinion."

"That's crap! Barn and I were like brothers! Who said that? I have a right to know. Oh, shit!" He waved Hawthorne away as an idea struck him. "Lora Lee's been talkin' trash, ain't she? Goddamn that woman. She's looney over Barn. That's all."

Since it was Lora Lee who'd named Manny, Hawk kept his own counsel. He let Manny run on about Lora Lee for a solid fifteen minutes before he intervened. "So, who's this Vandeway?"

"Federal agent. Thinks he's hot shit on a gold platter, but he's a cold turd on a tin-can lid. He's your killer, I'm tellin' ya."

"Why would he murder Barney?"

"I told ya," Manny sputtered, frustrated. "Couldn't stand me and Barn bein' successful, y'know. Hey. C'mere. Let me show you something."

Manny headed deeper into the forest. He stopped by an old-growth tree Hawk couldn't instantly identify, but as soon as he stripped off some of the bark, Hawk knew he was looking at a Pacific yew.

"Takes a shitload of this stuff, but they pay good."

Hawk rubbed the reddish bark between his fingers. "You're telling me that a federal agent killed Barney Turgate because he didn't like it that you and Turgate had permits to harvest bark on federal land?"

"That's what I'm tellin' ya," Manny agreed stubbornly.

"Have you and Turgate been in other deals together?"

Manny blinked. "Sure."

"Legit and otherwise?" Hawk guessed.

"Hey, I'm not sayin' nothin' that'll get me in worse shit."

"Turgate's been murdered. I don't think there is worse shit," Hawk pointed out with a certain amount of irony.

Manny pondered that heavily, checking its merit. "Okay, we've poached a little, and pulled some strings, but those permits are one hundred percent real. That's all I'm gonna say about that."

Hawk nodded. "How long are you planning to stay out here?"

"'Til you catch the bad guys, Detective."

"Would you consent to a polygraph test?"

"Yes, I fuckin' would!" Manny declared heatedly. "I wanna catch this guy's bad ass. I'm not shittin' around."

"So, what do I have to do to convince you to come to the station?"

"I—"

Manny never got any further. Hawk barely had time to register the blast when yew bark flew from the tree as a bullet whizzed between him and Manny. *Blam.* Pain ripped through Hawthorne's shin. A burning sensation. He toppled over. A scream sounded in his ear. Manny's—as he crashed like a bull elephant through the undergrowth.

Faint acrid smoke. Pain so intense it caressed him all over. Hawthorne inhaled deeply. His senses swirled. He dreamed. "Joey?" he asked.

Footsteps followed Manny. The unseen sniper. Hawk tried to lift his head, but he felt trapped in a body that wouldn't move.

Then there was only silence. That ungodly stillness that had fallen after Joey's shattered body slipped from his kidnapper's limp grasp into the arms of death.

Liz sat in an orange molded plastic chair in the waiting room of Woodside General Hospital. Rhythmically, she squeezed and unsqueezed her empty Styrofoam cup. The self-serve coffeepot was empty and no one looked about to refill it. There just wasn't a lot of personnel about. Woodside Hospital was small, friendly, and reasonably efficient, and the doctors were able, if not brilliant, and most common problems could be taken care of locally.

A broken leg caused by a bullet fell into that category— at least Hawk's did. No artery had been severed, and the bone, though chipped a bit, had broken clean. Woodside General Hospital had operated, reset, and casted his right leg, then sopped up the remaining mess.

Detective Hawthorne Hart was A-OK and would be released this afternoon or tomorrow morning at the latest. His excellent health should speed his recovery, but his attitude was piss-poor. Nurse Friendly hadn't said those exact words, but Liz, being the crack professional psychologist she was, had picked up the implied message.

She'd gotten the word about Hawk from Tawny, who'd heard that Jesse's dad was in the hospital from Brad. Without a thought to convention, Liz had grabbed her woven bag and driven straight to Woodside General, belatedly conscious of her denim shorts, sandals, and white tank top, and only caring then because the air-conditioning in the waiting room was likely to freeze her to death.

She'd been here for three hours. Hawk was in recovery. Jesse was somewhere; she'd seen him cruise by and had waved. What he thought of her vigil she couldn't say. She didn't know what she thought of it herself.

School was starting in thirteen days. Tawny's dance recital was even closer. But the man she loved had nearly gotten himself killed.

The man she loved. More like the man she loved to hate. She'd had some bad moments rethinking that night on Hawk's couch. This physical attraction thing was downright pathetic.

She hated herself. She loved him. She wanted to make love to him. She hated them both.

Ripping off a piece of Styrofoam with her fingers, she tossed the little scrap into an ashtray, glancing up to the NO SMOKING sign to verify the rules. Talk about your mixed message.

She stared at the carpet. Gray. With little wavy sections that reminded her of water. She concentrated, but all she saw were Hawk's biceps as his arms enfolded her, the tautness of his stomach and his happy trail, that feathering of hair leading from his navel down to his groin.

She rubbed her face with one hand, hating the memory and her reaction to it. Good God, she could get turned on just thinking about it and the man was lying in a hospital bed with a hulking cast on his leg.

Not enough experience as a teenager, she determined. A few groping encounters and then Hawk. Magically. Wondrously. Only he'd fouled up what should have been a lot more groping encounters until she found her perfect soul mate.

Except . . . except . . .

She bit into her lower lip until she tasted blood, seeking to shut off her thoughts. *Well, now, isn't this just great?* she thought, feeling like an utter fool. Self-inflicted physical torture. As if this mental torture wasn't pure and terrible enough.

But it didn't matter. She was consumed with the memory of that night. The rhythm of his body atop hers. The wild eagerness of her own to be possessed. The touch of hard, male body and wet, thrusting tongue. His heated breath. Soft moans. The anticipation at the brink of penetration as his body sought entry and hers opened in eager, breathless—

"Miss Havers?"

Liz started guiltily, her thoughts naked. But the nurse before her smiled a greeting and directed her to Hawk's room. Chastised, Liz slung her bag over her shoulder, ridiculously embarrassed and angry with herself. She had to get over this obsession.

Jesse stood to one side of the bed where Hawthorne, appearing unfairly healthy with beard shadow rakishly darkening his chin, turned toward Liz. Her internal femininity responded to him despite herself.

"Hey there," she said.

For a heartbeat, she thought she saw his eyes warm with welcome. But then he remembered himself and charged gruffly, "What are you doing here?"

"I just came to see that you're all right."

"Don't bite her head off," Jesse said. He scowled at his father and flipped his hair from his eyes. "God, what a grouch."

"You don't have to be here," Hawk snapped, turning away from Liz.

The snub hurt. It shouldn't. She couldn't expect him to embrace her, especially with Jesse so nearby. But, hell yes. That was what she expected. After those hot moments on the couch she'd believed he would treat her differently.

But nothing had changed and she'd better damn well remember that.

"No, I don't have to be here," she agreed.

He cleared his throat. "I don't want you here."

Now that couldn't be ignored. Jesse's face registered shock at his father's rudeness. Liz reslung her purse over her shoulder. "Okay. I won't dare to ask what happened," she added stiffly as she turned toward the door. "I'm just glad you're okay."

She was in the hallway, fighting the burn of unformed tears, when she heard Jesse call to her.

"Hey, Ms. Havers!"

It took all her willpower to cool the evidence of Hawk's rejection and pull herself together, but she managed to do it. And the smile she threw her son was easy to find; she just felt that way about him.

"Hey, don't listen to him. He's hurt and he's just trying to cover it up. That's why he's acting like a jerk-off."

"I know." Then, feeling the need to explain, she added, "I talked to him about some theories about why Mrs. Brindamoor's yew trees were cut down. When I heard he'd been shot . . ."

She'd nearly gone crazy. Her knees had sagged and she was in her car and driving before she'd damn near taken a second breath.

"Yeah, I know. Jeezus." Jesse shuddered. "He's a pain in the butt, but I've only got one parent left. Be weird if they both died. I don't think I could take it."

Liz counted her own heartbeats. "I didn't realize your mother was gone, too," she said slowly.

"She died in a car wreck. Dad nearly went nuts. He really loved her, and he's never gotten over it." He shrugged. "At least that's what everyone says."

"Do they?" Liz murmured.

He'd confounded her. Of course Hawthorne would spin that tale. Why not? Few people knew the truth and they were spread far and wide or long gone, like Liz's own parents. No wonder Jesse seemed to have no curiosity when it came to his mother.

No wonder Hawk didn't want her to tell him who she was.

"I guess some people love real deep like that," Jesse added, eyeing her cautiously, for Liz had subsided into a tight silence. "Cobain was married and had a kid. He loved 'em both a ton."

"But he committed suicide," Liz reminded him. "That's selfish."

"Ah, no. He was a heroin addict and he had chronic stomach trouble and he couldn't handle the fame. It wasn't *him*." Jesse was earnest. It was important to him that Liz understand his hero. "He grew up in Aberdeen, so even Seattle was a monstrous city. Then the next thing y'know, he's world famous. He couldn't take it. But he loved his family."

His bangs flopped in front of his eyes. Liz ached to brush them aside, but that would be too forward, too close. She was getting more of Jesse than most. She had to stay content with that.

"Do you want to be a rock star like him?" Liz asked.

"Hell no! I'm tone deaf."

"That doesn't seem to be a limiting factor," Liz said dryly.

"See . . ." Jesse shook his head and pursed his lips. "You're all the same. Your own music's great. The best. But you can't say a nice thing about anyone else's, and you don't even know it."

"You're right. I can't judge it because I've never heard it."

He perked up. "Want me to bring you a Nirvana CD? I've got 'em all."

"Um . . . sure."

"I'll be by the Fieldings' this afternoon. I'll drop off a couple."

"Okay." Liz smiled. Well, here was a clear path to getting to know her son.

"Thanks for seeing Dad." Jesse headed out the doors to the parking lot and a waiting bike. Liz followed and offered him a lift, but he shook his head. There was no way for the Miata to haul his bike.

"He's not always a jerk," Jesse added as he rode away, and Liz amusedly realized he was trying to hook her up with Hawthorne.

Oh, if you only knew!

"Damn it, Perry. Belding's around there somewhere," Hawk growled into the hospital telephone. A nurse showed in the doorway. Young. Unsure. Hawthorne scowled his meanest scowl and she scurried away. "He was *running*. He might have got hit."

"I know. I know," Dortner said wearily. Hawk had been a broken record from the moment he'd called in on his cell phone and explained where he was and why he was incapacitated. Pain or no, Hawk had given directions to his location and Perry himself had found him straight off.

"Find Belding," Hawk demanded now.

"That's what I'm trying to tell you. We found him."

Hawk's stomach sank. "Dead?"

"Yep. But not by a bullet. He was at the bottom of a ravine. Looks like he just fell over the edge. Probably running away and he just didn't see it."

Hawthorne shook his head to clear out the cobwebs.

Damn those painkillers. He was numb all over, especially his brain. "He couldn't have fallen."

"Well, he did. And it looks like an accident."

"Accident! Someone was *shooting* at us!"

"Your surgeon showed me the bullet," he said dryly. "But Belding's body wasn't hit. He died of a blow to the head, probably hit a rock at the bottom."

"Then he was chased," Hawk declared stubbornly.

"He could have been." Perry was noncommittal.

"Are you trying to piss me off?" he demanded. "Because you're doing a bang-up job."

"I'm just telling you what is. That's all."

"Fine. Fine." Hawk hung up, impatient to get off the phone. He had another lead, one he'd decided to keep to himself for a little while. He knew Perry planned to yank him from the case, but he didn't want to be yanked. Not after taking a bullet in the leg. This was personal now.

All his years in law enforcement and he'd never been hit by gunfire before. It took a trip back to his hometown before he took one in the flesh. How ironic.

And it didn't help to have Liz Havers be a part of that.

Gnashing his teeth, Hawk shifted uncomfortably. The cast bugged him. He hated being fettered. Damn it all to hell, why did he have to let Liz Havers consume his thoughts? He had an investigation to continue. Someone had very nearly killed him and he was an inch away from losing this case entirely because he was now infirm.

Yet the memory of Liz's smooth skin and whispery sighs kept swinging from the edges of his mind to the heart of it. One moment he was considering Manny Belding, the next he was envisioning himself rubbing against her soft curves, and it was enough to drive him crazy.

Why? Of all the women, why her? He'd spent so many years hating her or trying to hate her or determined to forget her existence. Why did it have to be Liz that he wanted?

Hawk inhaled through clenched teeth. He wasn't naïve enough to believe she wanted him the way she'd once professed. No, no. She wanted Jesse. She'd made that very clear. And if it meant a few hot sessions with Jesse's father, so be it. People worked from their own needs and no amount of candy-coating the truth ever made it go away.

Not that she was averse to him; she'd been right there, joining in. But her motives were tainted, and hell, his own probably weren't much better.

A bout of self-evaluation just made Hawk's head feel swathed in cotton. He didn't know up from sideways right now. Damn drugs. He had to get out of here.

Struggling with the rollaway table, Hawk nearly flung the whole contraption away, then thought better of it. He couldn't bear having to ask the young nurse for help.

He'd gotten the number for Federal Agent Don Vandeway through a little deception: He'd told Perry to call the man and ask some questions about Forest Service land, then had changed his mind and asked for the number. He hadn't mentioned that Manny Belding had fingered Vandeway. He'd only told Dortner that he thought Sarah Lister's boyfriend was a poacher and he was following up. All he'd told Perry about Manny and Barney was that they were connected and whatever they were into probably got Barney—and now Manny—killed and Hawk shot.

Perry was more cautious about those theories. He'd told Hawk to stop worrying about the Brindamoor tree case—an underling could handle it. Hawk's job was to recover. Period. But Hawk had rejoined that just because he sported a cast from his goddamn thigh to his ankle didn't mean he was completely useless. He might need a less-involved case. The Brindamoor yew case, for example.

This had, naturally, piqued Perry's interest. It was so unlike Hawk to relinquish the tougher assignment. But Hawk had kept his head lopped against the pillow and his eyelids at half-mast, looking as pathetic as he could while he fought to keep a clear head. Perry, viewing his right-hand man, had come to the only conclusion he could: Hawk was too weak to argue. Why not let him keep the yew trees? No one else wanted to help the formidable Mrs. Brindamoor anyway.

So, Hawk had Vandeway's number and a clear path to the one man who might lead him to Barney's killer.

"Detective Hart!" a deep female voice boomed. "You need to rest."

Attilla the Nurse. Hawthorne thought about challenging her, but she sailed in with such force he decided gallant defeat was his only option.

"You said it." He grinned hugely. "I'm wiped out."

"No more phone calls. No more visitors."

"I thought I was getting sprung from this place."

She sniffed. "We'll see when the doctor gets here."

"Good idea." His body might be numb, but his leg throbbed. He couldn't feel pain, just pressure. A bad sign. Closing his eyes, he sighed and let his body relax. Attilla fussed around a bit and he could feel her staring at him, but eventually she had to leave.

As soon as she was gone, he grabbed for the phone. She'd pushed the table farther away, but Hawk managed to drag it back by an attached cord. Feeling like a thief, he listened hard to make certain someone else wasn't about to burst into his room, then furtively placed a call to Federal Agent Don Vandeway's private line.

* * *

"I don't understand how that's all connected," Tawny said, frowning as she tucked a strand of blond-streaked hair behind one ear. It was a familiar gesture, but just now, Jesse found it took on erotic overtones. God. He was obsessed.

Tawny was sitting cross-legged on her couch as Jesse paced around the room. Her mom was in the kitchen, humming softly as she made dinner. He was glad she was feeling better.

"I don't know exactly either. And I couldn't ask 'cause I was eavesdropping," Jesse admitted. "But that dead guy, Turgate, and another guy were involved in some scheme. My dad went to meet the second guy—"

"Manny Belding," Tawny put in, to which Jesse smiled. She wanted him to know she'd been paying attention.

"Yeah. And he got shot. My dad, that is. Belding fell off a cliff or something and he's dead, too."

Silence. Jesse didn't like the echoing sound of his own voice. Death was another being in the room with them, hovering around. Tawny shivered and said, "I'm so glad Mom's okay."

"Yeah, me too." He sank down beside her. To his consternation, her eyes filled with tears. He didn't want her to cry. Not like in his dream.

Awkwardly, Jesse drew her toward him. Tawny unfolded her legs and slid into the circle of his arms, resting her cheek against his chest. He stroked her back, but his earlier ardor had been checked by her emotions. Silent tears dampened his shirt. He stared off into space. Sometimes he felt like crying himself, but there was no way on God's green earth he would allow even one betraying tear.

"You'll come to my dance recital, won't you?" Tawny's

voice was muffled against his shirt. He could feel the heat of her breath.

"When is it?"

"August thirty-first."

"I'll be there."

"Jesse . . ."

"Hmmm?" Intuition told him she was about to say something important. Inadvertently, he tensed. She hesitated.

Come on, Tawny, say it. Go for it.

He could almost feel when she changed her mind. She was afraid to risk it. To say how she felt. Instead, she murmured softly, "You really think Aunt Liz'll listen to your CD?"

"She's cool enough to."

Tawny chuckled and snuggled closer to him. Jesse let his eyes drift shut and concentrated on keeping a rein on passion, something he was pure shit at. Ah, well. Sweet torture was better than indifference.

He just had to make sure she didn't feel his growing interest because his role today was best buddy.

What a bunch of bullshit!

With an effort, Jesse concentrated on a memory of swimming in the ice cold Pacific Ocean, a vision that generally had some effect, although he figured it was plain useless right now . . .

"Who's beating you?" Liz asked Carrie bluntly. Direct confrontation was generally an ineffective tool, but Liz was at her wit's end with the girl. New bruises only confirmed her suspicions. It was time for action.

"No one." Carrie flushed and glanced over her shoulder. Her mother, Sarah, was late for the appointment, as usual, and for once Carrie looked like she wanted to see her.

"Come on, Carrie. I'm going to have to alert Child Services."

"Go ahead. You'll look like an idiot. I'm just clumsy."

"They'll come to your house and assess what's going on."

"Nope. Not if there's nothin' goin' on."

Carrie knew the system. Most kids who came to see Liz did. Still, Liz could file her suspicions and leave it there. She'd hoped, however, to get at the heart of the problem with Carrie first.

"Your mom seeing someone?" Liz guessed. Most often it was a male familiar to the household.

"Yeah. He's a great guy." Her tone was sarcastic; her dark gaze filled with hidden messages. She might not want to be a rat, but she did want to tell, Liz realized with renewed hope.

"What's he do?"

"You mean work?" She laughed without humor. "He's a mooch. Brags all the time about gettin' somethin' for nothin'." Her expression grew cagey. "You know Jesse, right?"

Liz's heart skipped a beat. "Jesse Hart?"

"He staked him out one night. Brad told me. They want to catch him in the act."

"In the act?"

"We all kinda think he stole those trees, y'know? Jesse wants to catch him, then shove it all down that old lady's throat. She hates all teenagers." She shrugged. "We hate her right back."

"Ah . . . What's your mom's boyfriend's name?" Liz asked.

"You can ask her when she finally gets her fat ass here. He's a mean son of a bitch."

"So I gathered," Liz said dryly, her gaze following the line of bruises up Carrie's arm.

"I'm not gonna say nothin' about anything, so you can just forget it. Jesse'll get him." Hero worship slipped into her voice.

So, Jesse thought Sarah's boyfriend had taken the trees. Liz didn't like the idea of him getting involved at any level. Maybe she could sow the seeds of caution if she brought the subject up just right to him.

Sarah breezed into Liz's office, her hair flying. Twin spots of color brightened her cheeks. She was irate. "Goddammit!" she yelled. "I can't take off work like this. I'm sick of this whole damn thing. She's not coming here anymore."

"Carrie still has a few hours of counseling—"

"I don't give a shit! I could lose my job. They're looking at me all the time, and I have to lie."

"She could come by herself," Liz pointed out, but this met with a spate of renewed fury.

"Yeah? And have you yap, yap, yapping at her? You're all the same. A bunch of nosy do-gooders who don't know a goddamn thing. What did you say before I got here?" Sarah demanded, glaring at her daughter.

"Nothin'!"

"She's a liar," Sarah bit out to Liz.

"What are you afraid she'll say?" Liz asked.

"I don't have to take this. I'm her mother, and though she might not like it, tough! I call the shots."

"I'm concerned about the bruises on her arms. I'm concerned that someone could be abusing your daughter. I asked Carrie if you were seeing someone, but she was reluctant to tell me the man's name."

Sarah's lips tightened into a white line. "You've got a lotta nerve, lady."

"You've got a daughter in harm's way," Liz rejoined softly.

"Screw you."

She whipped her index finger in a circle, signaling Carrie to leave. With a last look at Liz, Carrie slunk from her chair and preceded her mother out the door. Liz half-expected Sarah to launch one last volley, but she practically ran out of the room after her daughter.

Chapter Twelve

Sweat beaded on Hawthorne's brow. Exertion. Pain. Frustration. He banged his crutches against the door to the bathroom and nearly toppled to the floor. His doctor had suggested a home nurse for his first few days because he had no wife or significant other to care for him, but Hawk had rejected the idea straight out. Now, hobbling around the log cabin, he realized the idea had some merit.

Not that he had any intention of following through.

It took all his will to make it back to the couch. Flopping down, he jarred his leg, bit back a howl of pain, and ran a running argument through his brain about whether to try another painkiller or not. They made him fuzzy. He detested being fuzzy. Especially since he'd given up alcohol.

Because it made him feel better, he systematically barked out every four-letter word he knew into the empty room. By the time he was finished—for it was a considerable list—the pain had subsided and he was ready for action.

Phoning Federal Agent Don Vandeway for perhaps the twentieth time seemed an effort in futility. But shock of all shocks, the man actually answered the phone this time, then tried everything he could to disconnect from Detective Hawthorne Hart of the Woodside PD.

"This isn't a matter for the local police department," Vandeway told him superciliously. "We have bigger fish to fry."

"I'm the one with a bullet in his leg," Hawthorne reminded him. "As far as I'm concerned, it's a matter for the local police."

"You don't understand—"

"Then enlighten me," Hawk cut him off bluntly.

Vandeway sighed. "Look, I know how you feel, but believe me, we're handling the situation. And it's a lot more delicate than you know."

Yeah, yeah, yeah. Hawk had dealt with bullshitters and charmers and murderers and thieves. "Belding said you killed Barney Turgate, and now Belding's dead. Doesn't sound that delicate to me."

"Am I under investigation, Detective?" Vandeway asked primly.

"You bet you are," Hawk retorted. "Now, are you going to meet with me or not?"

It took a certain amount of extra coercion, but Vandeway, proving he was smarter than he sounded, seemed to get it that Hawthorne Hart wasn't going to give up. Muttering about the importance of keeping his investigation pure, he reluctantly agreed to meet Hawk at an out-of-the-way roadside bar in Willoughby, the nearest town of any size to Woodside. Hawk, however, wasn't in the mood for concessions.

"I'll be at the Elbow Room at four p.m.," Hawk told him. "It might be worth your while to make it."

He hung up while Vandeway sputtered protests. Hawk didn't like him on instinct. It was too bad he had to hide his activities from Dortner because he could have used the help. But he knew Perry would have a shit fit over Hawk's continued involvement. Better to fly solo for a while.

Vandeway showed up right on time. He wore wire-rimmed glasses and a prissy expression that made his lips seem perpetually puckered. Maybe they were. Tight-ass, Hawk thought inconsequentially.

"Detective Hart," Vandeway greeted him, biting off each syllable as if it tasted bad.

"Federal Agent Vandeway." Hey, he could be as friendly as the next guy.

Vandeway surveyed the cast, which stuck out across the worn red carpet. No more cabbage roses from the days of the Candlewick Inn. A small pang of regret slipped through him. Nope, he wasn't going to think about Liz now.

"You really took it," he observed.

"Mmm," Hawk shrugged.

"So, what do you want to know, Detective? I'm sure someone else would be better equipped to find your sniper, but if I can help in any way—"

"I'm going to tell you a story," Hawk broke in. "It's one of those fill-in-the-blank things. When I stop, you fill in the blank."

"Well, if I can." He sniffed.

"There were these two guys, Barney Turgate and Manny Belding. They had a neat little deal going. They alone held one of a handful of permits with the Forest Service to harvest yew bark off national forest land." Remembering his buddy Ed's comments about how Manny had connections, he added, "Belding was tied in by a relative of his. I'm not sure how."

"What does this have to do with me?"

"Belding fingered you. And all you can talk about is some 'delicate' operation. It's this yew bark thing."

When Vandeway didn't immediately start filling in the

blanks, Hawk went on impatiently, "So, something goes sour and somebody gets pissed off and blam! Barney Turgate's history. Then Manny goes the fugitive route, and whoosh! Falls over a cliff. Except that he talked to someone he shouldn't have first."

At Hawk's pause, Vandeway said in a bored tone, "You?"

"Good guess." His gaze on Vandeway, Hawk thunked his cast with his finger. "So, Barn's dead, Manny's dead, and I've got a bullet hole in my leg. Good old Manny laid all the blame at your feet."

Although Hawk hadn't believed it was possible, Vandeway pursed his lips even tighter. Without managing to unwrinkle them, he said, "So, that makes me guilty?"

"It makes you involved. So, what's it all about?"

For about thirty seconds Vandeway wavered, then he said, "You seem to know enough to be dangerous."

"Thank you." Hawk's voice was ironic.

"They did have a legal permit. Belding had a relative who works for ChemTek. Ever heard of them?" Hawk shook his head. "Big Midwest chemical company interested in yew bark for the production of Taxol."

"Go on."

"This relative worked it so Manny was the liaison out here and the relative facilitated the contracts. Manny got the permits in his and Barney's name, using his connections with ChemTek. Then he befriended a secretary at the Forest Service who helped keep the arrangement trouble-free."

"So, Manny and Barney could harvest yew bark and sell it to ChemTek."

"Manny and Barney were nearly the *sole* permit holders. They were one of the few legally allowed to harvest Pacific yew bark off U.S. Forest Service land. They were damn near *it*. A monopoly, Detective Hart. Forest Service land is where all the yew bark is, and they were practically the only ones allowed to strip the bark."

"So, why were they chosen?"

"Connections. They had a sweet deal. Got in when no one was looking and milked it. And it gets worse."

Hawk lifted a brow. "Worse?"

"ChemTek's got an exclusive contract to collect yew bark for one of the nation's largest pharmaceutical companies. This pharmaceutical company then inked an exclusive deal with the National Cancer Institute to be the one company producing and testing Taxol in the whole damn U.S. of A. for the next ten years. *Ten years.*" Vandeway was working himself up just relating the story. "The problem is: everything's *exclusive*—right down the line. Nobody wants anybody else to get a piece of the pie. So, it all funneled through Manny and Barney. It was—golden."

"So, where do you fit in?"

"I complained. I warned the Forest Service this would set up a gold-rush mentality, with everybody jumping in and pushing their poached bark through Manny and Barney. I said they'd steal it from all over and send it through that one legitimate route."

"Okay . . ."

"And that's exactly what happened," Vandeway went on in disgust. "Now we've got poachers all over the place who sold to Manny and Barney because Belding and Turgate could claim they harvested the bark off Forest Service land, and then show the goddamn permits to back themselves up."

Hawk thought it all through. He could see that some poacher had stolen Anita Brindamoor's trees and probably sold the bark to Manny or Barney. Except Barney had already been dead . . .

Or maybe it was the cause of Barney's death . . .

"Belding and Turgate were morons," Vandeway added, breathing out heavily through his nose. He was big into nose noises. "They fell into a sweet deal by virtue of this relative who only wanted to get Manny off his back. I talked to the man. He had no idea how big yew bark was going to get. I mean, yeah. Who would know? It's like the lottery, and once in a while, some undeserving schmuck scores big."

Vandeway clearly resented the fact that Barney and Manny had been suddenly prosperous. He seemed to keep forgetting that both men were dead, probably as a result of this extraordinary windfall.

Hawk rubbed his chin and glanced around the bar. He wanted a drink, a rare urge these days. Maybe he should have swallowed the painkillers. It might have helped after all. "So, Barney and Manny were the funnel, and they weren't averse to taking yew bark from others, no questions asked."

"Correct."

"Then why would someone kill them?"

"I don't believe they were killed because of this deal," Vandeway said firmly. "Belding fell to his death. An accident, by your department's own account. And Barney Turgate was a womanizer from way back. Probably wound up on the wrong end of some husband's gun."

It was Hawk's turn to snort his disbelief.

"Would it make more sense that *I* killed Turgate?" Vandeway wanted to know. "Like you just said, to what purpose?"

"You were pissed that they were making a killing," Hawk suggested, aware of how lame that motive sounded but unwilling to give up.

Vandeway trilled out a scale of laughter. "Oh, yeah. Sure."

"Someone shot at me while I was looking at yew bark,"

Hawthorne reminded him grimly. "It wasn't an accident and it wasn't some jealous husband." When Vandeway had no response to that, Hawk added, "I'm going to check with the Forest Service to see who else owns permits."

"There's hardly anyone."

"Well, fine. I want to know who they are."

"Stay out of it," Vandeway suddenly warned, leaning close to Hawthorne. If he were a different kind of man, Hawk may have felt threatened. But instead, with Vandeway, he was merely interested. "There are undercover agents involved in this deal, searching out poachers," he hissed. "Your meddling could jeopardize their sting. Hell, you already got yourself shot."

"Ah, so you don't think it's a jealous husband," Hawk drawled.

"I just want the local cops out of it, and that includes you."

Oh, there was no way Hawk was going to stay out of this one, but he was on thin ice with Dortner already and he didn't need Vandeway running to the chief and whining and complaining. "I'll let you know before I do anything," he said, lying easily. He didn't like Vandeway on principle.

"Don't *do* anything," Vandeway warned, picking up the tab for the two soft drinks they'd ordered. "Understand?"

Hawk had to refrain from saluting the man.

Liz held the phone away from her ear as if touching it to her skin would cause irreparable harm.

"Are you there?" Avery Francis asked, his voice sounding thin and far away because she'd stretched the receiver the length of her arm. She had to force herself to bring it back.

"Um . . . right here," Liz murmured.

"Would you care to have dinner with me?" he repeated, a smile sounding in his voice. He was so sure of himself, so smug. She'd gone from thinking he was fine to flat-out not liking him.

Still waiting around for Hawk?

She forced herself to say, "Dinner would be great."

"I'll pick you up at seven."

Wonderful.

Long moments later, Liz considered whether she'd actually answered Avery or if she'd hung up without a word. She truly couldn't remember. She couldn't decide whether to be horrified or amused, for she'd prided herself on her sensibility, practicality, and basically being a good person ever since she'd screwed up her life so horribly when she was in high school.

Of course those moments on Hawk's couch weren't exactly sensible and sane. They were, in fact, *insane.* And what was worse was the way she played and replayed them in her mind, over and over again.

She'd fallen in love with him half her life ago, for Pete's sake. It was high time to get over it.

Especially after what a bastard he'd been to her at the hospital.

Ten minutes later she was in the Miata, driving toward the police station with some vague idea of confronting Hawk. Ridiculous. He wouldn't be there. But she couldn't stop herself from cruising by and was, once again, helped along by fate. Hawk had just pulled to a stop in front of the station and was struggling to get out of his Jeep.

She made the colossal mistake of trying to help him. She grabbed his upper arm when he was turned toward the seat, hobbling on one foot, reaching for a crutch. She surprised him. He jerked around, lost his balance, nearly crashed down on her before looping one arm over the door and hanging, practically ripping his arm from the socket in the process. A spate of swear words followed.

"I'm . . . sorry," Liz breathed, embarrassed.

"Just—leave me alone."

She felt terrible. He was really hurting, and she couldn't seem to do anything right around him. "Want me to get that crutch?"

"No."

"I know you're angry. I'm sorry. But I just . . ." She squeezed around him and dragged the crutches from the Jeep, one by one. Holding them out to him, she tried to meet his eyes, but he was staring at the ground.

All she could think of to say was, "I'm sorry," but she'd already tried that twice, to no avail. Hawk's forehead had broken out into a sweat and she felt even worse. "Here," she said, thrusting one crutch under his free arm. The other still hung over the door for support.

"Thanks." His ironic tone would have cut except she knew he was hanging on by a thread.

"No problem."

She waited in silence as he mustered the strength to balance his weight on the crutches and swing himself up the two steps to the station and inside the front door. Heads turned, but upon spying his expression, everyone quickly went back to work, even if it meant only shuffling papers. No one wanted their head bit off.

"Holy moly," Chief Dortner greeted him, his friendly freckled face mock-woeful. "Look what the cat dragged in. Hello there," he added for Liz's benefit as she walked in behind Hawthorne. "You should be home," he said to Hawk in an aside.

"Hmph," was Hawk's answer.

Dortner quirked a brow at Liz and pulled out a chair next to Hawk's desk.

"No, thanks. I was just . . ." What the hell was she doing? ". . . checking in. I wanted to see how Detective Hart was faring."

"Detective Hart should be on medical leave," Dortner said, his gaze pointedly on Hawk.

Hawk's eyes were closed, his cheeks white, his lips colorless. He'd overdone it and it was obvious.

"I'm going to have someone take him home," Dortner added, moving back toward his desk.

"No!" Hawk protested.

Chief Dortner called over one of the junior officers. A brief argument ensued. Liz knew Hawk was steaming inside, especially having her as witness, and while they were sorting through "who" was going to do "what" to get Hawk "where," the door buzzed open and a woman walked in and stood beside Liz.

She was in her late thirties or early forties, with that worn-down look of too much work and too little joy. As she was closest to her, Liz might have asked if she could help her, but the newcomer's eyes were fixed on Hawthorne.

"I heard Manny Belding's dead," she rasped, as if her voice were overworked or she hadn't slept in a month.

Liz glanced to Hawk. He'd managed to get over the worst of the pain and recover his composure enough to keep Dortner and company at bay. Now, he focused on the woman, and to Liz's surprise, his expression softened a bit.

"Yeah. That's true."

"I can't say I'm sorry. It's Manny's fault, y'know," she

said. "Barney'd be here if it weren't for him. But there are others."

"What do you mean? Who?" Hawk gave her all his attention.

"There were a bunch of them, all trying to screw each other over." Her mouth turned down in distaste. "Scumbags who'd do anything for a few bucks. They took him from me."

So, this was Barney's girlfriend, Liz realized. She radiated pain. Hawthorne clearly felt it, too, and he motioned her to a chair, to which she shook her head.

"We'll keep working on the case," Dortner put in, but the lady cared only for Hawk's opinions.

"When will you get them all?"

"As soon as we can," Hawk promised.

"When?"

"Lora Lee," the chief said, holding out his hand to guide her back out the door, "it will be as quick as humanly possible."

"I want Detective Hawthorne."

"He's had a bit of a setback," Dortner began.

"You've got me, Lora Lee," Hawk cut in at the same moment.

That seemed to finally get through. She nodded bravely, glanced at Liz blankly, then gazed once more at Hawk. "They got my Barney all turned around on that deal. They need to pay for it."

"They will." Hawk was positive.

In silence, they all watched Lora Lee shamble out the front door, stand on the street for a moment in confusion, start one way and then turn back and head another.

"Barney's death's sure done a number on her," the chief said.

"She loved him," Liz said. "She's lost in grief."

"Is that your professional opinion?" Hawk asked coolly.

"Why, yes, it is," Liz shot back.

Perry Dortner held up both hands and looked from one to the other of them.

Liz had had enough. "I'm sorry I bothered," she said, and marched out of the station, telling herself she would never, never, never, ever, seek out Hawthorne Hart's company again.

Casually, oh, so casually, Jesse reached around Tawny to switch off the lamp. Images flickered across the TV screen, lending some light, and the moon was doing its romantic best to sparkle a trail of bluish illumination across the heartwood pine floor.

It was the first time Jesse had brought Tawny to his house and he was enjoying the intimacy. His dad was at the Dortners'. Perry's wife had insisted Hawk have dinner with them and she'd called Jesse to come also, but because he'd had a chance to be alone with Tawny, Jesse had bowed out. That had been an hour ago and he figured Dad would be gone a while longer.

Which left the two of them alone.

They were sharing a bowl of popcorn. The buttery scent couldn't quite eclipse Tawny's perfume—which was somewhere around the flavor of ripe berries and made his throat ache with wanting.

Jesse shook his head. He was getting downright poetic.

"Do you like this show?" Tawny asked.

Jesse glanced at the TV without interest. Reruns from one of last year's midseason replacement series. "No."

"Would you like to do something else?"

His interest piqued. "Like what?"

"I don't know. Listen to music."

Quick as a cat, Jesse was off the couch and turning the dials on his dad's ancient stereo. Okay, it wasn't ancient. But it wasn't from this decade, so it was by his standards. Hawk didn't care a whit about music, but at least there was a CD player.

His first inclination was to put on Nirvana. Kurt, after all, was the master. Then he thought about Kenny G. He detested jazz, but chicks seemed to go for that mellow instrumental stuff. Still . . .

"What do you want to hear?" he asked, searching through his father's CDs, a pathetically small collection and all bad. He made a mental note to buy his father some decent music.

"Nirvana?" Tawny suggested, and Jesse grinned his pleasure.

Putting the music on ridiculously low, he flopped down on the couch beside her, touching shoulders. He wanted to lean close to her and did so because, damn it, he couldn't help himself. She didn't seem to object.

"How're things going with your mom?" he asked.

"She's still doing okay. My father's coming for my dance recital." Her voice darkened. "I wish he'd just stay in Seattle."

"Yeah. I wish my dad had stayed in California."

"Then you wouldn't be here either."

Jesse turned his face into the glory of her hair. Strawberries. Or raspberries. The smell went straight to his head. "Yes, I would. I was destined to be here." He blew in her ear and she scrunched her shoulders and giggled.

"Why?"

"Because we were meant to be together."

"Oh, sure."

"You think I'm kidding?" He pretended affront. She

elbowed him and they started wrestling. Before long, Jesse had her pinned on her back and was staring into her golden eyes, reading the sudden wariness there. Instantly, he released her, jumped to his feet, and crowed, "I won! You're a wimp. I won!"

She leaped up beside him and pushed him before he knew what was happening. He sat down quick, flung against the couch cushions. "I won! I won!" she mimicked him, teasing.

That did it. Jesse reached for her hand and with a muscular twist brought her onto his lap. They grinned at each other, and he leaned forward and kissed her. She responded cautiously. He took his time, though a beat in his head told him to hurry, hurry, hurry, before she changed her mind. Girls were tricky. Especially nice girls.

They remained kissing. Jesse kept his hands to himself. He might skip school as much as he could get away with, but he wasn't stupid. He let her set the pace and it was excruciatingly slow. By the time they were half-lying on the couch, it felt like a millennium had crept by.

"I don't know if I should be here—like this," she whispered.

Jesse leaned on an elbow, watching the play of moonlight across her worried face. "I think this is great."

"You're supposed to think it's great."

"Well, how do you feel?"

"I don't know."

"Do you want to quit?" *Please, God, let her say no!*

"I don't know."

"I don't want to quit," he murmured, kissing her cheek. He would have liked to run his tongue across the hill of her cheekbone—he'd seen that in the movies and it seemed like a damn good idea—but he sensed that would send her running.

Tawny seemed content to let him kiss her. Her lashes fluttered closed, and with difficult detachment, Jesse kept his kisses light and gentle. Every once in a while, he tried for a deeper kiss, but he could feel her tense up.

"I have to go home soon," she said. "My mom thinks I'm with Liz."

"Can you tell her you're with me?"

"She'd ask me if your dad was here."

"Can you lie?" Jesse suggested.

Tawny drew in a breath and shook her head. "I don't think so."

"How much time have we got?"

"Just a few more minutes, then I've got to start walking."

"Jeezus, I wish I could drive."

"You'd have to become a model son and student for that," she said, her voice threaded with humor.

He gazed into her laughing eyes. Sometimes she took his breath away. He swooped in for a kiss, this one deeper, and for once she went with it, winding her arms around his neck and holding his face close to hers.

Jesse heard the thumping outside but was too entranced to connect what it was.

A second later, the door flew open, the light switched on, and his father hurled his crutches onto the floor and collapsed against the wall. Tawny and Jesse froze. A moment passed, then Hawk growled, "So, what's going on here?"

Tawny whimpered and Jesse, inwardly groaning, sat up to face the music.

Liz had spent a so-so evening. Not as bad as she'd feared, not as good as she'd hoped. Avery's company was fine, but now all she wanted was for him to drop her off at her door and disappear.

But it wasn't going to happen.

"You have the most unusual color eyes," he said as they stood together on her tiny porch.

"Mmm." She'd never been any good at handling compliments.

"Kind of like a Caribbean sea," he said.

"Aquamarine," Liz said. "That was my mom's description. She had the same color."

"So, it runs in the family. If you had a daughter, she'd have the same beautiful eyes."

And if I had a son he'd have the same beautiful eyes as his father.

Fidgeting, Liz searched her mind for a polite rejection. Avery either wasn't picking up the signals or chose to completely ignore them. He inched a half step closer and Liz could feel the heat of his skin.

"Avery . . ." she murmured in protest.

"What?" He had the audacity to tip up her chin with his index finger and gaze deeply into her eyes. She wondered if he practiced this move in front of a mirror.

"I think—" she began, only to have him steal a kiss, his movements so quick that his mouth actually stifled her gasp of surprise.

She handled the kiss stiffly, half-annoyed that she still was as unreceptive to other males besides Hawthorne Hart as she'd been at seventeen. She advised others to get over their relationships that didn't work, yet she couldn't seem to swallow the same medicine she dispensed so freely.

Since she didn't immediately push him away, Avery's arms tightened. His kisses continued, and finally, Liz gently turned her mouth away from his avid lips. "I'm not ready for this," she said.

Reluctantly, he pulled back. He didn't leave, however, and Liz had the disturbing feeling that he was debating how serious she was. Very serious, her eyes told him when their gazes clashed. Mustering a smile, he said good-bye and strode back to his car, so tense he could have had the proverbial broom up his butt.

"Brother," Liz muttered to herself as she stepped inside her cabinlike home. Moonlight striped the floor, arresting Liz's arm in midmotion as she reached to snap on the switch. It was beautiful, and her senses were starved for beauty. With a growing feeling of melancholy she didn't quite understand—but sensed was somehow related to Hawthorne—she slipped into the kitchen and pulled a bottle of white wine from the refrigerator, the only illumination the light bulb inside the door.

She was pouring herself a glass in the dark when stumbling footsteps up her porch stairs sounded. *Blam, blam, blam!* A fist pounded her door and Liz jumped, spilling the wine. Choked gurgles. Crying. Hard breathing.

"Who is it?" Liz asked, moving through the dark.

"Tawny!"

Recognizing her voice, Liz flung open the door and Tawny fell into her arms, sobbing. "What happened?" Liz cried, imagining terrible scenes.

"Jesse's dad is horrible! He yelled at Jesse. And then he started drinking and he screamed at both of us. I could just die! He scared me! He's so mean!"

"He scared you? What happened?" Liz led Tawny to the couch. Her body trembled like a newborn lamb. Reaching around her, Liz flicked on a lamp. Upon seeing Tawny's white, frightened face, she pulled her into her arms. "Oh, babe. Are you okay?"

"No." Her lower lip quivered and she buried her face into Liz's neck. Liz stroked her hair and Tawny silently cried, finally heaving a great sigh and pulling back, scrubbing her tearstained cheeks. "Can you tell me now?" Liz asked.

"I was with Jesse at—at his house. We weren't doing anything," she added hurriedly. "Well, we were kissing, but it wasn't—" She broke off.

"I understand. It's okay."

"Then *he* came in the house, and he was so *cold.* Started demanding what Jesse was doing. I felt terrible. It was awful." She began to shake anew at the memory.

"He was mad because . . . ?"

"We were on the couch." Tawny swallowed. "Kinda lying down."

"Ahhh . . ." The scene unfolded in Liz's mind and she didn't know how to feel. She was a bit touched at their youthful romance, an even tinier bit concerned based on her own mistakes, and a lot more amused. But she couldn't show that to Tawny.

"He just went nuts! Told Jesse to take me home. Jesse can't drive, but he did something kind of stupid, and that's what really started things."

"What did he do?" Tawny hesitated, and Liz said again, "Tawny, what did he do?"

"He took his dad's keys and said he'd drive me home. And his dad just started yelling!"

"Jesse's father just got out of the hospital and it hasn't been a great day for him," Liz said. "I saw him earlier. You know adults have problems, too."

"He's a crazy maniac." Tawny was having no excuses.

Liz debated on explaining a bit of Jesse's history; she knew enough about her son from Brad's confessions to understand Hawk's position. After all, Jesse and Brad hadn't been above hot-wiring vehicles in the past. But gazing into Tawny's tear-drenched eyes, she thought better of it. Her information was given in private; Jesse would have to tell Tawny all the details of his colorful past himself.

"He told Jesse to get rid of me. They had a terrible fight and then Jesse and I left and we ran here."

"Tawny, that's miles away!"

"I know! And now my mom's probably crazy with worry, but I'm afraid to call her. And Jesse just took off!"

Liz picked up the phone and put a call in to Kristy, allaying her fears with a terse explanation that Tawny and "her boyfriend" had had a fight and that Tawny was finding solace with Liz. Kristy was too relieved to be jealous that Tawny had turned to Liz instead of her, and Liz thanked the fates for small favors when Kristy herself suggested that Tawny spend the night with her.

"Want a cup of cocoa?" Liz asked, enjoying the thought of an evening by the fire with her favorite "niece." She poured the wine back in the bottle and set a kettle on the stove.

"Jesse was worried about his dad drinking," Tawny said when Liz brought them both a steaming cup.

As well he might, Liz thought, wrinkling her nose. Her memories of Hawk's drinking days weren't that far away. He'd been less than useless then—although undeniably attractive—and the only good thing from that period was the conception of Jesse Hart.

As Tawny recovered her composure, she told more. "They had a rip-roaring fight and said terrible things to each other."

"People do that when they're mad,"

"Jesse wasn't going to take it," she said with a touch of pride. "He told his father—a thing or two."

"And how did that go over?" Liz asked. She could well imagine.

"Not very well." Tawny half-laughed. "His dad threw him out of the house."

"What?" Liz asked in a deceptively calm voice. From neutral third party, she was fast becoming emotionally involved.

"He and Jesse were yelling and then they were in each other's faces." At the memory, Tawny huddled inside herself. "They were swearing something awful!"

Liz's own blood began to boil. To hell with his injury; Hawk really should have more common sense. What kind of parent was he anyway?

Working up righteous indignation was just the tonic Liz needed for her nebulous woes. She *wanted* to be mad. Hawk had no right to treat Jesse like some sex-crazed maniac just because he had a girlfriend—Tawny Fielding, no less!—over for a couple of hours.

"Dads can really go nuts sometimes," Liz muttered, thinking of Guy Fielding's no-compromise stance.

"No kidding," Tawny breathed. "Jesse's dad's a policeman and he doesn't know when to quit!"

"Boy, is that ever the truth," Liz agreed. Yep, this being mad thing was lots better than worrying about whether he cared about her even a smidgeon and whether he thought about their time on the couch—the same couch, by the sound of it.

"He called Jesse a bastard," Tawny revealed in a small voice.

Simmering anger boiled over. Liz jumped to her feet, infuriated.

"Where are you going?" Tawny asked, surprised.

"I think it's time someone pointed out to Mr. Hawthorne Hart just who the bastard is."

"Aunt Liz!"

"Don't worry. I've got this."

Hawk ran his hands over his face and wished he were anywhere but Woodside, Washington. He'd been deluded to think he could come back here and make a home for himself and his son. There was too much baggage. And damn it all to hell, *Liz* was here.

Okay, she'd followed him; she'd confessed that much. So, it hardly mattered where he was because she was bound and determined to fit herself into Jesse's life. He just hadn't expected to want her to fit into his as well.

The alcohol sloshed in his brain. He was coherent enough to know that. That was what always happened. *Slosh, slosh, slosh.* He might not be a flaming alcoholic, but he definitely had a drinking problem and he was never—after the debacle of this evening—ever going to drink again. But the evening wasn't over yet . . .

Attempting to raise two fingers for the Boy Scout code of honor required way too much effort for the task. With a sigh, Hawk sank onto the couch and wished he'd been calmer with Jesse.

But spying him lying atop the Fielding girl had been a hard slap to the face. He'd made those mistakes in his youth—and beyond—and he'd be damned if he'd see sex and fatherhood added to Jesse's list of youthful transgressions.

Please, please, let him have a whit of common sense!

It was fruitless to pray for it now. It had been fruitless when he was young to tell *him* anything. But he wanted more for Jesse. Better. And the fact that Jesse was fighting him tooth and nail on all these issues just made Hawk more determined.

With a head already throbbing, Hawk reached for the tall-necked beer he'd uncapped in the kitchen. He'd uncapped a few this evening; cleanup tomorrow would be a bitch.

They'd taken off together, Jesse and the Fielding girl. For the life of him, Hawk couldn't remember her first name. He'd half-expected Jesse to take the Jeep—he'd certainly threatened to—but they'd hoofed it to their destination, wherever that was.

Wincing, Hawk asked himself if he'd caused the very situation he'd hoped to avoid: maybe they were making love right this very moment. He shouldn't have overreacted.

A roaring engine filled the silence of the room. Headlights scanned the walls. The motor switched off, then sharp footsteps sounded up the porch steps.

Hawk lifted his head. It was nearly eleven. Who would be coming to see him at this hour?

In a whirl of fury and a hot autumn wind, Liz Havers suddenly burst through the front door.

"Who the hell do you think you are?" she demanded.

Chapter Thirteen

Hawk struggled to his feet. He detested the cast and his infirmity, and it was a hell of a problem to have any dignity at all when you teetered on one leg. "What are you talking about?" he demanded, bracing a hand against the wall.

She was beautiful. Anger tinted her cheeks a warm pink and her eyes glimmered a hot blue. He'd always known about her beauty, but it had been something he'd denied. He'd needed to lessen her affect, belittle her power, keep himself distanced because it wasn't fair to Laura.

His first reaction was pleasure, but the look on her face brought him up short.

"You're the bastard," she told him in a tight voice, raking her hair away from her face in a gesture Hawk could only describe as sexy.

"I'm the bastard?" he repeated.

"Not Jesse."

At sea, Hawk blinked several times, trying to make sense of this. Dimly, he realized Liz had somehow gotten involved in his and Jesse's fight. Had Jesse confided in her?

"It doesn't take a professional to know how dangerous

negative labeling is," she spat out through clenched teeth. "You've been a parent for years. Haven't you learned anything?"

"What label did I use?"

"You can't even remember!"

Hawk shrugged.

"You called him a bastard," she said, her eyes sparking with maternal fury.

"I did not call him a bastard."

"Oh?" She didn't believe him.

"He called me a bastard," Hawk corrected her, "and a few other choice names when I told him he couldn't have sex in my house, or something to that effect." The fight was a little fuzzy, but Jesse's reaction to the stricken look on his girlfriend's face was memorable. He'd practically grabbed Hawk by the throat and hadn't only because of his broken leg. Remorse had settled over Hawk until Jesse's language deteriorated, and then he'd grabbed his son's forearms and they'd been locked in a battle of wills that far outstripped the frozen clamp they had on each other.

That Hawk had been balancing himself was something they'd both understood even in the heat of anger. Jesse had released him and Hawk had collapsed against the wall again.

"They took off together," he said shortly. "But I guess you've seen them."

"I saw Tawny." Liz's voice was steel. "She was destroyed."

Tawny. That was it. For a moment, Liz seemed at a further loss for words, but then she took a deep breath and, to Hawk's chagrin, started in again.

"What is it about parents of teenagers? I swear, I've

seen hundreds of them and it's as if the child hits a certain age and the parents lose all their brains. They just spill right out of their heads. What are you trying to do? Force them into bed together?"

"I was exercising a little parental control," Hawk growled, hiding his feelings. It was a direct hit. He'd just been asking himself the same questions. But he didn't need Liz Havers, psychologist, throwing judgments on him. "Stay out of it."

"And let you deal with it? You're doing a crackerjack job already."

"Like you know a damn thing about it."

Liz flushed. "I never had a chance to be a mother."

"You tried to throw that chance away. Permanently!"

"Not my choice. It was against everything I believed in and wanted, and luckily, it didn't come off!"

"Only because I intervened."

"Well, I see you've turned to your favorite anesthetic," she said scornfully, adroitly dodging the issue.

Hawk, however, was sober enough to catch her. "Is that what you learned in psychologist school? If you don't like what you're hearing, change the subject?"

Liz glared at him. She wore her jeans and a cream shirt, but the swell of her breasts seemed highlighted within the buttery soft cotton fabric. He wanted to touch her. He didn't want to fight her. He wanted those lips soft for kissing, instead of tight with accusations.

"You're drunk, aren't you?"

"Not enough," Hawk corrected. He'd like to be stinking drunk, then maybe he'd get over his fascination with her.

"Where's Jesse?"

"Still out. The last I saw he was with Tawny." Hawk swallowed a long swallow of beer and wiped the back of his hand across his mouth. He could feel her gaze drilling into him.

"You really scared her," Liz told him. "And she's already scared enough of men." At Hawk's questioning look, she explained, "Her father's demanding custody. He's planning to take her to Seattle this weekend, something he's never done before. I just talked to her mother."

"What's your relationship to her?"

"Kristy and I are friends. Tawny's like a daughter to me."

"You're just chock full of maternal feelings, aren't you?"

"You can't keep me from my son forever. One of these days, I'm just going to haul off and tell Jesse the truth."

"Not yet," Hawk bit out.

"You're paranoid," she declared, shaking her head, her lustrous mane of hair shimmering in the light. "And I'm tired of playing by your rules."

"You tell him, you'll be sorry."

"You're threatening me?"

"I just know how Jesse'll react. He felt abandoned by Laura, and she couldn't help not being there for him. He won't forgive you."

He spoke the truth, and though she didn't know it, it cut him a bit, too. Her face registered her conflicting emotions.

"You owe Tawny an apology," she said unevenly, fighting for control.

"Yeah, well," he muttered gruffly. "She shouldn't have been here."

"They didn't do anything wrong."

"How do you know?"

"Tawny told me the whole story."

Hawk lifted a brow. "Like you told your parents the whole story when you were sneaking off to see me?"

Liz drew a shaking breath. "I was young and stupid when you and I had our affair, but you were old enough to know better. I'm sorry for everything, but by God, you'd better look in the mirror before you start hurling accusations because your face is just as guilty!"

Her words were darts. Hawk swilled back more beer.

"I know you were in pain. But you were also drunk most of the time we were together." She added, "I don't even know how much you remember."

"I was aware," he lied.

"You called me Laura," Liz said bitterly. "That's how aware you were."

"Well, I sobered right up when I found out you were aborting my child."

She shook her head. "You're just trying to divert blame."

"Damn right I am!" Hawk admitted, finishing the beer. He tested the weight of the bottle in his hand, then hurled it at the river-rock fireplace. Pieces of glass flew in all directions.

Liz remained unmoved. He expected her to rail at him some more, but she didn't. "You can't hurt me anymore," she told him flatly. "I won't let you."

"I've hurt *you*?"

"You've nearly annihilated me," she murmured, turning away. "But it's over now."

"Wait." He struggled toward her, catching her elbow at the door, his fingers closing over smooth skin. She pulled back, attempting to release his grip, but he hung firm. She refused to look at him and all he could see was her profile. An upturned nose, a generous mouth currently tight with disapproval, a defined, downy cheek, and a sweep of thick lashes.

"Don't touch me," she ordered, but there was no heat to her words.

"I don't want to fight."

"I don't want you—to touch me," she said again. "All I want is to see my son. And I want Jesse to know I'm his mother."

Hawk didn't answer. He resisted on principle.

"You told him Laura was his mother," she accused, and the hurt in her voice was as huge as the ocean.

"I wanted Laura to be his mother," he admitted. God, her skin was sleek. His thumb caressed her arm.

She trembled and tried to pull back, but Hawk held on. It was a replay of his scene with Jesse, but with a far different driving emotion.

She pressed her lips together, then burst out, "I can't do this. I don't want to feel that way again."

"What way?"

That way. Like when I was seventeen."

"I want you," he admitted, almost surprised by his own admission. "I don't want to, but I do."

"I want Jesse."

His leg ached and his head ached, too. Suddenly, he just needed to collapse into bed—with Liz. "I want to make love to you."

Liz's answer was a strangled sound that could have meant anything. He stared at her and slowly, ever so slowly, her eyes turned to meet his. Their gazes remained locked for long moments in which Hawk counted his heartbeats and Liz's lips parted.

Slowly, he bent forward, delicately balanced, and kissed her deeply, his mouth melding to hers, his tongue searching inside that warm crevice as Liz's hands found his arms, holding him at length even while her kiss reached out for him.

* * *

The view down the short hallway caught the front door, part of the wall, and a glimpse of the corner of the fireplace. Jesse was a statue, his gaze riveted. He'd heard the fight as soon as he slipped inside his bedroom window and he'd tiptoed forward into the hall, wondering what in God's name his father was saying about him and Tawny to Ms. Havers.

Words jumped from their hot fight . . . *I want to know my son . . . mother . . . affair . . . abortion . . . I want Jesse . . . I want to make love to you.*

Jesse's head was thick. Too much information.

Ms. Havers was his mother?

He backed away as if he'd been burned. Maybe he had been. He felt as if he'd turned to ash. A pillar of salt. Like that Bible story—he'd looked back. By mistake. To a past he hadn't known existed.

His mother.

A lurch to his stomach. Jesse melted back to his bedroom. Years of long practice saved him from screaming out his feelings. He knew how to hide. To run. To escape the forces of law and order and deadly emotion.

Silent as a ghost, he slipped back outside the window. Metal glimmered in the bluish moonlight. The handlebars of his bike. In a heartbeat, he was on the vehicle and circumventing the house, his father, and the shrink's car.

His mother.

"God," he whispered into the darkly shadowed night.

She shouldn't let him touch her. She shouldn't let him get close enough for the air to tighten between them. She shouldn't *be here* with him. Liz opened her mouth to say as much, but it just provided entry for his tongue. Her knees quivered. Resolve seesawed. Her fingers clung to his arms as if it were she who needed the support.

"Hawk," she murmured against his lips.

More kisses for an answer. Hot, short invitations driven from a deep hunger. Her shoulders sagged. She was losing. His body drew closer, more of a leaning because he couldn't put all his weight on his leg.

Then she was pressed against the wall, his weight deliciously hard against hers. Her brain disengaged. She gave up. He wanted her and she wanted him just as much.

"Liz," he said thickly somewhere near her ear.

Distantly, she thought, *he got it right this time.* The memory scoured inside her head. It bothered her.

"I can't!" she burst out. "You're just doing this to keep me from seeing Jesse!"

"No," he growled through tight lips. Abruptly, he shoved himself away from her, overbalanced and crashed to the floor.

"Hawk!"

She bent down, scared at the white pallor to his face. His lashes were closed. For a second she worried he wasn't breathing before she realized he was holding his breath against the pain.

"Are you okay?" she asked, touching his face lightly. "Hawk?"

"Get away."

The words were forced out. Liz, who'd shown no inclination to listen to him yet, didn't budge an inch. "I'm sorry."

"Don't . . . say anything," he expelled again, this time with more fury than pain. "*Damn* it."

Out of nowhere, Liz was struck with humor. She pressed a hand to her mouth, fighting a half-hysterical giggle. Hawk chose that moment to lift his lashes and eye her with those intense blue-gray eyes that missed nothing.

He was too humiliated to join in her amusement at his expense, but his lips twisted as if he, too, recognized how ridiculous they both could be.

With unusual lack of inhibition, Liz bent down and kissed him lightly on the lips. "I really am sorry you're hurt," she whispered. "I don't want to fight."

Hawk groaned and closed his eyes again. "Don't tell Jesse yet," he said. "Please."

"All right."

Her sudden capitulation threw him. "All right?" he asked cautiously.

"I'll be patient. I'll wait."

Now he stared openly at her. Liz's heart started a slow, sensual beat as she stared into the cool depths of his eyes. They were his most beautiful feature. She'd been seduced by them once; she could be seduced again.

Her hair fell forward and Hawk automatically reached up to brush it back. He didn't release her. "Come here," he said a bit fatalistically and Liz understood because she felt the same inexorable pull.

The floor was harder than the couch. Liz scraped elbows on the hardwood and complained, and Hawk and she struggled to their feet. She slung his arm around her neck rather than reach for his crutches and, as if they'd had their movements choreographed, they moved as one down the hall to the bedroom that was his.

Barren and male. That was how Liz saw it. A king-size bed with a navy spread. A pine nightstand and chest of drawers. A black Tensor lamp and a closet with too few clothes on the hangers and only two pairs of shoes.

This she took in at a glance as she lowered Hawk onto the edge of the bed. "You look like hell," she told him, aware that his pallor had yet to return to normal.

"You've got dust all over you," he returned, and Liz glanced down at her sleeveless blouse, snorting a bit as she realized he was right.

"When do you think Jesse will come home?"

"When he's darn good and ready," Hawk said. "He won't be back tonight."

"He could be."

Hawk's eyes were heavy-lidded. He lay back on the bed, but his hand drifted toward Liz. His tanned fingers restlessly played with the hem of her blouse. "He could be," he agreed in a voice that said the likelihood was very rare.

Liz knew she should leave. She'd had ample opportunity already. Sleeping with Hawthorne Hart would only add to her problems, not alleviate them. But he looked so helpless just now, and though it was partly his helplessness that had gotten to her in the past, she couldn't tear herself away.

His fingers crept downward, to her knee, gently massaging in a way that dug beneath her skin. If his hand drifted to more intimate areas she didn't know what she'd do. Bolt? Gasp? *Guide him?*

"Hawk, I—"

"What?" he asked when she broke off. Those fingers. Those damn fingers were stealing upward. It was so bold. So intimate. She could only wait in a sort of breathless anticipation.

"I—can't think."

His hand reached the juncture of her thighs. He caressed her and she collapsed against him. Now there was no holding back. She squirmed against him, as close as she could be. At some level, she was conscious of his cast, but because Hawk seemed completely unaware as his hands groped for her, Liz concentrated on the angles of his body that meshed with hers.

"I want you," he muttered, and that was all it took. No more waiting. He pulled her atop him and she went down like wax. Then they were touching and exploring, only their heartbeats and ragged breaths punctuating the still night.

Hawk slid Liz's blouse from her shoulders. His hands molded her breasts. Dimly, she worried that she shouldn't be here with him, but her own hands removed his shirt. His pants were split to the thigh to accommodate his cast and Liz undid his belt buckle with expert fingers. This touched a far corner of her mind, for her inexperience was something she took for granted. That she could be so adept was almost funny. But when Hawk's mouth covered her bare nipple she swept in a sharp breath, all humor gone in the suddenness of pure sensation.

His mouth was hot and moist. Frozen, she braced herself on her arms, stunned by the urgency of her need. Quickly, her hands helped him remove the rest of their clothes until they were both naked and dragging each other close.

"Your leg," she gasped at one point, to which Hawk only doubled his efforts to keep them both at the frenzied brink of sexual fulfillment. His mouth explored all of her, hot and wet and trailing along her skin until she melted from the inside out. When he found the deepest part of her she moaned and thrashed on the pillow, her fingers digging into his hair. She climaxed so fast she let out a cry of shock and pleasure.

When he slid inside her, she grasped his buttocks and pulled him hard and close. He tried to hold back, but she started her own campaign of pleasure, kneading his skin, circling his legs with hers, her own kisses deep and strong and sliding from his ear to his mouth. His groan of torment was surrender. Deep within her, he pumped rhythmically, Liz's breaths echoing the hard thrusts.

"Liz," he groaned thickly.

She didn't care. Her eyes were squinched shut. Her body peaking again. She moved fast and he matched her thrusts until they both cried out in ecstasy together, worlds colliding. Liz's head was thrown back, throat arched, body quivering as she felt Hawk's hot climax.

An eternity later, she opened her eyes. Hawk's arm was thrown possessively around her, his lips a hairbreadth from her ear, his face covered by a tangle of sleek brown-blond hair. He lay on his back, his casted leg out straight, but apart from this covering he was naked and Liz's gaze feasted on his male beauty.

She loved looking at him. She loved all the sinewy muscles and smooth skin and the dusting of dark chest hair. His hip bones and thighs and legs were totally masculine. She could even rhapsodize about his feet, though one was showing definite signs of discoloration from the blood that had drained down his leg post-operation.

He was everything she wanted in a male. Everything. Harshness and humor and sometimes scathing irony. He was tough with elements of weakness, the kind only visible to a female, the kind his type of man would abhor.

And he was hers. From long ago. She'd tagged him as the man she loved and nothing had changed in over sixteen long years of separation.

So, why was her heart so heavy? Why did she feel the need to guiltily pull on her clothes and slink into the cloak of night?

Because he didn't love her.

The answer was so simple her flesh broke out into goose bumps. She tried to talk herself out of it, tell herself it didn't matter, but she'd never been good at fooling herself for long.

Hawk murmured a protest as she slid from his embrace. Now that she was rational again, a thousand worries crowded her mind. Jesse could return at any moment. Worse yet, he might never return. Tawny was home alone at her house.

She hadn't used any protection.

Frozen with shock, Liz broke into a cold sweat. But . . . this wasn't the time of the month for a pregnancy. She'd known that in the back of her mind. She was regular enough to set a clock by. Even so, how could she be so reckless?

How could *he*?

She yanked on the rest of her clothes as Hawthorne surfaced from his alcohol-supported stupor and demanded, "Where are you going?"

"Home. Away. I don't know." He didn't argue with her. It upset and infuriated her that he didn't even try, and she knew that was ridiculous, but . . . "I must be out of my mind," she railed softly, her voice strangled.

"Don't leave."

"Hawk, for God's sake . . . !"

"Wait until Jesse gets back."

"Oh, sure. Great idea."

"Come here . . ."

His pleading did her in. She took a step forward, wanting so badly to climb back into bed with him, she felt weak from the effort of holding back.

"Just for a moment," she told him, hating herself a little as she slid into the cradle of his arms once more.

* * *

His lungs ached. His throat burned rawly. Legs pumping furiously, Jesse rode blindly to Tawny's house, throwing down the bike and running toward her window in one lithe movement. He banged on the pane, heart thundering, ears ringing,

Ms. Havers was his mother!

The thought lanced his brain. A second later, he sank against the siding, sliding down until he was kneeling beneath Tawny's window, spent. It couldn't be. It made no sense. He didn't understand how it could happen.

The front porch light blinked on. Jesse shrank into the shadows. A woman's voice. "Tawny?"

Jesse hunched his shoulders. He'd made Tawny's mom check the noise and he felt bad. But it gave him an answer: Tawny wasn't home.

That meant she was still at the shrink's house.

His mother.

Shivering, Jesse stealthily picked up the bike and rode as fast as he could toward Liz's. He had to be fast. He sure as hell didn't want to run into her, and there was no telling how long she'd be with Dad.

Dad. And Mom.

He swore violently and spat between his teeth, pumping the pedals harder.

"Where do you think he is?" Liz asked. It was dangerous lying here beside Hawthorne. If Jesse returned, she couldn't hide that she was in Hawk's room, locked bedroom door or no. How could she explain it? Yet she was paralyzed, unable to leave this warm comfort. The real world was out there waiting. Let it wait a bit longer.

"Halfway to Timbuktu. He'll come home when he's good and ready." Weariness edged his voice. Failure. He didn't like being the kind of parent who doesn't know where his kid is.

"I've got to call Tawny. She's waiting for me."

"Tell her you won't be home."

"No, Hawk. I can't."

He turned toward her, fiddling with the buttons down the front of her blouse. Liz's fingers covered his, stopping him. "I don't want to think about anything," Hawk said in that low voice that always made her heart hurt.

She was weak. Wanton. Without will. In slow motion, her clothes came off for a second time and she moved into the rhythm of lovemaking with far too much eagerness and not enough sanity.

The shrink's house was lit by a single lamp in the living room. There was no black Miata in the driveway and he already knew the garage was full of boxes, no room for a car. So *Mom* wasn't home yet. Good.

Jesse slunk through the shadows to the window, spying Tawny's blondish hair tucked onto a pillow on the couch. He tapped on the pane. She lifted her head instantly, clearly not sleepy in the least. Signaling to her, he saw that she recognized him. Her lithe form slid from the couch and she opened the front door.

"Hey," she greeted him, worried. "Haven't you been home?"

"Yeah." He was tongue-tied. The events of the evening had left him empty and unconnected. "I've been there."

"Was Aunt Liz there?" Tawny's eyes were huge. "I told

her about your dad and she got really mad and just tore out of here. Did she talk to him? Was he there?"

Jesse couldn't respond. *I want my son . . . I never had a chance to be a mother . . . I want you . . .* He shook his head. It felt like something had broken loose inside. Everything was rattly and jangling.

"Are you okay?" Tawny's fine brows drew into a line of worry.

"We gotta leave," he burst out. "Right now. We gotta get outta here."

"What do you mean?" She drew back instinctively, into the security and light of the little house.

But Jesse was outside. On the porch. In the heat of summer and the wildness of night. That same raffish desire to be untamed and defy all rules swept over him and he embraced it. "Come on," he urged, unknowingly seductive in his urgency. Tawny hesitated, eyeing him, a part of herself she'd never known existed heeding the cry.

"I—can't. Aunt Liz . . ." she protested, her eyes begging him to understand.

"Aunt Liz isn't who you think she is," Jesse replied scornfully. "She's . . ."

"She's what?"

"C'mere." Jesse stepped toward her, taking her hands in his, staring down at her through the curtain of his hair. She tugged one small hand free and brushed back silken strands. Within her amber gaze was a message he read clearly: convince me. He kissed her without a second thought, drew her against his fast-beating heart and held her tightly. "You've gotta come," he said roughly into her hair. "Your dad's coming to take you away."

"What?"

"I heard—Aunt Liz—say he's coming this weekend. You can't stay or I'll never see you again."

"I won't go! I won't."

"Then c'mon. Now. Don't think, just do it."

Her lashes swept downward. Her body was tense as piano wire. Indecision lasted a split second, then she slid a glance upward and he read rebellion in the set of her jaw. "Do you have money?"

Jesse expelled air through his teeth, furious with himself. He should have stripped his father clean. Tawny put a hand on his arm. "Give me a minute," she said, and disappeared to the back of the house.

She was gone so long he grew anxious, worried she'd changed her mind. But when she returned she had sweatshirts for both of them, a roll of bills, and a flashlight.

"Jeezus." Jesse was impressed.

"My life savings," she said ironically. "For saving my life. I keep it with me all the time. I guess I kinda thought I might need it someday."

"I'll pay you back."

"I'm not worried."

He kissed her once more, hard and fast. The phone started ringing at that moment and they both jumped guiltily. Tawny hesitated, then tucked her hand inside Jesse's, and they slipped away into the waiting arms of night.

Liz ended her phone call and tucked one hand beneath her chin. She glanced out the front window. The moon was high now, illuminating the grounds but not sliding fingers of light into the house.

She was fully dressed, unwilling to succumb to the warm pleasures of being Hawk's bedmate again, aware that it would only hurt her in the end. He was asleep. Exhaustion had erased the lines beside his mouth and only a tiny furrow remained between his brows as he breathed deeply. She'd wanted to trace that small crevice with her finger but had resisted. Instead, she'd dragged on her clothes for the second time and headed for the door.

A quick call to Tawny and she was out of here, or so she'd thought. But she'd rung the house twice now to no avail. Could she be sleeping through?

Maybe Jesse's with her . . .

That thought galvanized her into action. Without further ado, she drove back to her house, way too cognizant of the man she'd left sleeping so soundly. She shook her head in amazement. She had to get over this.

A light burned from the back of the house. The bathroom, Liz realized, as she entered the front door. Glancing at the couch, she realized Tawny wasn't there. She must have decided to climb into Liz's bed. Strange, but then, she'd been pretty upset.

Liz flipped on the light to the bedroom. Nothing. Except Tawny's small pile of belongings, a pile that seemed to ebb and rise depending on how much time she spent at Liz's, had been rifled through. Liz knew because she'd neatly arranged it after Tawny's last visit.

With a growing feeling of dread, Liz checked the kitchen and finally the bathroom. She gasped at the lipsticked message on the mirror.

I'm with Jesse. I can't go with my dad. I'm sorry.

"Oh, Tawny," Liz whispered, sick with dread.

Within seconds, she was speeding back to Hawk's cabin.

Chapter Fourteen

Hot-wiring cars was a Hawthorne Jesse Hart specialty. At the edge of Woodside, a decade-old red Ford sedan looked beat-up, neglected, and lonely. Jesse tinkered beneath the dashboard while Tawny held the flashlight.

"I feel like a criminal," she whispered.

"Don't think about it." Good advice. He wasn't thinking now. He was running on pure adrenaline.

"Where are we going?"

"Aberdeen," he told her, to which she made a noise of recognition.

Touching wires together, he heard a satisfying fizz and zap with a tiny burst of fiery connection. Jamming down the accelerator with his left elbow, the little car revved excitedly.

"C'mon," he ordered, scrambling behind the wheel. Tawny jumped in beside him, eyes huge.

"You sure you know how to drive?"

White teeth gleamed in the moon's glow. "Been doin' it for years," he assured her, and with a quick jerk of the stick shift, the car leaped forward and they were out of town.

* * *

"She wrote you a message in lipstick?" Hawk questioned, frowning.

"On the mirror," Liz reaffirmed, pacing around Hawk's kitchen. He was perched on a stool, wearing only boxer shorts, his casted leg stretched straight. His hair was mussed and his eyes were lazy with sleep and sensual fulfillment. No amount of anxiety on her part could get him stirred up. "I guess she knows Guy's planning to pick her up this weekend because she specifically said she wouldn't leave with him."

Hawthorne rubbed his hands over his face, trying to remove the effects of alcohol and lovemaking. He wanted to be sharp here. He hadn't been sharp all night.

"Did she know her father was picking her up before? Why'd she get so upset now?"

"Maybe Jesse talked her into leaving," Liz guessed.

"Has she done this kind of thing before?"

"No. She would never leave her mom. But then, Guy hasn't been so persistent. She's scared he'll take her away."

"So she left before that could happen."

"What are you trying to say?"

Hawthorne wasn't completely sure. "She came to you because I upset her. She poured out her heart. Did she mention the worry about her father?"

"No . . ." Liz felt the thrum of a deeper worry. Hawk was picking at it and she didn't like it.

"Maybe she just wrote that to give herself an excuse to be with Jesse," he said.

"But she was already with him. Why come home at all to talk to me? They could have left after you had your fight with them." Now Liz picked up his train of thought and fretted over it even worse. She sucked in a sharp breath. "I know Kristy didn't tell her about Guy because she didn't want her to know yet."

"And you didn't tell her?"

She shook her head emphatically. "The only person I told was you."

"Well, I didn't tell her," Hawk pointed out reasonably.

"Jesse," Liz whispered.

The last vestiges of sluggishness evaporated in Hawthorne's brain. Crystal connections. Obvious answers. "Jesse came back and overheard our fight."

"Oh, *Hawk*!"

"He knows," he whispered, clenching his jaw at his own stupidity. "He sneaks in the back window sometimes."

Liz moaned in pain, a hand pressed to her mouth in horror.

"He went straight to Tawny. He talked her into leaving with him."

"Where . . . where are they?" Liz choked out.

Hawk was grim. This wasn't a question he could answer because Jesse was notoriously hard to read, especially when he thumbed his nose at adult expectations and responsibility, an action less evident of late but never, as Hawk had just been reminded, that far out of range.

"We've got to find them," Liz declared. "We've got to find them. Kristy! Oh, God. I can't tell her."

"Calm down. They'll be fine. Jesse's—resourceful," he finished after a long moment of searching for the right word.

"Well, thank God for small favors," Liz responded with an edge.

"You should be proud."

"Damn you," she said, near tears. "We should have told

him from the start. Oh my God. What if he does something rash?"

"Something rash?" Hawk repeated in disbelief, lifting a brow. He couldn't help it. He was starting to get amused. And though he sympathized with her anxiety, he'd been here so many times before that he'd learned to cope.

She flushed. "Stop patronizing me."

"There's nothing to do but wait."

"Send out the police! Do something!"

For an answer, he slid off the stool and hobbled toward where she was currently standing in the doorway from the kitchen to the living room, her hands in her hair as if she wanted to rip it out by the roots.

"I've got to call Kristy," she moaned. "I've got to tell her."

"Wait 'til morning. They could be back any minute."

Liz closed her eyes and leaned her head backward. Her lashes dampened. "You were right. I'm no kind of mother. This never would have happened if I'd been more careful."

"Oh, for God's sake," Hawk snapped, growing impatient. "Anything can happen when it comes to our son."

Our son. It echoed into the sudden silence. Hawthorne had never fully addressed the fact that Liz was Jesse's mother—unless he was denigrating her. Liz opened tear-starred eyes and regarded him gratefully, and he regretted being so harsh these intervening years. He hadn't been fair, he realized now. He had put all kinds of judgment calls on her.

"Do you really think they'll be back soon?" Liz asked, fragile hope in her voice.

"I don't know." He wished he could tell her differently, but he couldn't. "If it's any consolation, Jesse's a good man to be on the road with."

She choked out a laugh. Hawk found himself almost

smiling, which was ridiculous considering the situation. He was afraid to tap into his feelings for Liz Havers just yet—apart from lust, which he had to admit was definitely part of the mix. But the rest of it . . .

"How do you do it?" she marveled, shaking her head. "How do you wait for him to come home?"

"You can't do anything else," Hawk answered.

"He knows, Hawk. He knows."

Because she couldn't stop bouncing from one crisis to another, Hawk was powerless to console her. Still, she was right here. Right in front of him. He reached out a hand and dusted his knuckles along the hill of her cheek. She swallowed hard.

"I feel completely lost," she whispered.

Gesturing to the couch, he followed after her in his ungainly manner. When Liz sat down, Hawk sank next to her. Their relationship was tentative at best, and now, with Jesse's probable knowledge about the whole affair, it was bound to get stickier.

As he'd already said, nothing to do but wait.

Aberdeen at dawn. Coastal. Gray. Depressing. Dark older buildings that to Jesse's youthful eye looked ancient and decrepit stabbed into a thick, hovering sky. The only color were streetlights; shots of red and green in an otherwise homogenous slate-colored day.

Tawny lay asleep in the passenger seat, her smooth brow clear and untroubled. Jesse eased his stolen wheels to the side of the road, cut the engine, and leaned over to kiss her forehead. She stirred and opened one eye. Memory washed over her and she sat bolt upright.

"Where are we?"

"Aberdeen."

"Did we just get here?"

"Nah. I've been drivin' around a while, just lookin'."

Tawny blinked several times, yawned, and finger-combed her hair. Her expression grew grim. Jesse knew how she felt.

"I shouldn't have left," she said in a worried tone. "What was I thinking? Mom'll have a heart attack."

Jesse gazed out at the gray day and stated flatly, "I'm not goin' back."

"Why not? What happened?"

"I just hate it there, that's all."

She gazed at him searchingly, her amber eyes way too knowing. He half-turned away, aware that she could see right through him. "Something terrible happened."

He shrugged.

"Something with your dad?"

Jesse chewed on the inside of his cheek until the pain penetrated.

"Tell me or take me back," she said, watching him closely.

"I can't take you back! This car's been reported by now. We gotta drop it and get the hell out of sight."

"What *is* it?"

He turned on her, furious, wanting to bite her head off and anyone else's within range. But it was only Tawny there. His friend. The girl he loved. The fire flamed out of him and instead, a lump filled his throat, choking him. To make matters worse, she reached out, touching his arm, curling her fingers in the sleeve of the sweatshirt she'd given him, which was too small and nearly choked him but helped keep him from freezing to death.

"Aunt Liz . . ." he struggled, his voice thready and uncertain.

"Aunt Liz," she prompted.

"She's"—Sucking in a breath, he exhaled in a rush—"my mother."

She waited. Simply waited. The words didn't compute, so she waited for further explanation. There was nothing more to say, so Jesse waited as well. He could almost see the words penetrate through the wall of her brain and travel along a nerve to reach that part of her that assimilated information and drew conclusions. It was a slow process. The brain threw out thousands of roadblocks to the truth.

"I don't understand," she mumbled, frowning. "What do you mean?"

"I overheard my dad and her fighting. She's my mother. My dad's wife, Laura, never was. It was all a big lie."

"Are you crazy?" she demanded, angry.

"No!" Jesse threw open the door and charged into the chill morning air. He wanted to run, but there was nowhere to go.

"You got it wrong!" Tawny declared emphatically, climbing from her side of the car and slamming the door. "That's all."

"I know what I heard," he rounded on her. "Don't you get it? Your wonderful Aunt Liz is my mother and I hate her. I hate 'em both. They lied to me and now *Aunt Liz* wants to be my mommy. A little goddamn late! Well, I'm not stickin' around. I'm outta there. Forever."

Tawny inhaled and exhaled several times, hard. Jesse hunched his shoulders, afraid of histrionics. He was no good at this. God*damn* it.

"I'm going to faint," Tawny said in surprise, staggering.

Jesse ran around the car and scooped her into his arms just before she crumpled to the ground.

Woodside Police Station looked cold in the early glow of fluorescent lights without the warmth of day to over-come that eerie illumination. Liz sat huddled in the chair next to Hawk's desk while he checked with the night staff on sightings of teen runaways.

"A car's been reported stolen," he told her, handing her a cup of coffee, presumably from a pot located in a back room. She was surprised how good it tasted. She rarely drank it black.

"You think Jesse took it?" she asked, hoping against hope he was wrong.

Hawk gave her an ironic look. "Yes."

Liz nodded. Not that many stolen cars reported in a town the size of Woodside, and Jesse had a history, after all.

And motivation, she reminded herself. She shuddered, wondering what he was thinking of her now. If only she'd had a chance to tell him the truth face-to-face.

"I need to go tell Kristy," she said, rising to her feet and feeling like an old, old woman.

"I'll go with you." At her look, he pointed out, "He's my son, too."

Liz stood by the back window of Kristy's house, lis-tening to Hawthorne's deep voice answer Kristy's ques-tions with patience and apology: patience because he was a policeman who dealt with these issues on a regular basis; apology because it was his son who'd talked Tawny into leaving.

A detached part of Liz was impressed; he was doing a better job than she could, given that it was Jesse and Tawny, two of the most important people in her life. Maybe *the* most important. And Kristy was taking the news well. She knew enough about Jesse and Tawny to believe in their safety.

"What should I tell Guy?" she asked in a small voice. "He's coming down tomorrow to pick Tawny up."

"That's one of the main reasons she left," Liz pointed out.

"Will he call first?" Hawk asked.

"Probably."

"Then tell him the truth."

"Should I do that now?" Kristy asked, her face reflecting her reluctance.

"Wait 'til he calls," Hawk suggested. "We could know something by then."

"He'll blame me," Kristy said.

"Don't let him," Liz broke in. "He doesn't know anything about Tawny or any of this."

"He'll use this as an excuse. I know him. Once he made up his mind to have Tawny, it was just a matter of time before he got his way." She smiled wanly. "He's probably sorry I'm in remission."

"Kristy . . ." Liz ached for her.

She waved her off, too many emotions weighing them all down. "He doesn't have to know until he phones, and maybe I can put him off a while longer."

Hawk, who'd been fidgeting and looking itchy, nodded and said, "Your daughter's never done this before. It's likely she'll be back before you know it. This is really Jesse's problem, and she won't want to deal with it."

"Do you think he told her?" Liz asked, swallowing against a dry throat.

Kristy glanced at her sympathetically. "They seem pretty tight."

"I know, I just . . ." Liz could well imagine that scene. Betrayal. They would both feel it, and the thought made her feel small and cheap.

Hawk clambered to his feet and leaned on his crutches. "I've gotta go."

"What?" Liz demanded, her head snapping up. "Where?"

"To work."

"This *is* work," she reminded him.

"Sitting around fretting isn't work." He headed for his Jeep. Now she knew why he hadn't offered to drive her; he'd wanted her to have her own car.

"Where are you going?" she asked, following him outside.

"I've got some other cases to get back to."

Liz stared at him in amazement. "There's still a lot to talk about, you know. It's not just Jesse and Tawny."

Visions of the night before invaded her thoughts, and she could tell he was reliving a few moments himself; his lashes swept downward, concealing his expressive eyes and Liz recognized the evasion.

"Yeah, well . . ."

"Hawk," she warned softly, sensing he was escaping.

"Damn it, Liz. Not now."

She was offended that it was suddenly her problem. That she was keeping him from his work. "That's so like you," she whispered angrily. "Take what you want and never give anything back."

"Well, what do you want me to say?" he asked through his teeth.

"I want you to say last night was wonderful. I want you to say you're glad Jesse knows the truth now. I want you to say that it's all great because we can start anew."

"That's what you want?"

"Yes." But her voice reflected her own doubts, ones she hadn't even known were there.

"I've got an appointment," he said after a tense moment.

If ever Liz wanted to kick his crutches out from underneath him, it was that moment. Choosing a more adult approach, she turned on her heel, marched inside the house, and slammed the door behind her until the crystal in Kristy's dining room hutch clattered furiously.

The Forest Service office was a small one-story building with shake siding painted forest green—appropriate, Hawk thought as he struggled out of the Jeep, cursing invectives to an empty afternoon where shadows crawled over the other two cars in the gravel lot.

But it was a walking cast on his leg now. He hadn't forgotten this morning's doctor's appointment during all this nonsense. Amid growling by the doc that he wasn't quite ready, Hawk had patiently waited while he'd been switched to a cast that ended at his knee.

Now he hobbled through the front door, glad for the improvement, chafing that it was still going to take weeks before he could move the way he wanted to. Inside was a long, narrow room that sported one desk and a lot of wood samples in a case. Behind the desk sat a hard-eyed brunette with permed hair. No niceties needed here, he decided. She looked tough enough to chew nails.

When she glanced up he swept in a startled breath: *Sarah Lister*.

Messages sizzled inside his skull. Conclusions. Don Vandeway's voice. ". . . then he befriended a secretary at the Forest Service who helped keep the arrangement trouble-free . . ."

"So you were Manny and Barney's connection," Hawk said.

"I don't know what you're talking about." Her voice was smart, but her eyes dilated despite herself.

"Your boyfriend's a poacher who used Manny and Barney's permits. Who is he?"

"You don't have any right!"

"That's where you're wrong." Flipping out his ID, Hawk drilled out, "I'm interested in the list of yew bark harvesting permits."

"I can't give out that information without authorization."

"This is your authorization," he pointed out, tapping his identification. It had been a long night and was turning into a long day, and he didn't have a lot of interest in waiting.

"You'll have to wait."

"Then I'll wait." Letting her see how much of a struggle it was for him, Hawk settled himself into one of the green Naugahyde chairs, stretching his casted leg and crutches toward the woman at the desk. She glared at him and he held her gaze.

Placing a call on his phone, he waited for someone at the station to pick up and give him an update on his misplaced son.

Liz hung up Kristy's phone, fighting to keep her expression neutral.

"Well?" Kristy asked, nervously clutching a throw pillow to her chest.

"Guy's coming tonight."

She sank onto the couch, forlorn and lost. "Oh, God, I knew it. I don't want him here."

Liz sat down beside her and clasped one hand. Kristy had handed her the phone as soon as she'd heard Guy Fielding's voice on the other end. By unspoken understanding, it was decided that Liz was Kristy's advocate as well as Tawny's. The only time Liz spoke to Kristy's ex-husband was on Tawny or Kristy's behalf, so as soon as Guy heard her voice he bristled and grew prickly and difficult.

"Where is she?" he demanded when Liz explained that Tawny was unavailable.

No amount of pussyfooting around was going to help. "We're not sure. She's taken off with a friend of hers."

That brought on an explosion to rival TNT. Liz actually held the phone away from her ear. Twice she attempted to soothe and placate, but Guy had simply bellowed that he was driving to Woodside that instant and Tawny damn well better be back by the time he arrived.

"You know, I really feel like a loser when I realize I loved him once," Kristy declared. "How could anyone love such a pompous ass?"

"He gave you Tawny," Liz reminded her, calling on the rationale she'd fallen back on for years.

"And now he's trying to take her away."

Liz half-laughed. "Jesse took care of that first."

"I'm not really worried about her with him. Are you?"

Kristy never ceased to amaze Liz, who shook her head in agreement. "That's not what's got me worried either."

"It's that Jesse knows."

Liz nodded.

"I don't think his father's such a bastard." Kristy managed a wan smile. "He was good to me."

"Hawk's . . . got his good points," Liz admitted, though it was likely to kill her to admit it.

"You still love him, and I understand why."

"No, I dislike him intensely."

Kristy actually laughed. "Will you be here when Guy gets here?"

"You know I will."

"It's for you," Sarah Lister announced coldly, holding up the receiver to her landline.

Hawthorne, who'd been in a state of semi-sleep, roused himself and frowned. He hadn't told the station where he was, so no one knew he was here. The taciturn Ms. Lister must have spilled the information to whoever was so desperate to talk to him.

"Hello?"

"Damn, you're a fucking nuisance," Don Vandeway's voice spit out. It was almost humorous, the way he swore with that perfect, snotty intonation. "You could kill someone through your negligence. Didn't I tell you you're screwing up this investigation?"

"Yeah, I think you did."

"You're not good at listening, are you?"

"I don't feel reasonable when someone's been shooting at me."

Silence. A moment of serious thought from his buddy, Don Vandeway.

"Okay, listen," he confided. "You've already met one of the agents I told you about."

"Oh?"

"I'll give this information, but then I want you to butt out."

Hawk wasn't promising anything, but if Vandeway wanted to name one of his so-called undercover agents, Hawk was willing to listen. "Shoot," he said with a certain amount of humor.

"He's a legitimate Pacific yew farmer."

Hawk's brows lifted. Avery Francis? "I see."

"Belding and Turgate were accepting stolen yew bark from poachers and claiming it came legally from federal land," Vandeway explained quickly. "After all, they had the proof of their permits. Our agent has been slowly collecting names of poachers. Your interference could jeopardize his efforts and his health."

"You believe that's why Belding and Turgate were murdered, then?"

"Belding's death was an accident," he stated firmly once again.

"Bullshit," Hawk said softly.

"Just stay out of the investigation," Vandeway warned before he hung up.

Feeling Sarah's avid gaze on him, Hawk said to her, "Don Vandeway's a friend of yours?"

"What do you mean?"

"You called him and told him I was here. Thanks for the help. I think I got what I needed."

Her perplexity turned down the corners of her mouth and she swore rather crudely under her breath as Hawk thunked his way out of the office. His buddy, Ed McEwan, had told him first that Belding and Turgate were being helped out by an employee of the Forest Service. A secretary. He was going to have to check in with Ed again.

* * *

By the time Guy Fielding finished his ranting and
raving, Liz was suffering from a pounding headache
and Kristy looked done in. Stiff and unrelenting, he'd
made certain they knew what foolish *women* they were
and that he'd come to straighten them out.

And he didn't even know Jesse was Liz's son.

She debated telling him. The pure moment of pleasure
it would bring to see his judgmental face burn purple with
apoplexy would be worth a lot. But Kristy didn't need any
further drama in her life right now.

"Tawny would never miss her dance recital," she said
for about the third time. "She'll be back soon."

"She's run away," Guy bit out, looking down his nose.
"She won't be back for some pointless dance."

"It's far from pointless," Liz answered, nettled.

"Who *is* this boy who took her?" he demanded. "Does
he do drugs?"

Liz glared through narrowed lashes. Kristy shot her a
look of apology that Guy missed completely.

"He's probably a user," Guy went on in disgust. "I'll
string him up by the balls, the little asshole."

"He's not so little," Liz said coldly.

"And for all we know, Tawny asked him to leave with
her," Kristy put in for Liz's benefit. Liz moved to the
couch and sat beside her friend, holding her hand.

Guy pulled at his collar, which was way too tight for the
circumference of his neck. Affluence and power seemed to
have turned him from a reasonably good-looking man
into an overblown boor. Of course, in Liz's opinion, he'd
always been a boor, but at least he'd been marginally attractive. Now she found him damn near repulsive.

A knock on the door brought Liz to her feet.

"Tawny!" Kristy expelled happily.

Guy threw open the door, but it was Hawk on the front steps, balanced on a new, shin-length walking cast. The sweep of pleasure that flooded through Liz was totally out of proportion to the circumstances. *You don't like him all that much*, she reminded herself even as she crossed the room to help him inside.

"I haven't been introduced," Guy declared coldly, a bit of jealousy surfacing despite himself.

"Detective Hawthorne Hart," Liz responded. "Have you heard anything?" she asked Hawk anxiously.

"They found the stolen car in Aberdeen. Abandoned. We don't know if they took it, but—"

"Aberdeen! Yes, they took it!" she cried. "Aberdeen's Kurt Cobain's hometown. Jesse would head there in a heartbeat."

"Who is this Jesse?" Guy demanded, scrambling for control of the conversation.

Hawk said to Liz, "Cobain's that dead rock star?"

"Jesse's idol. He talked all about him and told me several times about Aberdeen. Of course he'd head there. No question."

Hawk absorbed the fact that Liz knew more about their son than he did with good grace. Too much was at stake to worry unduly about small issues now.

Guy, however, didn't like it one bit. "How do you know Jesse?" he demanded of Liz.

"He's my son," Hawk answered.

"*Your* son!"

Liz got her chance to see purple apoplexy as Guy came unglued and started sputtering unintelligible words. Hawk watched blandly, then asked him, "And you are . . . ?" although Liz was pretty sure he'd figured out where Guy fit in already.

"I'm Guy Fielding. Tawny's father!"

"Who hasn't been interested in his daughter until just recently," Kristy put in with a small shrug that pissed Guy to no end.

"What kind of police detective would have a delinquent son who steals cars and kidnaps young women? I demand to see someone else." With that, he headed to the phone. "I have a friend who works for the Seattle Police Department," he bit out importantly. "We'll see what must be done."

"Want to go to Aberdeen?" Hawk asked Liz and Kristy.

"Yes!" they answered in unison.

Guy slammed down the receiver in the middle of placing the call. "You're not taking over! I'll drive to Aberdeen and find them myself."

"You hardly know what Tawny looks like," Kristy pointed out sadly.

"We'll take my Jeep" was Hawk's answer. He glanced at Kristy and added gently, "It might be better if someone stays here in case she shows up."

"You're right," Kristy agreed. "Guy and I will stay."

"What the hell? You can't speak for me! I demand to find my daughter."

"Come on," Hawk said to Liz, and they headed to his Jeep with Guy on their heels, sputtering more demands as he decided whether to follow in his own car. Hawk backed out and Guy stood on the sidewalk, hands on hips, jaw locked in anger.

"I'm glad we're alone," Liz whispered, as if he might hear though they were yards away.

Hawk sent her a glance that melted something inside her. "Me too" was all he said.

Chapter Fifteen

"Trouble," Jesse muttered, standing beneath the streetlight and watching the approaching black Jeep.

Tawny lifted her head. She was seated on the ground, her arms wrapped around her knees, her cheek resting on her bent knees until Jesse spoke. Glancing around, she asked, "Where?"

"It's *them*!" he spat out.

"Who?"

"Dad and *Mom*."

Tawny jumped to her feet, dusting off the seat of her pants and gazing eagerly in the direction Jesse was looking. But he grabbed her arm and pulled her backward, into the shadows of a dour-looking brick building. She let him guide her, but as the Jeep whizzed by she leaped into the lamplight.

"Hey!" Jesse cried.

Tawny waved frantically, but when the Jeep was out of sight her shoulders slumped. Jesse glared at her. "What was that all about?"

"I want to go home," she told him, sounding suspiciously like she was about to cry. "I'm tired."

Jesse raked back his flopping hair and turned his face to the night sky. A cold moon looked back at him. He was tired, too. Tired of all the bullshit and lies.

"This is going to sound dumb, but I've got a dance recital that really matters to me," Tawny whispered. "It's coming right up."

Headlights arced at the end of the street. The Jeep was turning around. They'd been seen.

Like a prisoner in front of a firing squad, Jesse stoically waited for the end of his life. He didn't care. He didn't owe his parents anything.

Still, when the black Jeep cruised to an idling stop directly in front of them and Liz Havers, shrink extraordinaire, stepped onto the sidewalk, Jesse couldn't help the frisson of emotion that slid down his spine and invaded his gut.

"Hi, Mom," he said in a voice devoid of feeling.

The interior of Hawk's car was close and hot and Liz couldn't help counting Jesse's breaths as he sat directly behind her, so controlled and careful that it seemed as if he were regulating the inflation and deflation of his lungs. He probably was. She didn't trust her own involuntary reflexes to work.

Hi, Mom . . .

Shivering even as she sweated, Liz slid a surreptitious glance Hawk's way. He was bent over the steering wheel, his mouth a thin knife blade of tension.

Jesse had refused to get in. Even Tawny had been reticent, a clear sign that Jesse had told her his feelings about finding out his mother was alive and well and practicing psychology in Woodside. It had only been Tawny's pleading that had gotten to him. Now, as they neared the edge of town, where Hummingbird River wound its way near Tawny's house and then much farther down, past Hawthorne and Jesse's, Liz decided to speak the first word for thirty miles.

"I guess you were eavesdropping," she said into the silence.

No answer.

"You obviously learned the truth."

Still no answer.

Hawk glanced in the rearview mirror at his son. "Do you have anything you want to say?"

"Do you know who killed that dead guy yet?" Jesse asked with a trace of belligerence.

Liz bit her lip and forced herself not to mind too much.

"No." Hawk's terse reply sent the car into another round of deafening silence. Struggling to keep the conversation alive, Hawk elaborated, "I have a few leads, though."

"Like what?"

Liz was about to tell Jesse that his father probably wasn't at liberty to say when Hawk surprised her with some information.

"I think it all has to do with that yew tree theft. I think Barney Turgate and Manny Belding were paying off poachers and then using their legitimate federal permits to claim they'd harvested the bark from Forest Service land. From there, they'd sell the bark to a business, in this case ChemTek, at a much higher profit, and ChemTek would strip the bark of Taxol, a chemical substance in the bark proven to fight cancer."

In the rearview mirror, Liz could see Jesse's parted lips. He'd gotten a lot more information than he'd expected and was having a bit of trouble processing it.

Tawny said, "So, you think someone killed them for their money?"

"No. I don't think they'd made enough yet for that."

"Then . . . ?"

Hawk glanced back at Tawny, who sat in the backseat, kitty-corner from him. They hadn't made their peace yet, but Tawny was trying and Hawk understood.

"I think someone stumbled on their sweet deal and either didn't like it or tried to cut himself in. But everything went haywire, like those things often do."

"Got any clue to who that someone is?" Jesse asked, some of his animosity fading beneath curiosity. He still wouldn't look Liz's way, but at least the glower that had darkened his handsome face was temporarily lifted.

This was where Hawk grew cagey. Either he didn't know or his guesses were too dangerous to be thrown into the conversation. He merely shrugged and shook his head.

"What about Sarah Lister's boyfriend? Did you talk to him?"

"No . . ." Hawk was thoughtful.

That ended their conversation, and soon they were parked in the Fieldings' driveway and Kristy and Guy were hurrying toward the Jeep. Tawny slid out on one side, Jesse on the other. Hawthorne, protectively, stood by his son, and Liz climbed out to greet Kristy with a hug that embraced Tawny as well. Tears misted Kristy's eyes and Liz felt her own eyes burn. Tawny's small body shook and she gasped out a few sobs.

"I'll have you up on charges," Guy stated coldly, eyeing Jesse as if he were the planet's most-wanted criminal.

Jesse just stared him down and Hawthorne did the same. Their similarities clutched at Liz's heart.

"We'll talk about this later." Kristy's voice rang out authoritatively, surprising everyone. With that, she hustled

Tawny into the house, and Liz followed slowly, glancing back to Jesse and Hawk. Guy, after a second of indecision, strode after Kristy.

Hawk stared at Liz. She hoped all the love and worry and desire she felt wasn't written across her face, but she had a feeling it probably was. Jesse refused to meet her gaze. He glared down at the ground and scuffed at small rocks with the toe of his boot.

"We're going to work out the details of the stolen car" was Hawk's gruff way of saying good-bye, then he and Jesse climbed back into the Jeep.

Brad sucked on a cigarette so hard his face turned deep purple. Watching him, Jesse did the same. His lungs filled to popping and his head throbbed. He expelled on a small cough. No explosion or hacking fit this time, thank God. Too bad his eyes teared up.

"You're lame," Brad said conversationally.

"So are you."

"I'm unemployed. Lannie kicked my butt outta there."

"Why?" Jesse swiped at his eyes but tried to make it look like he was flinging back his hair.

Brad was too self-involved to notice. He flipped back his own scattered locks and talked with the cigarette hanging out the side of his mouth. It was supposed to look cool, but Jesse couldn't help wondering how long before the cigarette dropped to the ground.

"I'm a slacker." Brad shrugged. "They caught those other guys for stealin', but then it was just a lot of work and I kinda didn't do it anymore. Lannie yelled and bitched and I said a few things I shouldn't've. Y'know."

"Yeah, I know."

"So, I guess school's comin' up. Might as well give it one last try."

Jesse didn't tell Brad that he'd taken the job at Lannie's himself. He wouldn't have been able to fully explain the urge that had come over him. That he needed the money was only part of it.

The world, it is a'changin'.

Jesse smoked the rest of his cigarette in silence as Brad updated him on his flagging interest in Carrie Lister. "She's a pain. And her mom's a witch. Jeezus, they were always fighting, and that guy, the one who whacked her, y'know? He's around, but there's another guy, too." Brad sighed, the weight of the world on his shoulders. "Too much shit."

"I know what you mean," Jesse said with feeling. Tawny's parents acted as if he were a leper, although her mom was nicer than her dad. He understood why Tawny didn't want to connect with *him*. Bastard. He was lucky he didn't have parents like that.

The thought carried a tiny sting with it. He did have parents, however. Plural. A dad and a mom. He wasn't sure how to feel about it, but he knew he couldn't just turn around and pretend to be happy.

Sliding a glance Brad's way, Jesse considered confiding in him. But somehow, he couldn't. Tawny was the person he wanted to talk to, but since the escapade to Aberdeen she'd been locked away with her folks. God, what a mess.

"I gotta go," he suddenly said, turning to jog toward home before the words were fully past his lips.

"Why?"

"Somethin' I gotta do," he mumbled. There was one person he probably could talk to, though he didn't really want to. A person he'd talked to in the past when everything was less complicated. The one person who could answer his questions, if he could actually formulate and utter them.

Might as well give it a try. Better than standing around burning up his lungs smoking.

Hawk hadn't seen Liz for the better part of three days. Straightening out Jesse's mess took a ton of energy and he wasn't certain he'd gotten it right yet. The guy whose car had been stolen wanted Jesse in jail for the rest of his natural life. Hawk couldn't blame him. People were sick and tired of teen crime going unpunished. Jesse, however, showing remarkable restraint and remorse and initiative, had suddenly gotten a job to pay the man's time and expenses for car retrieval and mental stress. Hawk had taken the usual, what-kind-of-policeman-can-you-be-with-that-delinquent-son-of-yours, abuse in stride. What the hell. If the guy wanted to rant and rave it was his right.

The more personal issue for Hawk was Jesse and his new situation with him. Knowing Liz was his mother hadn't improved Jessie's relationship with his father, although, in all fairness, it hadn't exactly worsened it either. In fact, it seemed as if Jesse had a deeper appreciation of the facts than he possibly could. Or maybe teenagers were less judgmental of social convention. That was certainly a given in Jesse's case, but it was borne of necessity because Jesse regularly thumbed his nose at anyone or anything he considered the establishment.

Still . . . they'd managed to get through the past few days with a degree of civility, and as Hawk climbed into his Jeep, he considered tracking down his wayward son and seeing if they could actually have a conversation on the subject. As if Jesse had picked up the vibes, he suddenly appeared on his bike coming down the drive. Hawk struggled back out of the Jeep, waving Jesse's silent offer of help aside as his son threw down his bike, and reached out a hand.

"Hey," Jesse grunted.

"Hey there," Hawk returned. "I was just thinking about looking for you."

"Why?" Suspicion reigned.

Hawk shrugged. "A lot of things to talk about."

Jesse considered that laconic explanation for a few moments and asked, "Why didn't you tell me about the shrink lady before?"

"Her name's Liz."

Jesse snorted. "At least you don't expect me to call her mom."

"I'm not completely stupid," Hawthorne said dryly.

And suddenly Jesse grinned. A wild, foolish, youthful curve of the lips that turned into a laugh. Hawk found himself smiling back. A moment. A connection.

Jesse said, "I guess I'm gettin' used to it."

It felt as if a monumental load had been lifted off his back. Hawk clapped Jesse on the shoulder. They grinned at each other for a few moments before Jesse started looking uncomfortable with the emotion. To save him, Hawk turned back to his Jeep, his thoughts happy. Might as well get on with the yew bark case, and that meant a trip to search out Avery Francis. The guy was in this thing neck deep. Time to hammer out the truth.

His son watched him leave with a more mature expression than Hawk had ever seen. *I love you* . . . Hawk thought inconsequentially and drove away before he could embarrass them both by actually voicing his feelings.

* * *

The dance performance came upon them rapidly. One minute it was a dream sparkling in Tawny's bright eyes; the next it was an event ready to open at the local community theater house, which was really a renovated church. Liz had had no time to connect with Jesse, and Tawny was immersed in her program, as if it were her lifeline to a sane world. Guy's presence put everyone on edge, but he didn't seem to notice. His new wife didn't like that he was in Woodside one bit and called every two hours. It all put Liz's teeth on edge and by the afternoon before the recital, she was ready to bite someone's head off if they said the wrong thing.

And it didn't help that Avery Francis had insisted on coming by. Now, as Liz finished up some nagging paperwork for her job, the doorbell rang. She groaned inwardly. She'd hoped he'd gotten the not-interested message earlier, but apparently, he hadn't.

"Hello there," Avery greeted her in his friendly fashion, but beneath his easy tone there was tension.

"Hi" was all she could think of to say. In truth, her mind was full of other issues: Jesse, Tawny, Kristy, not to mention Hawthorne Hart . . .

"We haven't seen each other in a while, and I thought maybe we could go out for a quick drink or something."

"I can't," Liz declined, letting regret slip into her voice. "I've got a billion things to do."

"Then maybe we can talk here. I've got a few billion things of my own." He let himself in without further invitation and rested one thigh on a chair around Liz's tiny table.

"Would you like a cup of coffee? Or a glass of wine or something?"

"Beer?"

"Sorry."

"Wine'll do."

Because he clearly didn't have a preference, Liz poured him a glass of chardonnay. She poured one for herself as well. Who knew what was coming?

It didn't take long for Avery to get to his purpose. "You know your friend's been overstepping the bounds of his authority."

"Oh?" She lifted her glass to her lips. "What friend?"

"Detective Hart. He's been digging into things he shouldn't."

Hawk's aversion to Avery at the park and vice versa came back in a flood of memory. And Hawk had said he believed someone involved in the yew bark scam had murdered Barney and Manny. "What things?" she asked carefully.

"I think you already know."

Was that a threat in his voice? Liz's throat was cotton. Hurriedly, she took another gulp of wine. This was no answer. She'd probably get drunk and leave herself open to God knew what. With a slightly trembling hand, she put the glass down on the counter.

"I'm an undercover agent in a federal sting," Avery suddenly blurted out, throwing her for a loop. "Hart's been talking to a fellow agent, Don Vandeway, who's been trying to get him to keep his nose out of it."

"Unsuccessfully?" Liz asked in a strained voice.

"You got it. I was hoping maybe you could help. He's a cowboy. Won't listen to reason. He's going to get himself killed, I'm afraid."

A cold feeling settled in the pit of Liz's stomach. Avery's tone was light and menacing. Had he been the one to shoot at Hawk and chase Manny Belding to his death?

"I could call him . . . ?" She moved toward the phone.

"Don't" was his soft command.

They stared at each other and Avery drained his glass, silently holding it out for more. Obediently, Liz complied.

He patted the chair next to his, but she couldn't bring herself to move. The doorbell rang at that moment.

No Avery Francis at his farm. No Sarah Lister at the Forest Service. And surprise of all surprises, Don Vandeway was out of the office. Their little triumvirate had taken out Manny and Barney; of that Hawk was certain. How and why, exactly, were still a mystery, but it was fast becoming a plot that Hawk, in his handicapped state, couldn't handle alone. Perry would have his head anyway. Might as well come clean and take the abuse straight up and then they could forge ahead.

As Hawk considered heading for the station, an image of Liz Havers crowded his mind. His leftover feelings of joy over Jesse's acceptance couldn't be denied and he decided to make a side trip first.

Not that you want to see her or anything, he admonished himself.

So what? Jesse's acceptance was the real hurdle, he realized now. His own feelings for her had always been there, whether he cared to admit them or not.

Sarah Lister stood in Liz's living room, her eyes full of suspicion and something else. Jealousy? Possibly. But there was an element of fear inside their angry depths, too, and Liz wasn't quite certain why.

"You followed me here?" Avery repeated, his voice tense. Liz stayed quiet. She already mistrusted Avery, and this new wrinkle couldn't possibly help the situation she'd been thrust into.

Sarah tucked her arms around her waist, looking defiant. "What was I supposed to do? Wait for you to call?"

"We don't have to talk about this now," he said tightly.

"Don't mind me." Liz sidled toward the little kitchen.

"That policeman came by and harassed me and you don't care! I'm not taking the fall!" Sarah wailed. "And then you come here and what am I supposed to think? Does she know about you? Does she?"

"Shut up," Avery bit out.

Intimidation, however, didn't work well on Sarah. She'd built up a head of steam and she was venting furiously. "You two-timing bastard!" she cried, then turned to Liz, pointing an accusing finger at Avery. "It's because of him. That's why Barney's gone! Because of the yew bark permits."

Liz regarded Carrie's mother carefully. She fervently wished Hawk were there. "You work for the Forest Service . . . and you helped Barney and Manny get the permits?"

Sarah nodded fiercely. "That's right. And then Avery came around, wining and dining and making me think everything was great. But y'know what? It was all a lie!"

"You're overreacting," Avery declared tiredly as Sarah's eyes brightened with the telltale sign of unshed tears.

She blinked rapidly several times. "You're a fuck," she declared. She stared him down. Avery met her eyes squarely, sending hidden messages, but she was past his influence.

Hell hath no fury like a woman scorned . . .

"How do you think Carrie got those bruises?" Sarah asked Liz, never releasing Avery's gaze.

Liz darted a look Avery Francis's way but could tell nothing from his reaction. He simply shook his head in disgust, as if to say Sarah was way over the top and he couldn't be bothered to deny her allegations.

"You think you can just dump me?" she cried, losing

the last shreds of her control. "I'll go to the feds. I'll tell them the truth! You can't do it without me! You killed Barney Turgate."

"Oh, for God's sake, Sarah. Get a grip!" Avery sounded more exasperated than scared.

"It's all his fault He's behind it all. Barney's problem was having too big a mouth, that's all. Manny warned him to keep his mouth shut, but Barney loved to brag. *He* couldn't take that," she added with a sneer. "So he blew him away."

"You're crazy." Avery finally tore his gaze away from her. He shrugged to Liz. "It's because I'm here with you. That's why I'm getting the blame."

"I'm telling the truth!"

"I didn't touch either of them," Avery declared, losing patience. He went on for Liz's benefit, "She thinks because she helped wax those federal land permits for Turgate and Belding that somehow it'll benefit me."

"You're worse than both of them together!" Sarah ranted.

"Why don't you tell her who really gave Carrie those bruises?" he suggested coldly. "I'm not the only bed warmer around, am I?"

Sarah's mouth dropped open. She clearly hadn't expected this counterattack. "I don't know what you're talking about!"

"I don't give a rat's ass what you've got going. But get this straight: I was *investigating* Barney and Manny, for God's sake. I wouldn't just rub them out for the hell of it. I had nothing to gain and it would blow my whole investigation, which, in fact, it's done. Whoever killed 'em is sitting back with a big laugh."

Liz hovered by the wall to the kitchen, fascinated and frightened. Sarah blinked several times, a broken woman.

Avery's arguments were too strong to go against, and it was clear he'd made some painfully true suggestions.

After a long, long time, Avery got to his feet. "I don't think Ms. Havers wants to hear any more of this."

Liz expelled her breath in relief. Tension had infected her from head to toe.

He waited for Sarah to rise, but it took her a while. The stuffing had been knocked out of her. He threw open the door, but in his distracted state he didn't immediately see the figure on the porch. Hand raised to knock, Hawk took in the situation in a sweeping glance, his gaze thoughtful as it landed on Sarah.

Liz's heart swelled with joy and relief.

Glancing around, Avery met Hawk's gaze and said, "Oh . . . shit . . ."

Chapter Sixteen

Hawk's arrival acted like a collective gag. Sarah and Avery clammed up, as if Hawk were judge and jury and any spoken word would incriminate them—which, indeed, it might. Liz had formed a picture of the whole yew bark scam and found the players to be almost sad and pathetic. Barney and Manny had tried to make a few quick bucks and landed six feet under. Sarah, who may or may not be interested in a windfall, was desperate for a relationship with a man. Avery Francis was her first choice, but she clearly wasn't his. Liz, herself, seemed to be Avery's pick, and that had set up this little scenario.

And so the world goes 'round . . .

"I've been meaning to talk to you," Hawk said conversationally to Avery.

"I have nothing to say to you."

"Sarah here sicced Vandeway on me," Hawk said, shooting Sarah a look that could have meant anything. She set her jaw and glared at him. "You seem to all be pretty cozy with one another."

"Don told me what he told you," Avery retorted frostily. "No need to play coy."

"Is that what I'm doing?" Hawk asked.

"Did you come here looking for me?" Avery parried. "'Cause I'm not interested in talking to you."

Hawk gave Liz a look, and something in the depths of his eyes started a flutter in her stomach. No, he hadn't been looking for Avery. He'd come to see Liz.

Suddenly, she wanted Avery and Sarah and everyone else out of her life. There was only room for Hawthorne and Jesse right now, and this was the time to put everything back together that had been torn asunder for so long.

"Maybe you could leave us alone," Liz suggested softly, her gaze encompassing Sarah as well.

Avery looked as if he might argue the point, but Sarah was more than willing to hustle him out of Liz's range. They stood together for a moment on the porch, and in that interval, you could have heard the proverbial pin drop. After they were gone, Liz glanced at Hawthorne, who seemed to be thinking about what he wanted to say.

Liz said, "I feel—weird."

Hawk nodded. "Yeah." He cleared his throat and asked, "So, what was going on with them?"

"God only knows. Sarah had some kind of relationship with Avery that's gone sour. She followed him over here."

"But he'd come to see you," Hawk finished, to which Liz shrugged. "What are your feelings for him?"

"Avery? Nothing."

"He's up to his eyebrows in this yew bark thing," Hawk muttered.

"I know. And it's connected to Barney Turgate's murder, isn't it?"

Hawk's brows lifted. "You know?"

"Too many pieces fell into place." With that, Liz related what information she'd put together and Hawthorne listened in moody silence. Eventually, he explained a little of his own themes. They talked until the subject was exhausted and then looked at each other. They had more pressing business that neither of them knew how to address.

Eventually, Hawk said carefully, "I talked to Jesse."

Liz's heart beat fast. "Oh?"

"He's . . . coming around. He's changed over the course of the summer. For the better."

"He's a good kid, despite everything. You did a great job raising him."

The look he sent her was full of dark amusement. "Yeah."

"No, I mean it. And you were right to wait to tell him about me. It was good to get to know him first. You know, he might even talk to me again someday," she added lightly.

"Sooner than you think."

"What? Why?"

"He's—accepting."

"Oh, Hawk . . ." She swallowed against a growing lump in her throat.

"I probably should have told him the truth right from the beginning. Maybe it would have helped."

"No, no. You don't know."

"God . . ." He closed his eyes and she slipped her arms around him and let him sway against her for support, and he supported her as well. Her heart swelled. Moments ticked by in her mind.

For his part, Hawk could only accept that Liz was in his arms. The future was murky. He was afraid. Passion simmered beneath the surface, and all he wanted to do was make love to her. Jesse's mother. The lover from his past.

To that end, he turned his lips into her hair. Liz responded with a soft, submissive sigh, and that was all it took. In his ungainly way, Hawk led her to the couch, where they tumbled together and made love as if it were their last night on earth.

Jesse stood on a small rise. From this vantage point, Woodside spread out in two directions—west toward Hummingbird River; east toward town and then a stretch of rural homes and farms that finally petered out and edged onto Forest Service land.

Jesse had never been much of a thinker. Not that his brain wasn't adequate. He just wasn't the reflective type, generally speaking, and he realized with new adult thinking that neither was his father. Hawthorne Hart acted first and buried emotions he refused to acknowledge. He'd blamed himself entirely for the death of that boy and he'd nearly imploded from the effort, his soul nearly destroyed.

But something had changed, and Jesse was astute enough to realize what it was: Liz Havers. His *mother*, for Christ's sake. His father's secret love.

He didn't have all the details. This was no chance meeting back in the old hometown. No, the shrink lady had come here on purpose. She'd followed him and Dad because she wanted to reconnect. And then Dad had been such a mess. It was amazing, really, that they'd come to this point.

Sighing, Jesse closed his eyes and pushed all those thoughts aside with an almost physical effort. Tonight was Tawny's dance performance. Talk about eating away at the soul. Jesse was bound and determined to be there and her parents could just bite it. He would grab Brad and they would sneak in the back so they could watch.

A thought hit him like an arrow: Maybe he could wax his way in with the shrink lady first.

Jesse headed down the hill. He would go to her house

and just get an idea of how he felt. He didn't have to go in, but there was no harm in checking it out. With thoughts of bolting and running as a Plan B planted firmly in his mind, he headed down the hill to Liz's.

"You incredible ass," Perry declared, throwing a file at Hawk. Papers flew everywhere. Torn between amusement and annoyance, Perry demanded, "What kind of cowboy are you anyway?"

"I didn't feel like being benched," Hawk responded.

"You're injured, for God's sake. Let somebody else do the legwork."

"That's why I'm telling you now," he pointed out reasonably.

Including Perry had been a necessity. Hawk had done everything he needed to do on the yew bark case. It was over. And it had served its purpose. He'd come back to the land of the living. Okay, sure, his leg was still casted, but the quest for peace that everyone had told him he needed to take—and he'd adamantly refused to embark on—was over before he'd even known he'd set off on the journey.

Now, all he wanted to do was concentrate on his family. Jesse.

And Liz? an inner voice asked.

"You said this Vandeway character warned you off," Perry went on. "And he is what he said he was, a federal agent."

"But I don't trust him."

"You don't trust anybody."

"Is this your way of saying you won't follow up?"

Perry rolled his eyes. "I'll follow up, but I might just let them do their job. If it turns out to have something to do with the Turgate murder, I'll even step in. But I might just step a little more cautiously than you."

"Keep after Francis. He may not have taken out Turgate, as Sarah Lister claims, but he's in deep. I can feel it."

"He's an undercover agent. They're always in deep."

Hawk shook his head. There was just something wrong about the whole thing, but he was tired of it. Glancing at the clock, he felt a lift to his senses. Close enough to quitting time to start thinking about the evening ahead. With Liz. Even if it was some hokey dance recital for her adopted niece.

"I've just got one more stop," Hawk told Perry as he headed for the door. "Sarah Lister's boyfriend. I think he's a poacher."

"Watch your backside."

"Always."

Hawk left the building and was congratulating himself on how much more gracefully he could climb into his Jeep these days when a hand reached in the window and touched his upper arm. He twisted violently, heart slamming, prepared for battle before his brain had connected the danger. Lora Lee Evans shrank back with a gasp, clutching her throat with both hands.

"Sorry," Hawk muttered. His pulse still ran at breakneck pace.

"Have you got them yet? The killers?"

"We're close." Hawk hesitated. "Why do you think there's more than one?"

She shook her head. "Manny was the one. He might be dead, but there are others."

"Other killers, or other poachers?"

Lora Lee gazed at him as if his message hadn't fizzed into a chemical connection in her brain yet. The sadness in her eyes looked lifetime deep. She'd been around this town a long time and it appeared she'd be here for decades longer. She was a fixture. A small-town spinster whose man was always out of reach, whether living or dead.

"Poachers . . . ?" she asked blankly.

Hawk asked, "Who's Sarah Lister's boyfriend?"

"Sarah Lister?"

"Do you know her?"

"Oh, sure. I know most everybody who's been around town for long. It's Ed McEwan," she added. "Although that new guy's been around, too, but he doesn't really like her. Everybody knows that."

Ed McEwan. Quick with information and muscle-bound as a steer, Hawk remembered their meeting at the bar. "Does he beat her or her daughter?"

Lora Lee turned a face up to the heavens and closed her eyes, drawing in a breath and sighing as if to remind the fates of their senseless cruelty. "Barney never hurt any-body, but Ed's mean."

Shifting his Jeep into gear, Hawk waited until Lora Lee stepped away from the car. Looked like he had one more stop before the recital.

Liz paced the living room like the proverbial caged lion, waiting for Hawthorne. It was strange. Like a real date. A first date, and she sensed the progress much more profoundly than the fact that they were merely going to see a high school dance recital together, but waiting was hard. After all these years of separation it would seem a few more minutes wouldn't matter, but, apparently, they did because she felt nervous and itchy.

When the bell rang, Liz jumped in surprise. She hadn't heard Hawk's Jeep. Cautiously, she opened the door, then gasped, "Oh!" on an intake of breath. Jesse stood on the front stoop.

"Hey," he greeted her, shifting his weight from one foot to the other.

"Come on in," she invited. If she'd thought she was nervous before, the sight of her son with so much unsaid between them turned her insides to a mass of jelly. "I was waiting for your father."

"Oh? Yeah?" Jesse gazed around the room distractedly.

"Are you going to the recital tonight?"

He threw her a look screened by his errant hair. "Yeah, I'm going."

"Kristy knows you and Tawny are together," Liz babbled, wishing she could calm her butterflies. She could really use a glass of wine, but it didn't seem like a good idea to gulp liquor in front of her son. Instead, she stood behind the couch, gripping the back of it for support.

Jesse shook his hair from his eyes, then raked his hands through his hair in a gesture reminiscent of his father. Without the protection of those brown-blond bangs, he looked like a young copy of Hawk, his eyes so blue they seemed to pierce through Liz's protective armor. She felt naked and vulnerable. Jesse had the power to hurt her in ways she hadn't known existed. She waited for him to say something more, to let her know which way he stood.

"I overheard you and Dad," he admitted in a gruff voice.

"I know." Liz clasped and unclasped her fingers.

"He should've told me." Liz didn't respond, so Jesse added, "Or you should've."

Nodding, Liz said in a strangled voice, "I didn't know who you were at first. You were just Brad's friend Jesse. Then, when Hawk came to Kristy's and you were there, it was just . . . hard to believe. I know I didn't handle it well.

But I was glad it was you," she added, daring a direct look at him. "That you were my son."

His gaze slid away.

"I liked you right off the bat," Liz continued doggedly. "And then, when I realized it was *you*! It was—like a gift. And then I wanted to tell you, but . . ."

"You could've just said it."

"That would have been better?"

A hesitation. "Yeah."

"Then I'm sorry I didn't."

A roar of an engine and the crunch of gravel. Headlights swept the room. Hawk had arrived.

Instantly, Jesse's demeanor changed. All diffidence was gone. The smoldering rebel still lingered, and as Hawk knocked on the door, Jesse said, "So, don't think we're just one happy family now."

"I would never," Liz admitted, holding up her palms like a suspect under arrest. Jesse slid her an uncertain look, then threw open the door and bolted toward his bike.

"Hey!" Hawk called after him, but Jesse was gone before his father's "Be careful!" could even reach his ears.

"You're late," Liz said, plumping a pillow to cover up her rampant emotions.

"Okay, let's go" was his response.

Liz gazed at him in surprise. Hardly an auspicious beginning for their first real date.

The theater lights burned brightly on stage, but the rest of the house was as dark as midnight. Liz and Hawk sat several tiers away from Kristy, who'd graciously given Guy her extra ticket for the seat beside her. Even from her vantage point, Liz sensed Guy's uptight personality: it was evident in the thrust of his shoulders, the tautness of his neck, the push of his jaw. With a feeling of unreality, she glanced at Hawk, who met her gaze questioningly. His handsome face was serious, and he, too, was tense. But it was the same tightly strung sensation Liz was feeling, not the judgmental quality of Guy Fielding. In the candid moment, while they silently searched each other's gaze, Liz touched her fingers to his. Hawk's eyes swiftly glanced down at the heat of that contact, and a second later, he linked his fingers in hers.

Music swelled. Dancers appeared. Miniature tots in tutus and makeup like war paint. Wildly flinging legs and tapping toes. Class after class appeared on stage and strutted their stuff, to the amusement of the crowd as a whole and the teary-eyed pride of the angels' parents.

Liz could only feel Hawk's touch. She floated in sensation that was nearly X-rated while barely making contact. Ridiculous. Wonderful. Sublime. God, she was *nuts*! And then Tawny came on stage in a red leotard with a flowing, shimmery gossamer skirt and began a dance that was half jazz movements, half ballet, and Liz held her breath, stunned by the beauty and fluidity of her body.

In the back, back row, Jesse ground the heel of his boot into Brad's foot until his friend growled out in pain. "Watch it!" Brad whispered harshly.

"You light up in here and the goddamn fire department'll come down and haul our asses to jail."

"Did I say I was going to light up?"

"What are you reachin' in your pocket for?"

"A stick of gum, asshole."

"Sure."

"Look, I—"

Jesse elbowed him in the ribs, hard. "Shut up. There's Tawny."

Brad muttered on, but his voice trailed off as Tawny sparkled in a sea of red gossamer and hot white lights. Jesse, who'd never had much of an appreciation for the arts apart from alternative music, was moved to stunned silence. This dumb dance thing touched him inside. The whole production was more performance than recital anyway, and Tawny was just plain fabulous. His throat closed. His heart hammered. His head filled with noise. He felt as if he were running a marathon while standing perfectly still.

It ended far too soon to tumultuous applause. Jesse melted into the shadows at the back of the theater, while Brad gazed at him quizzically.

It was magnificent torture. Jesse knew he should leave, but he had to wait for Tawny. He wanted to touch her, to check that she was real and still part of his life.

Jeezus, life could knock you on your ass sometimes.

"You're breaking my hand," Hawk murmured, amused.

"Sorry." Liz relaxed her grip, swollen with pride.

"Do you mind catching a ride with the Fieldings? I'm going to have to leave early. I've got to stop by the Listers."

She glanced his way. "I thought you said you handed the case over to Perry."

"I think Sarah's boyfriend's someone I've met. I'd like to ask him a few questions about yew bark."

"I'm going with you."

"You're staying here and congratulating Tawny," he reminded her. "Tell her she was great."

Hawk left before Liz could do anything more. There were a couple of dances after Tawny's, nothing nearly as spectacular in Liz's biased opinion, then the lights came up. Liz moved with the herd to the outside deck, where tiny lights wrapped around bare-limbed trees provided illumination. The air was warm and sultry and thick. A hot August night.

She caught sight of Tawny's flashing red costume at the same moment she spied Jesse. They were together, and the look in Jesse's eyes made it clear he'd shared some of the same emotion that flooded Liz upon seeing Tawny dance.

Threading her way through the crowd, Liz lost sight of them for a few moments. When she was finally free again, she realized an ugly scene was in full play.

Guy was glowering at Jesse, whose back was to a railing, though he strived for nonchalance. Brad kept glancing between Jesse and Guy, flexing, as if he were about to jump on Guy if he twitched a muscle the wrong way. Kristy held Tawny's arm in a death grip, dragging her away.

"Guy, please," Kristy begged as Liz squeezed between a couple, the last people in the way. "It's all right."

"Stay away from my daughter. That's *all*," Guy growled at Jesse.

"Could you be a little more specific?" Jesse drawled with perfect insouciance. "I don't think I understand."

Guy bristled. Brad shifted his weight forward. Liz stepped between Guy and Jesse and placed a hand on Guy's chest. "You've made your point. Please don't make a scene."

"He comes near Tawny again, I'll have him arrested."

"Oh my God," Tawny murmured in agony.

"Guy . . ." Kristy was at her wit's end.

Liz said, "You're talking to my son, Guy. If you have

anything more to say, bring it to me or Hawthorne. Jesse's through talking to you."

A moment of electric silence. Guy blinked. His mouth opened and closed twice before he clamped his jaw shut. He reared back, staring at Liz as if she'd gone completely bonkers. "Your son? What's that? *What's that?*"

His stupefaction broke the tension of the moment. Jesse and Brad both snorted in amusement. Guy's neck turned red with embarrassment and fury.

"Stay away from her!" he ordered, stabbing at Jesse with his index finger. He moved stiffly toward the parking lot.

"Aye, aye, Captain," Jesse muttered, sketching a salute.

"Don't push it," Liz muttered. "He is Tawny's father."

"He has no control over me!" Tawny declared, running into Jesse's arms. Jesse, after a moment of surprise, held her close, and Liz turned to Kristy, hoping it was okay. Kristy didn't seem to know what to do.

Liz said to her, "Hawthorne had to leave. Please tell me you brought your car because I don't think I could stand to ride home with Guy."

Kristy tore her gaze from Jesse and Tawny. "I brought my car."

"Mom, we're going to walk to the ice cream parlor," Tawny said. "Lots of kids are. Can you pick us up later?"

Kristy nodded a bit blankly. Too much happening all at once, Liz concluded. Steering her away, Liz said, "They'll be fine."

"I know," Kristy agreed, sounding a little bemused. "I know."

"Jesse's a good kid down deep where it counts."

For an answer, Kristy gave Liz's arm a reassuring squeeze and they headed to her car together.

* * *

By the time Hawk reached Sarah's house he felt as if the cavalry had arrived ahead of time, heralding his imminent appearance. Sarah and Ed were standing on the porch, caught in the headlights of Hawthorne's Jeep. Before Hawk could stop the vehicle from rolling, Ed had hauled off and belted Sarah one right across the face.

The man was drunk as a skunk. Stepping between them, Hawk called reinforcements on his cell, then asked Sarah, who was crying and swearing at fever pitch, to go in the house, out of the range of Ed's drunken fury.

Not that Ed was even all that furious. He was just used to dealing with issues with his fists. He swung a few times at Hawk, cursed Sarah, who refused to heed good advice and just kept on blasting him with invectives while Hawk played referee. It was an almost comical dance they performed: Sarah behind Hawk; Hawk on the phone while keeping himself between the two of them; Ed staggering and swinging.

If Hawk had felt threatened he would have pulled his gun. After all, statistics proved that domestic fights were the most dangerous for policemen, and Hawk knew he was testing the fates by being handicapped himself. However, Ed was too far gone to do much damage unless he found another weapon, and at this point he was spending most of his energy just keeping his balance.

When the cavalry arrived to save the day, Hawk was surprised to see Chief Dortner himself step from the patrol car. "What gives?" he asked.

"Talked to Vandeway," Perry said cryptically. "Did you find out if McEwan was a poacher?"

"Not yet. He's drunk and raving. I tried to ask him a few questions, but he's surly and doesn't care."

"He took that old lady's trees!" Sarah declared. "Just ask him."

Ed lunged at her, but now his hands were cuffed. Perry nodded for his men to thrust him in the back of the police car. He struggled furiously but was overpowered.

Watching, as they ducked his head into the backseat, Hawk asked Perry, "So, why are you here?"

"You stirred up a hornet's nest, my friend. Vandeway's at the station right now, incensed. He's named Avery Francis as an agent working both sides of the law, and apparently, Francis got nervous when he ran into you at Liz Havers's place."

"What?" Hawk was half-amazed. "I hardly talked to him."

"According to Vandeway, Francis had a thing for Liz until he realized you were part of her life. Since then, Francis has been hanging around trying to figure out what you know."

Hawk shook his head. "Why was he so worried about me? I told Vandeway all I knew."

"Well, it looks like Francis might be the guy who shot you," Perry explained with a grimace. "That's Vandeway's theory anyway. You spooked Francis and he's gotten real unpredictable."

Hawk thought that over. Avery Francis had shot him and then sent Manny Belding to his death? "Why's Vandeway gotten so chatty?"

"Because Francis is a loose cannon who could make him look bad. Vandeway's a tight-ass," Perry added with a snort.

"So where's Francis now?"

"Anybody's guess." Perry's face took on an earnest look. "When I heard you were in the middle of this fray, I decided to come see what was up. I wanted to make sure you were all right."

Hawk gave his friend a long look. "Francis isn't the only one who's spooked," he guessed.

"Vandeway said Avery shot you. I take that real serious."

So did Hawk. After a moment, he clapped Perry on the back, grateful for the concern even if he felt it wasn't really necessary. "I'll come down to the station and we'll take care of Ed."

"Vandeway's there already. You're the one he really wants to talk with."

"Surprised he cares about my health. We're not the best of friends."

"You're still not," Perry Dortner said as he headed for the patrol car with Ed McEwan inside. "But Vandeway's in a wringer where Avery Francis is concerned, and he's jumped to the winning side."

Chapter Seventeen

With a feeling of complete ecstasy, Jesse dived cleanly into the one decent swimming hole Hummingbird River had to offer. Down, down, down he cut until he sensed he'd better surface before his lungs cried for air and he swallowed a ton of dark green water.

Bursting through the surface, he shook his head like a wild dog. Grinning from ear to ear, he swam lazily on his back, staring into a star-studded black sky framed as if in a picture by the tops of the towering firs.

He was happy. He and Tawny and Brad had gone to the ice cream parlor and had laughed and talked and joked until Tawny's mom came by—without that jerk-off ex-husband of hers, thank God—and picked them all up and dropped him and Brad at their houses. Tawny had been in her dance costume with a sweatshirt thrown over the top, exposing her long legs. It had felt good just to be seen with her, and her dad's griping and bitching had only succeeded in drawing her closer to Jesse.

And her mom was cool. He'd been kind of nervous with her at first, her being sick and all. But she was okay and he was half-ashamed that he'd ever felt uncomfortable with her illness. It wasn't her fault.

As for *his* mom . . . well, he still couldn't think of her that way. But if he just kept in his head that she was Brad's shrink and a pretty cool person, it was okay. He hadn't known quite what to think when she'd jumped to his defense like that, but seeing old man Fielding nearly bust an artery had been worth it. Jeezus, that guy was a pain. Jesse cheerfully wished him nothing but the worst.

Jesse breathed deeply, content. But then he remembered finding the dead body not all that far from here, and his euphoria subsided a bit. Dad still hadn't found the killer, and hey, the guy was probably a total psychopath hopped up on fifteen different kinds of drugs. If he was found here, he was literally a sitting duck.

A few clean strokes and Jesse was out of the water, buck naked. He grabbed up his clothes and threw them on. They stuck to his wet body, but he felt safer being dressed. Skirting the darkest depths of the woods, he quickly trotted down the path that led to the edge of the road where his bike lay.

As soon as he was pedaling, he felt better. But he wasn't ready to go home. His dad was probably with the shrink. Liz, he reminded himself. He could never call her Mom. Not for real. But he could handle Liz. Maybe he'd just stop by her house and check in. Why? He couldn't think for the life of him, but he wanted to, so that was that.

Besides, he was hungry. Didn't moms always have food on hand for their teenage sons? It was a natural law of nature or something.

* * *

Bumping down the dirt track surrounded by tiny Pacific yews, Hawk asked himself why he even cared whether Avery Francis was at home.

Because according to Vandeway, the guy tried to kill you.

Hawthorne could feel his gun at his hip. His body was pumping adrenaline through his system, though he wanted to remain calm and detached. Could he believe Vandeway, or was the guy passing the buck? It was difficult to tell, so here he was on this midnight chase, though Perry hadn't wanted him to go.

"Damn it, Hawk. Aren't you listening?" Dortner had demanded, pacing the length of the station while Vandeway sat primly in the chair next to Hawthorne's desk. He'd turned to the tightly wound agent. "Explain it to him."

So, Vandeway, after clearing his throat, had decided to tell Hawk everything that was still left out. "I turned Avery in," was his first admission. "He came out here to ferret out the poachers, but when he learned about Manny and Barney's setup, he decided to cut himself in on the deal. He started his own legitimate yew farm, then began accepting stolen yew bark from poachers—such as your newest guest, Mr. McEwan—and fed it through Manny and Barney. It was a sweet little moneymaker."

"So, his farming was just a front?" Hawk inquired.

"Yes and no. Because of the five-year wait until harvest, Avery had to find another source of income. His government salary wasn't enough," Vandeway added dryly. "Of course Manny and Barney didn't want to share, so Avery moved in on Sarah, hoping to get his own permit. When she couldn't swing that, he threatened to prove that Manny and Barney had gotten their permits through a certain amount of string pulling and they reluctantly allowed him in."

At this point Perry, who'd listened quietly to this tale he'd already heard earlier, asked, "You're not saying that Francis took out Turgate and Belding. That's kind of like killing the golden goose, isn't it?"

"Belding had the permits in his name first. Turgate was an add-on. Belding had second thoughts about letting his old pal in on the deal. They fought, and he ended up killing Turgate."

"Bullshit," Hawk muttered. He'd only met Manny Belding briefly, but he'd bet his life that Manny hadn't undercut Barney.

"Francis figured it was just a matter of time until Manny came after him, so he shot at Manny and hit you by mistake. Then Belding fell to his death."

"You've got a lot of theories, but that's all they are," Hawthorne growled.

"Facts," Vandeway corrected, looking down his nose in that superior way that got under Hawk's skin. "I was with Francis when he shot at Belding and accidentally hit you," he admitted.

Hawk jumped out of his chair, on the verge of strangling the man, but Perry intervened. "We're checking into it," he told Hawthorne, seeking to calm him down. "Our buddy Don was a little late in coming forward."

"A little!"

"As I've said before," Vandeway declared loudly as Hawk and Perry were heading out of earshot, "it would be best for everyone if the local authorities stayed out of it."

With two ground-devouring steps Hawk returned to stand in front of Vandeway, bristling all over. "You're pretty damn close to being arrested yourself, *Agent* Vandeway."

Vandeway merely drew into himself, turning aside in affront.

"Now what?" Perry asked as Hawk headed for the door.

"Time to see our other agent friend."

Dortner's hand darted out and Hawk's arm was held in a vise grip. "Don't."

"I just want to ask a few questions."

"It could be a setup."

"It could be," Hawk conceded, determinedly loosening Perry's grip. "But we'll never know until we check."

"Call for backup if you need it," the chief muttered gruffly after a moment of wrestling with whether to allow Hawthorne to go to Avery's or not.

So, now, here he was, feeling alert and revved up in a way he hadn't for months. Years, maybe. The thought of facing off with the oily Avery Francis was part of it, his relationship with Liz another part. There were no more worries about the past where she was concerned. All that baggage was set aside. They'd both gone through all the mental postmortems and it was a relief to think about a happier future.

Hawk pulled up to the house, but he could see there was no one home. He knocked loudly on the front door, then circled to the back porch. The door was wide open. The hairs lifted on the back of his neck. His hand drifted downward, searching for his gun, but just feeling its hard surface gave him the willies. Visions. Pictures. Snapshots of Joey's death. He dropped his hand, cursed himself for his weakness, and stepped inside Avery Francis's house.

Liz hummed as she sipped her wine. Too bad it was so darned hot outside; she would love to set fire to the logs in the fireplace. Still, it didn't matter. There was already something cozy about the room: the buttery glow of yellow lamps; the faintest smell of autumn creeping inside; a cuddly feeling of contentment that made her keep smiling even while her lips were on the rim of her glass.

She expected Hawthorne. Nothing had been said between them at Tawny's recital, but it was understood. Touching hands with him—just thinking about it both embarrassed and exhilarated her.

She was chuckling a little at herself, really, when she heard the crunch of gravel outside. Thinking it was Hawk, she threw open the front door, but it wasn't a black Jeep. A second later she recognized Avery's car. She stifled the urge to run back inside and bolt the door; instead, she lifted a reluctant hand in greeting.

"Hi there," she said as he walked toward her, head bent down as if he were concentrating hard.

She stepped back into the house as he was coming fast. *What?* she wondered vaguely. He didn't stop. He barreled right into her, pushing her farther inside, slamming the door with his foot.

"What the hell?" she gasped.

"Shut the curtains." His voice was threaded with desperation. "Quick!"

Liz didn't hesitate. She did as she was bidden. Tremors infected her lower limbs, and when she was finished she stood by the fireplace, quaking a little.

This wasn't the Avery she'd come to know. This was someone else. Someone—unstable.

Avery Francis. Yew bark. Barney Turgate. She hadn't wanted to believe it, but it made too much sense. "You killed Barney," she whispered.

"No!" His head whipped up in surprise. Liz drew in a sharp breath when she saw the gun held loosely in his hand. *Oh God.*

Avery glanced down, seeming surprised that it was there. "No, I didn't."

"And you shot Hawthorne," she realized faintly.

"No, no, listen. You've got to listen to me. It wasn't like that. It's Vandeway. He's blaming it all on me, but *he's in it, too!* We're all in it; I'll take my share of the blame. But, but he's trying to make out like I'm some kind of cold-blooded killer and I'm not."

"You're not?" *Keep him talking. Buy time. Think!*

"I just wanted my part of the yew bark thing, that's all. I'm not a killer. I've got a few debts," he admitted. "Some gambling debts."

Liz nodded. Where was Hawk? He'd said he had a stop to make. To see some guy he'd met before.

His cell phone. With an effort, Liz dragged the number from the depths of her memory. She'd asked him what it was once, not long after his hospital stay. It had been a casual comment because she didn't want him to know how worried she was. Hawk didn't deal well with people being overly solicitous.

But she hadn't written it down. *What the hell was it?*

"I needed some cash kind of quick, and Manny and Turgate were rolling in it. It wasn't millions, but it was ample. I figured, why not? There's hardly an agent out there who isn't on the take, you know?"

"Okay."

"Belding was going nuts. I went to reason with him, that's all. But he took off screaming—" Here, Avery cut himself off.

"You didn't intend for him to die," Liz said in what she hoped was the right tone.

"That's right!" Avery averred. "He ran off and I shot and hit the wrong guy. What the hell was Barney doing there anyway? Stupid shit. He wouldn't stay out of it!"

"Manny's death was an accident?"

"Absolutely." Avery paced around the room, ending

up only a few feet from Liz. She felt choked by his proximity but knew better than to move away. "I've got debts to pay," he muttered, striding toward the kitchen. Belatedly, Liz realized he was opening the refrigerator door. She heard the wine cork open with a pop. Quick as a cat, she grabbed for the phone, dialing Hawk's cell number—she prayed to God!—and counting the rings, which matched five of her rampant heartbeats.

To her amazement, he answered in his policeman's voice. "Hawthorne Hart."

"Hawk . . ." she breathed.

Slam! The phone was knocked from her hand. A moment later, Avery's hand wrapped in her hair, pulling her close, yanking so hard tears formed in the corners of her eyes. "I'm not going to hurt you," he said through his teeth, as if struggling to convince himself as well. "But you can't call that boyfriend of yours again, understand?"

"Yes," she whispered. "I understand."

"Don't fuck around with me."

"I won't," she said and meant it.

He slowly released her. They stared at each other for several moments. "Now, all I want to do is get out of here with my money, and you're going to help me."

"How?" she asked through a taut throat.

He grimaced, sighed, and revealed his plan. "I need a hostage."

Jesse skidded his bike to a stop in front of Liz's walkway. Her black Miata was parked in its place, but another car sat beside it. Who was here? It wasn't his dad's Jeep, nor Mrs. Fielding's car.

Worried that it was Guy Fielding, Jesse tiptoed up the front steps and tried to peek through the curtained window.

That was weird in itself. Liz Havers didn't normally shut the front curtains because this little house was as private as prayer. With patience, Jesse waited for someone to walk through his line of vision. Moments later, his efforts were rewarded. A man cruised by.

Jesse sucked in a scared breath. His skin crawled. Was that a *gun* in the guy's hand? Good God, what was going on?

It took him half an instant to make a decision. With the rashness of youth, he decided to take the bastard on himself. Hell, he was six feet tall and strong enough to take any guy who made a nuisance of himself. Some of Woodside High's most obnoxious could attest to his strength if they were smart enough to form sentences, which, in Jesse's private opinion, they weren't.

There was a back door off the kitchen, but it was always locked; he'd learned that much from prowling around the times he'd been here. But there was a window off the bedroom that might be cracked open on these hot nights.

So thinking, Jesse crept to the side of the house where Liz's bedroom was. Just as he'd suspected, the bottom of the window was open and a soft wind blew into the room, fluttering the curtains. Carefully, oh so carefully, he pushed it upward until the space was big enough for him. With all the finesse his sixteen-year-old body could muster, he quietly heaved himself over the sill and into the room.

They were talking. The guy was explaining something, but it didn't sound right. The tone was whacked. Like he was trying to convince her of something he didn't believe himself. With his heart tattooing painfully in his chest, Jesse crept forward, wishing for about the thousandth time that his damn hair would stay out of his eyes just this once.

Crunch! He bit back a cry of pain with a supreme effort of will. Liz had placed a box on the floor and he'd banged his shin into it dead-on. Glancing around for a hiding place, Jesse heard the thunder of running feet a half second before the guy blasted into the room, gun swinging wildly.

"Jesse!" Liz screamed behind him, hitting the guy in a flying tackle. He twisted free and whacked her once on the side of the head with his gun. Jesse was on him before he knew he'd moved. He pummeled with all his might.

"Stop it!" the man wheezed. "I'll kill her. You'll make me kill her. See? See?"

The gun was waving in Liz's direction. Her eyes were on Jesse, scared but calm.

Jesse debated a nanosecond, then lifted his hands in the age-old sign of surrender. The man struggled to his feet, the gun aimed at Liz, his eyes on Jesse.

"Come on," the man growled, his gun signaling both Jesse and Liz into the living room.

Trickles ran down his neck. It felt like sweat, but it wasn't. It was something else. Electrochemical impulses running down nerves. Jittery messages. Déjà vu.

But it hadn't been like this with Joey, Hawk realized. Not at first. Joey's situation had been just another job until their worlds collided and suddenly Hawk was Joey's and vice versa.

Except this was Liz, and he had the gut-twisting feeling she was at the hands of Avery Francis.

There'd been no one home at Avery's. He'd tiptoed through the place like a thief. The place was quiet. That quiet that said there wasn't a soul around. Then his phone rang. He'd answered it without thinking, believing Perry to be on the other end because Jesse never called and no one else knew the number.

Except maybe Liz . . .

That thought penetrated as her voice came on, saying his name. SOS. He'd heard the message loud and clear, though she'd said nothing more.

And now he was tearing through the night at breakneck speed, unable to feel anything but pure fear. What if it was already too late? Why hadn't he paid more heed to Dortner when he'd called Avery Francis a loose cannon?

He pulled into the end of Liz's drive and cut the lights. Climbing from the car was easy; he was used to the walking cast. Making his way silently was another story. He wasn't as agile as he could be.

But he had Avery Francis to thank for the cast, too. With resolve, he checked his gun again, lifting it from its holster, drawing it forward so that it led him like a dark beacon toward the house.

He hated this position. Memories were black as the enveloping sky. Sweat rose on his skin and though the night was warm, his muscles felt cold and frozen.

He stopped short, heart jerking painfully. Ahead was a familiar shape. A glint of moonlight on handlebars. Jesse's bike.

Oh God.

"Don't move," Avery warned, his gun trained in Liz's direction. She stood by the hearth, a statue, her gaze on Jesse, who sat loosely on the couch, hands dangling between his knees. His eyes followed Avery's every move. He was thinking. Plotting. Not a good sign. She was scared to death he would do something heroic and get himself killed in the process.

"I won't," she assured him.

"Don't move," he ordered again, swinging the barrel of the gun in Jesse's direction.

"I won't." Jesse was as terse as Liz.

They stayed like that for eons, or at least it felt like it.

"What's that?" Avery demanded, glancing at the window. "A car?"

Carefully, he edged his way to the drawn curtain, peeking through a tiny slit. Liz glanced at Jesse, silently begging him to stay put. His muscles tensed.

No! Liz mouthed, but it went unheeded. Jesse launched himself at Avery like a bullet and both men crashed down in a punching, thrusting, yelling heap.

"Goddamn it!" Avery hollered.

"You goddamn sonofabitch. You sonofabitch," Jesse muttered furiously.

Jumping past the melee, Liz grabbed the phone, not certain whether she was going to place a call or use it as a weapon. Avery reared back, caught her legs with one of his, and tripped her. She went down with an "oof," then struggled up, but Avery'd ripped the landline phone from the wall.

Jesse had him on his back. "Drop the gun!" he yelled. "Drop the gun! Drop the gun!"

Avery lifted his gun hand. Liz screamed. With a hard slam, Avery smacked Jesse alongside the head and Jesse went down like lead.

"Jesse! Oh my God, Jesse!" Liz cried, bending over him. He was breathing. Knocked cold but alive. She jumped on Avery, all fury and hatred.

"Get off me or I'll kill him," Avery gasped, writhing

to avoid her clawing hands. "I mean it. I don't want to, but I will!"

"I'll kill you!" Liz yelled back. "If he's hurt, I don't care what happens. I'll kill you!"

"Get off me!"

Liz wanted to kick and gouge and maim his manhood. She panted and gulped air. Tears ran down her cheeks. Avery jerked an arm free and aimed his gun at Jesse's youthful cheek. Liz froze, gulping air. Jesse's lashes lay dark against his skin, a bruise developing along his jaw and toward his temple.

"I'm sorry," Avery whispered. And in that terrible moment Liz knew he was going to shoot Jesse right there.

"Move out of the way," a cold voice said from the direction of the bedroom.

Liz gasped, backed up automatically. Hawk stood like stone in the doorway, his gun trained on Avery with deadly purpose. "Put down the gun or I'll shoot," he said in a voice that sent chills down Liz's spine.

A hesitation. Avery's hand twitched.

Blam! The noise was deafening. Liz shrieked in fear, but it was Avery who was suddenly writhing on the floor, holding his shoulder and howling in pain. Jesse lay in blessed silence. Scared, Liz touched him, but he was merely unconscious.

"Hawk," she murmured brokenly as Hawthorne came forward, his hands touching Jesse.

"Is he . . . ?" he asked in a whisper.

"He's fine. No, he's fine. Really. He'll be fine."

She babbled and cried, and then cried some more when she saw the tears of relief reach Hawthorne's eyes. They collapsed into each other's arms and held on as tightly as they could as police sirens wailed in the distance— Hawk's backup.

* * *

Hours later, after the police had grilled and questioned and hauled Avery away and Jesse had been taken to the emergency room and diagnosed with a concussion, Liz and Hawk sat clasped together on the couch, arms surrounding each other, while Jesse slept peacefully in his bedroom. Tawny and Kristy had stopped by, stunned that so much had happened in so short a time. The good news there was that Guy was leaving in the morning, sans Tawny,

It was done. It was over. Vandeway was still being questioned, but with Avery in custody and the whole nefarious plan facing the light of investigation, the truth would come out.

"So, it was Avery who killed Barney," Liz stated, more fact than question.

"Mmm," he murmured into her hair.

Liz curled close to the heat of his body, relaxed and filled with awe that this moment had finally happened. Those seconds with the hot smell of gunfire and Jesse on the floor and Hawk frozen in the doorway were burned in her brain. But everything was all right now. Hawk was here, with her, and Jesse was safe.

In the hospital, Jesse had met her gaze with those beautiful eyes and smiled tiredly. Acceptance. Maybe even a hint of love. She'd been so moved, her throat ached. And then Hawk's arms dragged her away and back to his cabin, and they tucked Jesse in and tumbled onto the couch together, needing the closeness. Needing each other.

Now, drawing a finger down the length of his arm, Liz smiled against his cheek. He groaned and dragged her closer.

"You're crushing me," she whispered.

"Sorry."

"No, don't be. I love it . . . and you."

"Liz . . ."

A period of intense kissing followed until Liz couldn't help the curve of her lips. Happiness was infectious. Hawthorne's mouth answered in kind.

"I think we've loved each other a while," he said lightly, amazing her.

"I think we have," she agreed.

"When I saw Avery with the gun, and Jesse, and everything . . ."

She pressed a finger to his mouth. "But it's over now."

"Joey's death doesn't have its power anymore," he said slowly, as if the idea were just taking hold. "It's still there, but when I saw you two, it just crashed in my head. This is *real*. It's *now*."

Liz pulled his mouth to hers. She kissed him with all the depth of her desire, dragging another groan from his chest.

"We're staying here together in Woodside. All of us."

Liz nodded.

"We're a family," he added, as if it were a new flavor to be tasted. "Do you believe that?"

"Yes," she admitted happily, cuddling in the shelter of his embrace.

Long moments passed. Quiet thoughts in the shadowed room. Liz drifted, exhaustion taking its toll.

"When they test Avery's gun they'll see if the bullets match the ones found in Barney," Hawk said, yawning. "Then we'll know for sure." He turned his lips to Liz's crown and she closed her eyes and sighed.

"What if the bullets don't match?"

"Then there's another gun out there," Hawk answered.

He also sighed. "I keep thinking there's something I'm missing, but you know what, right now I don't care."

With a muscular twist, he flipped her on her back, kissing her all over until she was laughing and wrestling with him, enjoying the moment, filled with desire and love.

Across town, a tiny slit of September moonlight cut through the drawn curtains of a darkened room. It had been that way since sunset, for the occupant of the home didn't care for illumination of any kind these days. The light had gone out years ago. Snuffed out. But not quickly. Oh no, it had been slowly smothered out.

On the coffee table in the center of the room lay a snapshot. Football days. Glorious times. When youth was all that mattered and love was free of disappointment. The boy in the picture sported a huge grin, helmet tucked under one beefy arm, number seventy plastered across a massive chest. In the background, a group of girls cheered hysterically. Not the cheerleaders themselves. Just a group of nobodies who might turn into somebodies one day and have a chance at a guy like Barney Turgate.

The slit in the curtains shined a finger of light on Barney's face and diffused illumination over the rest of the picture. Picking up a pair of scissors, the figure seated on the couch systematically cut the photo in half, then half again, then half again. Love was strange. It could grow without nourishment. It could consume everything in its path like a holocaust.

A shaking sob rattled from her chest. She'd thought the pain would end. Barney's death should have ended it. She felt tears cascade down her cheeks; silent homage to the man she loved more than life itself.

Swiping at the tears, she pulled the hood of her gray

sweatshirt close to her cheeks, shivering a little. She wiggled her toes in her black Nikes. The finger of moonlight moved ever so slightly and struck a bluish glance off the handgun tossed on the coffee table.

Why wasn't the pain gone? Killing him should have ended it, but no, it was a thousand times worse. It wasn't fair. It shouldn't be!

Snatching up the gun, she pressed it to her temple, squeezing her eyes shut, counting her elevated heartbeats. With her free hand, she grabbed for the bits of picture, kissing them until they stuck to her lips and mixed with her drizzling tears and uncontrollable gasps. Cocking the trigger, she moved her index finger ever so slightly. A hairbreadth. A millisecond. One more everlasting moment . . .

With a cry, she dropped her arm, the gun slipping from her fingers and tumbling against the couch cushions. Just like always, she couldn't pull the trigger.

Like the old woman she'd become, Lora Lee dragged herself to a huddled, standing hulk. Maybe she would turn herself in. After all, what was left now? Maybe she would . . . maybe . . .